D0119316

A Sea of Troubles

By David Donachie

THE JOHN PEARCE SERIES

By the Mast Divided
A Shot Rolling Ship
An Awkward Commission
A Flag of Truce
The Admirals' Game
An Ill Wind
Blown Off Course
Enemies at Every Turn
A Sea of Troubles

Written as Jack Ludlow

THE REPUBLIC SERIES

The Pillars of Rome
The Sword of Revenge
The Gods of War

THE CONQUEST SERIES

Mercenaries
Warriors
Conquest

THE ROADS TO WAR SERIES

The Burning Sky
A Broken Land
A Bitter Field

THE CRUSADES SERIES

Son of Blood
Soldier of Crusade

a&b

A Sea of Troubles

DAVID DONACHIE

Allison & Busby Limited
12 Fitzroy Mews
London W1T 6DW
www.allisonandbusby.com

First published in Great Britain by Allison & Busby in 2012.

A CIP catalogue record for this book is available from the British Library.

First Edition

ISBN 978-0-7490-4060-4

Typeset in 12.75/16 pt Adobe Garamond Pro
by Allison & Busby Ltd.

The paper used for this Allison & Busby publication has been produced from trees that have been legally sourced from well-managed and credibly certified forests.

Printed and bound by
CPI Group (UK) Ltd, Croydon, CR0 4YY

To Nicolas James Prisco
Welcome to this world

CHAPTER ONE

Sleeping on the deck between a pair of cannon had drawbacks; the planking was hard and the ship rolled enough on the swell to require John Pearce to jam himself against the bulwarks. For all the discomfort it had two distinct advantages: the tiny cabin of HMS *Larcher* was not comfortable for two people seeking to avoid any kind of tactile contact, which he must do with Amélie Labordière, his passenger and one-time mistress. In addition, even if he was the captain, he was, on such a small vessel as an armed cutter, required to share the watch, which meant no more than four hours sleep and often not that if anything untoward happened.

The only other option, and one to which he had condemned *le Comte de Puisaye*, his other passenger, was to sling a hammock 'tween decks, which, in terms of space on such a cramped vessel made the cabin seem palatial, and that said nothing about an atmosphere replete with snoring and the all-pervading odour of endemic and malodorous flatulence – all the French aristocrat had to protect himself from that was a canvas screen, and John Pearce, needing to be quick on deck in an emergency, would not have been granted even that; besides, fresh air was so much more to his liking.

The night being cloudy, the heat of the day had been trapped and, unusually in the northern quadrant of the Bay of Biscay, if there was a decent swell coming in from the Atlantic the wind was no more than a zephyr. That meant, with a slight breeze on her quarter and few sails aloft, the ship was making little headway in what was a Stygian darkness. Pearce had added to the lack of light by shading the lantern that illuminated the binnacle. A candle could be seen at sea for miles in clear weather and they were in hostile waters, close in an arc of shoreline in possession of the enemy, and obliged to cross, on the way back to England, several well-worn routes to the major French ports, both commercial and naval, and that took no account of French cruising warships or privateers in search of prizes.

'Wake up, Captain.' The voice was soft yet insistent enough to penetrate a rather lubricious dream full of scantily dressed women and bring him to full wakefulness. 'There's something odd.'

Disturbed slumbers at sea went with the position of commander; while men could be left to con a ship set on an unchanging course, if anything untoward occurred, and very much so if danger threatened, only he could make the necessary decisions. The sleeper rolled up the cant of the deck and out of his boat cloak to look up into the ghostly face now inches from his nose, hoping that whatever was odd did not include the danger of a lee shore. As a man who knew his navigational limitations, Lieutenant John Pearce lived in dread of an error that would see his ship wrecked. Then he remembered that he had discussed the course they were sailing with his master, Matthew Dorling, who might be young but knew his stuff.

'What is odd?'

'Listen.'

All Pearce could hear was the groaning of the ship's timbers and it took a firm hand to get him upright so that he could allow such aural examination to extend further. The first slapping sound was unmistakable – the well-known thud of an object hitting a heavy body of water, and wherever it was coming from it was not the bows of the armed cutter. This reprised the fear of going aground, the second rhythmic slap doing nothing to bring about reassurance. Yet as it continued it carried with it none of the other sounds associated with waves cascading on a shore, no hissing of trapped water escaping over rocks. Then some timbers moved so seriously as to send a crack of strained wood out into the night and it was not off his own vessel.

'A ship?' Pearce hissed.

'Reckon,' came the soft reply.

Peering outwards Pearce looked for any glint of light, only to conclude there was none.

'Holy Christ, it could be a ghost ship.'

That whisper had an air of panic about it, reminding Pearce of just how superstitious was the average Jack tar, even if in this case it was no tyro but a leading hand.

The temptation to scoff was high – the man in command of HMS *Larcher* did not believe in spectral spirits – yet it seemed inappropriate in the circumstances so instead a firm hand was applied to a barely visible shoulder to induce calm.

'Steady now, man. I will take the wheel. Go below and rouse out the crew, but quietly. No bells, no drums and make sure they are silent as they ascend to the deck.'

'Aye, aye, sir.'

No sooner had Pearce got his hand on the spokes, having released the leather strap by which it had been secured, than the rocket went up, seeming to rise from nowhere, a red streak of flame shooting skywards to form a starburst as it exploded, that accompanied by the flash of a signal gun, he thought somewhere to windward. What followed was both astounding and alarming as all around the armed cutter great stern lanterns began to be lit over a vast expanse of sea, not in single figures, not even by the dozen, but to Pearce's vivid imagination by the hundreds, each one illuminating a small patch of deck on those he was close to, showing a sliver of white and phosphorescent wake, as well as the lower sails of what constituted an armada.

'Mother of Christ, if we're not in the middle of a fleet.'

Given the darkness of a moonless and starless night, it was like being placed in a candlelit galaxy, and if they were moving at a snail's pace, Pearce quickly realised the ships all around them were very obviously on an opposite course to his own. Even in the dark he knew the voice of the man who had uttered that curse to be his friend Michael O'Hagan; there was no mistaking that deep Irish brogue and the religious nature of his blasphemy. He also sensed that the required warrants had taken up their places beside him, which proved to be so when each one named their task so he would know they were present.

That was followed by silence as Pearce contemplated the dilemma in which they were trapped; given their location there was no way this fleet of vessels was friendly, but against that, from what he could see – and granted that was limited – they were not warships. They looked to be, certainly by the shape of their transoms and bluff bows, too squat for fighting, more in the line of merchant vessels, which in turn led to the deduction that this was a French commercial convoy, with the qualification that one of such dimensions must have an armed escort and very likely a potent one.

'Mr Dorling, we need find a reasonable patch of sea in which to come about, but very quietly. Can the hands do what is necessary without any calling out or shouted orders?'

'I would say yes to that, sir.'

The tone of voice in that reply was worthy of examination; much as he had come to like the crew of HMS *Larcher* and as much as he had seen their competence when sent about any particular duty, he still had areas of ignorance. It was as well to take into consideration that he was not their titular captain, but merely in temporary command from the mission upon which they had been so recently engaged. Dorling had sounded very assured and really there was no choice but to go with his judgement.

'Please relay the necessary orders, then come back to

inform me when all is in place. Also tell our passenger below on no account is he to come on deck. Gunner?'

'Capt'n.'

'Mr Kempshall, as soon as we are come about and have settled on a new course I want the flintlocks in place, the guns run out and loaded on both sides, bow chasers too, then hauled back in and left behind closed gun ports, but slowly and with minimal noise.'

There was a silence then, as the gunner contemplated the ramifications of that, for a trundling gun could be noisy and then there was the damage they could do. Fired at closed ports, which they could be in a panic, would cause serious damage to the woodwork and, in the dark, who knew where the splinters from such an act would go; they could easy kill or maim the crew and anyone else. Pearce misunderstood that long pause and remarked on what he thought was troubling the man.

'Difficult as it is, Mr Kempshall, I would rather have to worm them later than seek to load in an emergency.'

'Weren't that, your honour; I was thinkin' of the work I'd give my carpenter brother. I'll set my mates and the gun captains to work and get below and start preparing charges, sir.'

'Make it so. Michael, get the muskets out and loaded and every weapon we have available by the guns.'

'Jesus, we can't fight this lot.'

'They are merchantmen, Michael, and they will not fight, but if any of their escorts come snooping, then I must seek to use what little gunnery we have to get away. The best way to achieve that is to give them something else to think about, so when you have seen to the swords and tomahawks I want you working on some strong combustibles that we can sling at another ship.'

'A vessel ablaze will keep them busy, happen?'

That made Pearce smile in the dark; he had not been sure Michael would smoke his aim. He was about to say so when he realised the Irishman was gone. All around him men were doing likewise, going about their duties, and it was a testament to the efficiency of the Royal Navy and the massive amount of sea time the fleet enjoyed that they could do so without being able to see anything, albeit such actions were usually carried out with a great deal of noise. Not now; they were appreciative of the danger they were in, could see just as he could the myriad number of lights all around the ship, so the shrouds were climbed by touch; likewise, the way the men eased their bare feet into the foot-ropes and made their way along the yards was done in silence, and if they did call to each other it was in voices so low as to not even carry to the deck.

Somewhere forward and amidships Dorling was peering skywards, trying to see by the odd white flash of a bare foot that the hands were in the required places, sure that, on deck, those allotted to pull on the falls were standing by to release them from their cleats, prepared to haul hard and swing round the yards before sheeting them home once the cutter, aided by the hard-over rudder, was on a reverse course. On the wheel, Pearce would also take his cue from the master, a man so much more competent in the art of sailing than he.

The actual turn was far from noiseless, for with so many men employed in physical tasks such a thing was impossible. All Pearce could hope for was that the odd call or curse, the sound of ropes whirring through blocks or the creak of a swinging yard would not carry to the other vessels around them, and if it did, they would have few men alert at this time of night aboard a merchant vessel to hear them. Even if they were attuned to the danger of an enemy, they must surely feel safe in the cocoon of their armada. Added to that was the constant sound of their own timbers, which would be creaking and groaning as all wooden and rope-rigged vessels do.

Pearce sensed a presence. 'You with me, Michael?'

'I am.'

'Sneak into the cabin and find the flag locker – there's a tricolour in there. Don't unshade the lantern until the door is shut.'

'And if I wake the lady, who might need some comfort?'

'Tell her to stay off the deck,' Pearce snapped, for he could discern the trace of humour in his friend's tone.

There was no setting of a course; Pearce steered to keep an equal distance between two of the nearest vessels, only troubled by a series of flaring rockets and booming signal guns that were clearly imparting some message of which he had no knowledge, these briefly and partially illuminating the seascape, luckily not close by. That did tell him the escorts, who would seek to control the convoy movements, were way off to windward, a position from which they could protect their charges from interdiction, the added advantage being that should a threat emerge from another quarter, they had the wind with which to deal with it.

Time lost all meaning, which gave him a period to think, and once he recalled his previous course and where he had set out from the day before it seemed to suggest this fleet was heading for the mouth of the Loire, which would take them up to the main French commercial port of Nantes. The other thought which occurred was that such an event was of some importance. Given the overwhelming superiority in numbers that the Royal Navy could deploy across the oceans, this sort of convoy should, in theory, be impossible to assemble and even harder to escort to home soil. Given the size, it must have some bearing on the ability of Revolutionary France to continue the war, especially since he had been informed by one of the male passengers that the nation was in the grip of famine, not that he had entirely believed a man with an agenda of his own to pursue.

'The escorts will form an outer screen,' Pearce said, really thinking aloud as he included Michael O'Hagan in his ruminations. 'Something this size, I should think they are numerous, mostly with the weather gage to give them control, but I should not be surprised if there are warships bringing up the rear to scare off our cruisers.'

'Seems to me they might be the ones to give us worry, right enough.'

Pearce nodded, unsure if it could be observed. He asked Michael to fetch Dorling and, after a talk about their previous course and their likely location now, was obliged to conclude that the merchant convoy expected to make landfall early in the morning, possibly at first light. If their navigation was good then it would be the Loire estuary, but even slightly off it would be simple to correct and begin the next stage of the operation, which was to send the ships, one by one, upriver to the port of Nantes as and when the tide permitted.

'Which means we must not be in the same position then as we relatively are now.'

'Soon as it's light, sir, we will be spotted, and for my money that – a strange ship right in the middle of this lot – would bring someone to have a look-see.'

'Can't fault that.'

Looking out into the darkness as he contemplated Dorling's opinion, Pearce was suddenly aware that even in the pitch dark one of the nearby merchantmen had fallen off its course and was being brought closer to them by the leeway forced upon it by the current. Those lower sails, which had been ghostly, now had a more defined shape, there was no sign of a wake, while the stern lantern was no more than a glow hidden by the bulk of the vessel. Unsure if it was imagination or vision, he thought there was a bowsprit too close for comfort and possibly heading for his shrouds. Spinning the wheel he let the head of HMS *Larcher* fall away and spoke as soon as that had an effect.

'Take the wheel,' he hissed to Dorling, making for the side as soon as the exchange was complete, hands cupped to his mouth and about to yell. For a split second he held his tongue, as it came to him that to call out in English was unwise, so he did so in French, demanding to know what the *sal cochon* was playing at. That his words had an effect was obvious; someone on the merchantman's wheel was hauling hard on the rudder, this evidenced by the way the light from that lantern altered that which it was illuminating. Pearce, leaning over the side, was certain that if he reached out he could touch the bowsprit rigging of the other ship; he could certainly hear the noise of the bow itself breasting into the swell, the slapping sound loud in his ears. Then a voice called back.

'What in the name of Jesus does that mean?'

English, and with it an accent of some kind? Pearce decided to stick to French and informed the man on the other deck that he had nearly run them down.

The response was querulous. 'Have you got anyone aboard who speaks a proper language, you Gallic booby? And might I enquire, if you do, what in the name of creation you are doing sailing in the middle of this damn convoy with no light showing?'

'I speek a leetle English,' Pearce replied.

'Then get some lights aloft if you don't want to be run down, monsure.'

It was the last word that nailed the speaker as a Jonathan. What was an American doing in a ship off the coast of France?

'I pilot,' Pearce replied, wondering if that would make sense; no ship in this convoy would risk the Loire sandbanks without one.

'Well, monsure, you're not much of one, I'd say, but if you want all this goddamn grain and barley we have fetched over three thousand miles of ocean, you better have a care where you lay a course.'

'Grain and barley?' called Pearce, too surprised to think.

'Thousands of tons of it, friend, enough to feed the whole of France for a year and some left over.'

While they had been talking the voice had been fading

slightly, evidence that the merchant vessel was resuming a proper course, this while Pearce was trying and failing to calculate the kind of total cargo being borne by what ships he knew to be around him. Without another thought he raised himself up on to the bulwarks, then half climbed the lower shrouds and began to try and count the lanterns he could see, lit because the convoy was close to shore and clearly in no danger in the opinion of the man in charge of the escorts.

'Michael,' Pearce said, when he had jumped down and made his way back to the wheel. 'Have you got out that tricolour?'

'I have.'

'Then get it bent on and our ensign down and out of sight. Mr Dorling, we need to change course once more and get back on to the original heading. I do not want to be enclosed by this lot when the sky gets light.' That was followed by a sigh. 'And if you are a praying man, beg for a bit of a decent wind and from the right quarter.'

That manoeuvre was carried out with more noise than previously; clearly his crew had heard the exchange and thought they had little to fear from an armada of Jonathans, indeed there were one or two willing to suggest that they press a few into the King's Navy, given the high chance that many of them were deserters over the years and from that same body. Once on a new course and cursing the lack of that wind, Pearce steered by the light of those lanterns, sailing in line ahead, keeping HMS *Larcher*'s head equidistant between them. Being summertime the dawn came too early and they had not got clear by the time he could apply the standard naval test and see a grey goose at a quarter-mile. What he could see, off the stern of the last convoy vessels, was a pair of frigates beating to and fro, while to windward there were visible the higher topmasts of a pair of ships of the line.

That he was not immediately spotted was, no doubt, due to their concentration being to seawards, the area from where danger could threaten. It would take time, perhaps more than a day, to feed those merchant ships even into such a wide estuary. The rest, stationary and waiting their turn, would be exceedingly vulnerable to anything coming in from the wide Atlantic like a squadron of British warships, which would certainly save him and *Larcher*. Such a thing was too much to hope for: all he had was that tricolour and the hope that being a small warship sailing along with closed gun ports, he would be seen as no threat.

It was a risk to sail close to one of those frigates, to seek to convey an expression of unconcern, which he added to by raising his hat, too far off to be seen to be British, wise that such an action was not taken too far; he did not want to get within anything like hailing range. Sam Kempshall, as ordered, had loaded the signal gun and in time-honoured fashion Pearce ordered that the distant flagship should be saluted, an act that received a reply in what was, on both ships, a total waste of powder.

'Time to worm those cannon, Mr Kempshall, but I would beg you leave one of the chasers loaded.'

That took time – worming guns to get out the ball and the charges was a slow process, a period in which, even in light airs, the gap opened up substantially until any visible French warship was no more than hull upon the horizon. When all was ready John Pearce called for the ship to heave to and presented to his enemies a broadside view.

'Michael, put back out the ensign, if you please.'

The proper flag was bent onto the halyards and as it raced aloft and the tricolour came down, the temporary captain of HMS *Larcher* hauled on the lanyard that fired the flints of the three-pounder cannon. That he wasted a ball – it landed harmlessly in the sea – was of little consequence. The purpose was to alert those Frenchmen to what was happening, to let them see, as they trained their telescopes on what had taken their attention – the noise of a cannon fired and the billowing smoke that produced – that the vessel which had sailed so serenely past was one they would have done well to intercept. The nature of that convoy and what it might contain would soon be known in London.

'Your guests are desirous of being allowed the deck, Captain.'

'Make it so, Mr Dorling, and set us on a course for home.'

'Aye, aye, sir.'

CHAPTER TWO

Jahleel Tolland had not endeared himself to the hard-working folk at Buckler's Hard, but then, being a fellow of rough manner and impatient with it, he was not much given to being pleasant to any living soul; to his way of thinking these New Forest folk were too close-mouthed for their own good and a whip would not go amiss to get them to mind their manners and have them respond to his enquiries. Franklin Tolland had been found to be easier to deal with; indeed it was he who had elicited the replies to the questions the pair had come to ask.

Even if they had been previously supplied with information and from an unimpeachable source, such was the endemic mistrust of the Tolland brothers they needed to be certain of the facts. Yes, the armed cutter, HMS *Larcher*, had set out from Buckler's Hard a week past and was expected to return to the River Beaulieu in short order, though only providence knew when. And yes, the man in command was a lieutenant who went by the name Pearce, though they could not swear to his given name being John, for he had bedded down elsewhere and had not spent, if you added it all up, much more than an hour or two ashore in the vicinity.

To that was added a physical description, confirmation that the Tollands were in the proper place to lay by the heels the man they sought, and that had allowed them to mount their horses and return up the road to the town of Lyndhurst, where they had left the rest of their gang, each of whom, it was decided, would take it in daily turns to ride down to a point that overlooked the estuary of the River Beaulieu to catch the return of the ship.

To stay in Buckler's Hard itself was difficult given the lack of accommodation in what was no more than a maritime shipyard inhabited by those involved in construction, impossible without they arouse suspicion as to their motives for being in a place few visited. The Tolland name would likely not be known to anyone locally but that could never be certain, and when you lived outside the law, as these smugglers did, it was best to never take a chance on it being recognised.

'This Pearce bugger could be gone half a year,' opined one of the band, a near-toothless and bent-nosed ruffian called Cole, this after four days of waiting, during one of which the rain had come down in buckets to depress any high spirits with which they had come to the place.

'Never,' Franklin Tolland replied. 'We have it on good authority that he would be gone two weeks at best an' it could be less.'

'Weeks in which,' Cole hissed through his gums, 'we would see not a coin turned.'

'Stow it,' Jahleel growled. 'When did you ever earn a crust that me and my brother did not provide?'

'All I is saying, Jahleel, is that we are men of the sea wereselves.'

'So?'

'So we knows she is fickle, mate, an' if what you say is true, this Pearce feller is set to go ashore over the water and that be hostile, so he might get himself killed. Besides that, goin' there an' comin' back won't be easy on a sea crawlin' wi' French ships of war. We could be here till doomsday.'

Jahleel Tolland looked round the tavern table and assembled faces to see if there was general agreement with Cole, hard to discern with few of the others present prepared to catch his eye; to a man they were in fear of him which was just the way he liked it.

'Has you lost all recollect of what that bastard did? He stole our ship and our cargo from under our noses and damn near put us in the workhouse.' A gnarled hand slammed down on the bare wood of the tabletop. 'An' that's an act for which he has to pay and pay high. I want to see his bleached bones after he's told us what we need to know.'

'You mean to slit his gizzard?' asked one of the gang quietly.

'After he's told us where to find the rest of his gang and I've made him scream for death in place of what I will do to his carcass.' Jahleel Tolland produced a large knife and began to carve out marks on the tabletop.

'Happen I'll leave my name on him, afore I get to his throat.'

'It might be a bad idea to do him in, brother.'

Jahleel looked at Franklin, making a point of aiming his gaze at the red and far from fully healed scar on his younger brother's cheek, the result of a sword swipe given to him by the very same John Pearce. If the older brother was scarlet of face and, with his pockmarked cheeks, both intemperate and unprepossessing, Franklin was the opposite. He had always been a ladies' man, a comely-looking cove and proud of it, to which he added the manners of speech and behaviour of what he considered himself to be, a gentleman. Now, none would look at him, male nor female, without first seeing the scar, which would class him as villainous.

'And you with that face?'

'We don't want the law on our tail.'

'Christ, we live outside the law.'

'Smuggling is one thing, Jahleel, murder another.'

'You goin' soft, Franklin, for I don't recall you bein' shy of killing afore?'

Grunts of agreement greeted that comment; in a game where trust was unknown and acts of thieving and disloyalty common, Franklin Tolland had been as swift as the rest of the crew to take the life of anyone light-fingered, twice as much so when it was a sneak or a turncoat willing to dob them in to the excise for a cash reward.

'Never, but if we do in one of our own kind in the act of shipping contraband, who's to give a care? This Pearce might be as much of a scoundrel as any in our game but he is King's Navy too and that might get us a whole heap of trouble. They look after their own and the last thing we want is Jack tar seeking vengeance when we get back to our proper trade. We want them to pay us no heed so we can come and go without fuss.'

'Then it has to be out of sight,' Cole wheezed. 'Happen we let him land, an' take him when no soul is about. Plenty ground and soft round here to bury him in once you'se got what you want, then it be a mystery.'

'Never,' Jahleel spat. 'That sod has slipped me four times now, so he's getting taken up as soon as his feet touch soil.'

The door swung open and the eighth member of the gang bustled in. He had been doing his duty on the seashore by the hamlet of Lepe, which overlooked the deep-water approach to the winding River Beaulieu.

'I think I sighted that cutter bearing up for the river.'

'You sure?' Franklin demanded.

'Christ no, couldn't see her transom even if she does bear a name, but she has a naval pennant, the right lines and has two bow chasers and four six-gun ports a side, which fits what I was told to watch for.'

'Tide?'

'On the rise, and she was getting her sweeps out, given the wind don't favour her.'

Jahleel was already on his feet, his face even redder than normal with rising passion. 'Get the horses saddled up, all of you. I want us to be well hidden afore he makes the final bend.'

That accomplished, they gathered outside and mounted up, being just about to set off and take the road south when a shay came hurtling down the street, drawn by a single sweating horse. Sat under the canopy and being free with his long whip was an elderly fellow in the heavily braided uniform of a rear admiral, and if Jahleel Tolland had a high colour on his face he was well outdone by the sailor, who seemed able to match him in passion too.

'Stand aside there, damn you to hell!' the admiral cried, his protruding eyes raking the assembled horsemen who threatened to impede his progress. 'I am on the King's business.'

'You'll be on a funeral slab, you old bugger,' Jahleel shouted after him, having been obliged to haul hard on his reins to get his mount out of the way, while the shay had gone through a deep puddle left over from the heavy day's rain, an act which threw up a spray of mud-filled water.

'Quiet,' Franklin called, waving a hand to cool his brother's passion, a sideways glance showing that the good citizens of Lyndhurst had stopped to stare. What followed was a quiet hiss. 'We don't want our faces remarked upon.'

'Too late for you, Franklin, so let's get going and sort out that bastard who marked you for life.'

Pearce, standing on the tiny quarterdeck of the armed cutter, realised that the positive mood in which he had allowed himself to wallow since clearing that grain convoy was fast evaporating and that had nothing to do with matters nautical. Perhaps it was to do with the weather, for after a day of heavy rain in which he had required his oilskins it had turned sunny, which in itself seemed to mock his previous sanguine mood. Reality came home to roost as HMS *Larcher* sailed past the mouth of the Lymington, a river that took its name from the port to which it led. More tellingly, for his happiness as well as his future, Emily Barclay was there, waiting for him to return and this had forced him to revisit an unpalatable truth – to wonder how the person he loved would react to him arriving back from this short voyage bearing, as a passenger, a woman who had previously been his mistress?

Emily was somewhat prudish in an English county way. This had everything to do with her stable, parochial and provincial upbringing, which so contrasted with his own life of endless wandering in the company of his combative father, none more so than the formative years he had spent in Paris in the immediate aftermath of the French Revolution. The city, eighteen months after the fall of the monarchy, had been exciting and vibrant then, full of optimism, an air of adventure, gossip, the discussion of radical ideas and of course, beautiful women.

Coming of age there, tall and slim, with a handsome, unblemished countenance, John Pearce had caught a come-hither look in more than one female eye. With the exuberance of youth and eager for experience he had taken full advantage of what was very obviously on offer, finally settling into a more serious liaison with Amélie Labordière, this with the full cognisance of her understanding husband; a rich man and no hypocrite, he had his own pleasures to pursue.

Emily had experienced nothing of that nature: from her parental home she had gone on to be trapped in a loveless marriage to the odious Captain Ralph Barclay, a husband seventeen years her senior and a man Pearce saw as his mortal enemy. This was an encumbrance from which he was in the process of rescuing her, a task that had been fraught with many complications, not least Emily's own disinclination to acknowledge their mutual attraction or to succumb to his advances.

Circumstances had favoured his suit, though she had only become his lover in the few days before his departure and he knew such a position left her, even if she sought to hide it, with a residue of deep Anglican guilt. He suspected she would not readily take to the unexpected presence of the aristocratic and Catholic Amélie, while he also assumed that any attempt by him to explain it away as pure coincidence stood a very strong chance of being treated as so much stuff.

Yet it was nothing more than happenstance; he had been charged by the Government to undertake a mission to the Vendée to assess the state of the revolt there – was it worth supporting or should it be left to wither? He had come across Amélie in the company of those who were fighting the Revolution on behalf of their region, their religion and their monarchy, the latter two concepts ones to which John Pearce could only take exception. Nor could his undertaking be said to be a success, this exemplified by the other person he was fetching back to England.

In the few days the *Comte* de Puisaye had been aboard, and for some days prior to that, the man had become a sore trial to John Pearce and he was now wondering if keeping him below when they were in some danger – in the same way he had confined Amélie to his cabin – had as much to do with the man's insufferable nature as a need to ensure that any interference he might produce could have a negative effect. He had been raised by an extremely radical father to see the world as an inequitable place in need of change, where the fortunate few had an excess of money and land while many lived in poverty, where the twin pillars of the Church and the Crown ensured nothing was allowed to disturb the status quo. Good manners had obliged Pearce, many times, to bite his tongue.

Puisaye was an unreconstructed aristocrat whose sole wish was that life should return to that which it had been before the fall of King Louis. The *comte* could neither see nor accept that the world had changed, nor could he or his ilk seem to accept that they bore a great deal of the responsibility for what had befallen their class. If the guillotine was barbaric in the frequency with which it was now being employed, if the terror sweeping France was indiscriminate in whom it killed, the men who had occupied positions of power under the monarchy, by their indifference to the plight of the mass of their fellow countrymen, only had themselves to blame.

The count was likewise convinced that he and his fellow rebels in the Vendée held the key to the defeat of both the Jacobin Terror and the Revolution. All they required was that Albion support them with a massive injection of naval assets – warships of every size, regiments of infantry and batteries of artillery – plus several tons of gold to pay for their return to power. Given such aid they were convinced they could advance from their coastal swamps to overcome the forces sent from Paris to defeat them. From what John Pearce had observed they were living in cloud cuckoo land.

Puisaye was less of a pressing personal concern than Amélie Labordière; the fellow could be passed on to William Pitt and Henry Dundas to be dealt with, and those two politicos as well as the government they led were welcome to him. Less cheering was that Amélie, in the few conversations he had allowed himself with her – any hint of intimacy had to be avoided – had made it plain that she too held the same opinions as Puisaye, which left him to wonder how his discomfort at her stated views had never surfaced during the months they had been lovers. The answer was, of course, obvious: ardent youthful lust and carnal engagement took precedence over any concern for politics of any hue. John Pearce was too busy enjoying himself, added to that the fact that he had been far from wholly convinced of his father's opinions then and he still questioned some of the more outré notions now, not least the innate goodness of the human race.

Such thoughts recalled his last visit to Paris, a city much changed from that which he had enjoyed in the company of Amélie, and that dragged up, in turn, the memory of the last contact he had enjoyed with a parent known throughout England and Scotland as the Edinburgh Ranter. This soubriquet had been given him for his years of radical stump speeches and pamphleteering, all denouncing the privileges enjoyed by the monarchy, the Church, the aristocracy and the greedy mercantile class.

Adam Pearce had been hated by these pillars of the British Government for the way he stirred up discontent and sometimes even riot; a marginal nuisance for most of his life, all that had changed with the fall of the Bastille and the revolution that swept France. Suddenly his activities and growing fame – he called for a similar overthrow in his homeland and the notion was welcomed by many – presaged a potent threat, so much so that Adam and his son had been imprisoned for a short spell in the Fleet. Set free Adam had not kept silent; he had taken up his cause again only to be forced to flee to France from a King's Bench warrant for sedition, a crime which could be punished by hanging.

Initially welcomed in Paris as a famed supporter of republicanism, as well as a victim of reactionary justice, Adam Pearce had been feted and admired by the men then in power. But both that power and his welcome had begun to pall over each month; never one to hold back on what he saw as morally right, John's father found that the people who had taken over the revolutionary government had no more love of his honesty than the ministers of King George; in a city increasingly febrile, that was dangerous; there were no warrants in France, just arbitrary and revolutionary justice.

John Pearce had returned to England to plead for that King's Bench warrant to be set aside only to find himself being pursued by men intent on serving it and clapping him in gaol. On a cold winter night he had taken refuge in a crowded tavern hard by the River Thames, in a part of the city called the Liberties of the Savoy, much used by men avoiding the long arm of the law. Called The Pelican, it proved to be a poor choice in terms of safety; he had been illegally press-ganged into the King's Navy by none other than Emily's husband, Captain Ralph Barclay of the frigate HMS *Brilliant*.

As much good fortune as bad had attended his service since that night: he had been cast ashore and nearly drowned in a cutting-out expedition, got he and his companions back to safety and obliged Ralph Barclay to release him and them from the navy only to be pressed for a second time on the way home. The commander of his new vessel had promoted him as a way to stifle a troublemaker; he had then found himself obliged to take command of the vessel in the first successful naval action of the war and was hailed for that as a hero, which resulted in Pearce being given his present rank by order of King George.

In the interim, in Paris, matters had gone from bad to worse for his father. The party of the Girondins, who took control of the Government, cooled towards him and sought to still his criticisms by disapproval. The Jacobins, who overthrew the Girondins and sent their political enemies to the guillotine, imprisoned Adam Pearce to silence him completely. Appraised of this his son hastened to rescue him, finding him too ill to give any attempt a chance of success. Knowing he was near to death, Adam substituted himself in place of another prisoner, a fact his son discovered too late; he was already in the tumbrel and on his way to the place of execution by then. John Pearce failed in the race to seek to save him, instead witnessing a decapitation by that same infernal device which had lopped off the heads of so many before him, accompanied by the screams of a bloodthirsty revolutionary mob.

Duty came along to chase away such gloomy

recollections, for over the prow lay the sandbanks that protected the entrance to the River Beaulieu and those he examined carefully. He must take cognisance of the state of the tide, for he would need it to be rising or at flood to take him, on a north-westerly breeze, up to his anchorage at Buckler's Hard on what was a tidal waterway. Once there he would quit the ship and his temporary appointment. That brought its own feelings of regret; if he did not have much love for the navy, he had enjoyed being in command of the young men who manned this vessel.

As he looked along the deck at the hands that had been called up to their duty, he hoped they too had appreciated his being there, at least the majority, for the man he had replaced and who would return was a tyrant. There amongst them, chatting easily and causing the occasional ripple of laughter, was his good friend Michael who, if he came across as the jolly Irish giant, was a proper handful sober and could be fierce when inebriated.

On their first ever encounter, the same night when both had been taken up in the Pelican Tavern, Michael had been near blind drunk. Pearce had been obliged to duck a haymaker that, from such massive fists as the Irishman possessed, would have removed his head. Much water had flowed since that day when they and many others had been the victims of the press gang. For a small group, stuck together as messmates, the name of that tavern had given them their own soubriquet: they called themselves the Pelicans. Even if he was not truly a friend then, nor the cause of their subsequent troubles, John Pearce could not avoid feeling responsible for what had become of them since that night: old Abel Scrivens had perished in his place; Ben Walker was now a slave to the Musselmen, if he was not expired too.

For them he could do nothing, but his primary task once ashore, Emily Barclay and potential complications notwithstanding, was to get out from under the thumb of Ralph Barclay the two remaining Pelicans, Charlie Taverner and Rufus Dommet, with whom he and Michael had been press-ganged. First he must bear up for the river entrance and, given he still held himself to be short on experience, being a naval lieutenant by good fortune rather than long experience, Pearce thought carefully before issuing the necessary orders.

'Mister Dorling,' he called, 'prepare to shorten sail and, I think, given the wind is not favourable, we will need to employ sweeps to progress upriver.'

'We could warp her up with boats, sir.'

'No' Pearce replied with a smile, before taking off his blue coat. 'That would burden a few men. With sweeps we will all share the task, myself included.'

'Monsieur!' the *Comte* de Puisaye exclaimed when, minutes later, he saw John Pearce grab the end of a sweep. 'This is undignified for an officer.'

'Dignity be damned,' came the reply, in English, which made the crew chuckle.

CHAPTER THREE

Emily Barclay was sat on a stool, by a stream and under a wide-brimmed straw hat, at a place the Lymington locals called Batchley Copse. She had a brush in her hand, pigments on a trestle by her side, while behind her sat an elderly fellow, there to instruct her on the finer points of watercolour painting as she tried to capture the midsummer sunlight dappling on the water. Apart from walks and a nightly visit to Lymington harbour – there was some hope that John Pearce would come to anchor there rather than Buckler's Hard – this was part of her daily routine, clement weather permitting, which it had been most days, though the ground was still damp from when it had poured.

Concentrating, the image she was trying to get on canvas took her mind off a sea of troubles that seemed to grow in difficulty the more she gnawed on them, not least what kind of future she could expect with the man who had so recently become her lover. It was true that when her thoughts did turn to John Pearce and what they had enjoyed together, worries gave way to fond recall as well as a trace of a blush, for he had shown her what pleasure two people could enjoy when happily coupled.

But that did not last; such memories inevitably took her back to the previous experience of the same acts with her husband and they had been anything but pleasurable, having ranged from painful, through mind-numbing to, on one occasion, an act of downright brutality bordering on rape. This had shown her clearly that far from marrying a man of some stature and refinement she had become attached to a beast rather than a gentleman, and Ralph Barclay had become someone from whom she was determined to permanently separate.

As an act it had proved easy, she simply found somewhere to reside apart – but as a condition of living it was far from that. Emily knew only too well the world in which she lived and the mores of the society in which she had been raised: marriage was for life, a sacred trust, not something to be taken up and discarded on a whim. John Pearce might say and truly believe that society could go to damnation but it was not his reputation that would be shredded. Men were expected to be weak in the article of sexual temptation but no woman was allowed the same licence; to stray off the conjugal path was to be tarred as not much better than a whore.

It was impossible not to dwell on what their joint future might be and in truth that had barely been discussed, though they had the means to impose silence and acceptance on her husband. In their possession was a copy of the details of a court martial in which not only had

Ralph Barclay committed perjury, it provided evidence that he had induced or coerced others to lie as well, a document that could see him hanged. Now in command of a 74-gun ship of the line, he was presently at sea as part of the Channel Fleet and that was a position, his naval rank and responsibilities and his life notwithstanding, he would never let be put at risk; Ralph Barclay saw himself as defined by his rank as a senior post captain.

How foolish she had been at seventeen years of age, how easily she had allowed herself to be persuaded that a match to a man of such status was not to be missed. Only later had it occurred to Emily that the parental pressure, seemingly gentle but now perceived as persistent, had more to do with their comfort and happiness than her own. By marrying she had secured the continued possession of the home in which her mother and father lived and in which she had been raised, a dwelling entailed by inheritance to her soon-to-be husband. Had she refused him he might have taken his revenge on them by repossession, which would have seen the whole family on the streets.

'Might I suggest, Mrs Raynesford,' said her elderly instructor, 'that a deeper green be applied to show the more heavily shaded leaves.'

The use of that name made her jerk and move the brush too rapidly, smearing part of the work, for if Raynesford was her maiden name, it was not her wedded one. She turned her head away so he could not see any trace of her deep blush, for it was inclined to induce both shame and guilt; in a moment of indecision and under pressure that was the name by which John Pearce had booked them into the King's Head in Lymington as man and wife.

There was a sigh from behind her back. 'Perhaps another tree branch, even if you cannot observe one, will rescue the work, which has a degree of promise.'

'Yes,' Emily said, biting her lower lip as she sought to concentrate on what was before her eyes rather than behind them.

Ralph Barclay was sitting on the sunlit quarterdeck of the Third Rate, HMS *Semele*, the round-backed captain's chair lashed to ensure it stayed in place, watching as the crew worked hard to repair the battle damage she had so recently suffered. Underneath his uniform coat, left sleeve pinned to his chest because of his lack of an arm, he had been obliged to wear ducks instead of his normal breeches, making him feel improperly dressed. This was due to the wound in his thigh, sliced open by a musket ball in the encounter with the main French battle fleet, which had bled so copiously he had passed out. As a precaution against repetition, the leg was heavily bandaged.

Thus placed on his chair he was unable to see much of the rest of the Lord Howe's command as it sailed up the Channel towards Plymouth in the company of those French warships that had been taken as prizes. If the fleet was abuzz with talk of the victory, and it would be if it were anything like HMS *Semele*, then a large part of the conversation would be about prize money, that much favoured wardroom and 'tween-decks topic. Even the great cabin was not immune to speculation and Ralph Barclay could happily contemplate his own booty, for a great fleet victory brought reward not just in terms of glory but also in terms of wealth to the whole ship's company, the captain most of all.

That would dominate every waking thought now the dead had been committed to the deep, the wounded were under the care of the surgeon and the last vestige of loss, the auctioning of the possessions of the deceased, had been completed. Ralph Barclay had engaged in endless calculations of the various forms of payment in which he would be entitled to have a share, the hulls of the prizes of course being the most valuable. But there was the value of the stores they carried, as well as the rigging, the canvas, head money for the captured sailors, gun money for the weapons, both cannon and muskets – his only worry that those who decided such things would not properly take into account the sinking of the *Vengeur du Peuple*, the vessel with which he had been heavily engaged and the enemy that had inflicted the damage now being repaired.

A seventy-four like *Semele,* she could not have been crewed by much less than six hundred men, yet from what he could tally only just over half that number had been taken off alive. Beresford, third lieutenant at the start of the encounter, now, due to the expiry of the pair above him, the first, had recounted to a recumbent commanding officer what had happened after he passed out. It was plain that attempts at rescue had been hampered by the fact that many of the crew of the dismasted French warship had perished because, having broken into the spirit room, they had been drunk. That did not alter their worth; representations must be made in writing to ensure such men or their money value was not ignored just because they had drowned.

'Sir,' said Lieutenant Beresford, approaching his captain. 'The surgeon was wondering if you would be up to visiting the wounded. He is sure such a thing would lift their spirits.'

Spirits, Ralph Barclay thought, his face taking on a savage look; the only spirits those sods care about are the same ones that killed the Frogs aboard *Vengeur*. His next thought was that they were hardly likely to get any emotional lift from the sight of him either, for he was no soft-soul commander but a strict disciplinarian, a man who ran a taut ship and was as likely to flog a fellow as praise him. Yet it had to be, it was his duty.

Looking up at Beresford he saw how different the youngster appeared from the fellow he had been in his company prior to the contest, more sure of himself, and he could guess why. There would be promotions, especially for first lieutenants, even if they came to it by the death of their superiors. They would be entitled to become commanders and be given unrated ships, sloops and armed cutters of their own if they were lucky enough to have the influence to be granted a commission; even languishing on the beach that would mean prize money to spend, an increase in pay and a ready audience if they were called upon to regale their neighbours, not least the young daughters of the local gentry, with the story of the battle; many an advantageous match had been founded on less.

'I will require aid, Mr Beresford,' Barclay said, lifting his empty sleeve, 'for I am a one-winged bird.'

'Sir,' the lieutenant replied, embarrassed, for he had not contemplated the need.

'Add to which my wound—'

'Of course.'

'As you know, Devenow, the fellow I usually rely on, is one of those under the care of the surgeon.'

Beresford tried but failed to hide his distaste at the mention of that name; Devenow had acted as the captain's servant, a task to which he was wholly unsuited, which had raised questions of probity in the wardroom. He was a nasty bully and a man inclined to drink himself insensible, having threatened many of the crew to acquire their grog; what his captain was doing relying on such a creature escaped almost the entire crew.

'Perhaps we could ask Gherson?'

Ralph Barclay nearly spat out 'That dammed coward!' but he contained the temptation to abuse his clerk, for it would only diminish the man who chose to employ him, even if the accusation was palpably true. Gherson had tried to hide in the cable tier during the battle, needing to be hauled out by a midshipman and forced to stay in the place of danger; it was doubly galling that he had survived unscathed.

'I shall fetch a pair of hands to help you, sir.'

It was unfortunate that the two closest and barely occupied were Charlie Taverner and Rufus Dommet. Poor Beresford could not know that, if they were now volunteers, these men had once been press-ganged by his captain from a tavern set in a place where such acts were illegal. It took some time for Ralph Barclay to both look at and acknowledge them but when he did so his thoughts of prize money and what he could buy with it evaporated.

'Not that pair, damn you,' Ralph Barclay cried, for even if he was looking at them he was thinking of that scoundrel John Pearce, with whom they were associated under that stupid Pelican soubriquet of theirs. 'They would as like cast me down a companionway as help me.'

If Ralph Barclay had the right to fix the two men with a basilisk stare they did not have the freedom to respond in kind, for Charlie and Rufus were nought but common seamen, who lived at the mercy of such men as the ship's captain. Dismissed, without once ever matching his stare, they knuckled their foreheads and turned away as Beresford called forward two other souls to help the invalid.

'Chance gone begging there, Charlie,' hissed Rufus, his freckled face alight.

'Not half, mate,' came the whispered reply from Taverner. 'Nought would give me greater joy than to see that bastard take a tumble.'

'As long as it did for him it would be sweet.'

'Trouble is, Rufus, he knows who we are, an' that can't be to the good.'

'You sayin' he did not know we was aboard before?'

'Can't have done, Rufus, or I reckon we'd have stripes on our back by now.'

'Happen when we make port, Charlie, John Pearce will be waiting there to take us off.'

'Pray for it mate, for with Devenow and that bastard Gherson aboard as well, we've got three devil's on our tails, not just the one.'

In the great cabin, Cornelius Gherson was working on the endless logs required by the Admiralty and Navy

Board that gave evidence of the proper running of one of His Majesty's ships of war; every item of food, drink and stores consumed had to be listed and accounted for, while after a battle the repairs that required the use of canvas and rigging, ropes, pulleys and chains, as well as timber, nails, paint and even turpentine seemed to never end. This was a task for which he was well suited, though there was some sorrow that the various peculations he had carried out so far since HMS *Semele* had been commissioned would be required to be set aside.

The clerks who examined these logs had a fearsome and completely unjustified reputation for diligence; in truth they were as lax in the pursuance of their duties as any man who acted without too much supervision and was overpaid for their task, more interested in their privileges and the quality of their claret than their responsibilities. Most submitted logs got no more than a cursory examination, meaning that a certain amount could go missing without being spotted. A fleet action changed that and eagle eyes would scour the books for signs of sloppiness brought on by the euphoria of victory; those Admiralty clerks hated the notion that another might prosper.

Yet even as he added, subtracted and listed, Gherson's thoughts were on other problems, not least his relationship with Ralph Barclay; never entirely sound, it was now much diminished by his recent behaviour. Worse, over the horizon lay not just the coast of England but also the lies he had told to get him out of a tight spot. Tasked to get the copy of the court martial papers that would damn his employer, he had not only failed to even find them, he had assured Barclay that his mission had been successful and they had been destroyed by burning.

If he did not know where they were precisely, Gherson assumed they had to be in the possession of Emily Barclay and that presaged great trouble. That they could see his employer hanged if ever produced in a court of law was less of a consideration; Cornelius Gherson was only troubled by that thought in the sense that it would impede his own progress to where he wanted to be, clerk to an admiral either on a profitable station or in command of a fleet, a position from which could be extracted, by fair means or foul, a great deal of money. It might be time to seek another employer.

He had done well so far, going from press-ganged sailor at the outbreak of war to his present position, which he could hope to hold, given Barclay needed his skills to ensure he made the most of what could be procured by a little light peculation and the care of his investments. It was even better considering he had ended up at sea after an attempt at murder by chucking him off London Bridge, brought about by previous thefts as well as the seduction of the young wife of his then employer, the city nabob called Alderman Denby Carruthers.

He had survived the raging River Thames by dint of a strong hand on his shirt and ended up in the navy, obliged to mess alongside all those unfortunates taken from the Pelican Tavern. Still, for Gherson, in a life of continual ups and downs, its twin, good luck, had always followed misfortune, so he put aside matters of which time itself could only take care. He concentrated instead on ideas of how he could best extract personal profit from Ralph Barclay's sudden acquisition of increased wealth.

Alderman Denby Carruthers knew nothing about the construction of ships and was well aware that a devious seller would know how to use paint and putty to make look better some tub likely to leak through its timbers. No fool, he had engaged the services of an experienced old salt who was long past the age at which he desired to go to sea, a one-time ship's master who had sailed merchant vessels on the triangular passage all of his seaborne life. Not that he was in search of a true blue-water boat; the vessel he had been tasked to buy, specifications given to him by the Tolland brothers, required a shallow draught added to decently copious holds and it also needed to be dry and weatherly. No point in loading it with valuable contraband only to have it ruined by the seepage of seawater.

Even if he had never engaged in the illicit trade, Carruthers knew only too well that smuggling had ever been a profitable enterprise. That had only increased with a war going badly and that was doubly the case recently: the Duke of York had taken an army to Flanders, marched it to and fro only to begin to bring it home again, so he was now the butt of a wonderful ditty that had been composed on his return, a song that everyone was singing, much to the chagrin of his father, King George. Nor did it go down well at the Horse Guards building, the place from which the army was run.

Indeed he was humming 'The Grand Old Duke of

York' as he paced the deck, waiting for his old sailor to come up from the bilges where he had claimed the smell alone would tell him half of what he needed to know. The Tollands had said they did their trade out of Gravelines on the Flanders coast, now in the hands of the armies of Revolutionary France. His worry that such a force would impede the trade had been set aside; even Jacobins needed to trade for gold and the smugglers brought in that commodity while taking away the fruits of the luxury French trades. That they had lost their previous vessel he knew, if he was not aware of how; it mattered little – they were in need of financing and he had the funds to support them and that was all he would do. They would take the risks and between them they could share the rewards.

A very successful man of business he did not live a life without concerns, though none of that related to his business or his substantial wealth. His gremlins lay in the domestic sphere, for he now realised that it had been folly for a man of his age to marry a much younger bride, who had not only cuckolded him with the clerk he had once employed, but was now, he was certain, trying to make contact with the fellow again. That had him glaring at the River Thames, hard by which the vessel being examined was berthed, and it was as though that waterway had failed him. He had seen Cornelius Gherson, short of the fine clothing bought for him by Catherine Carruthers, his besotted paramour, chucked by two brawny helpers into the river at a point where the water flowed fast and deadly through the arches of London Bridge. How had the swine survived to come back and haunt him?

Then the second plan he had hatched to take care of

Gherson had failed and he could only console himself with the fact not every venture in which he had engaged returned a profit; that was the way of business. If anything, his scheme had added to his troubles by placing him in obligation to a low-life villain called Jonathan Codge, the man he had engaged to rid his world of Gherson; in fact he had sought to get shot of both of them in one fell swoop by dobbing them to the Bow Street Runners but somehow Codge had got out of that too, which left him having to buy the man off with a monthly stipend.

Still, matters were in hand to solve all his problems and if not fully formed they soon would be; if he was short on the kind of hard bargains who would see to his needs, he was fortunate to be related by marriage to a man who did know where to find them. Edward Druce, as a successful prize agent, knew the kind of men who made up the London press gangs and they fitted the bill when it came to muscle. Not only would he rid himself of Codge but also something had to be done about his wife Catherine.

He had forgiven her once, yet it would be folly to do so again – and then there was his new clerk: Gherson's replacement, Isaac Lavery, seemed to have taken her side. Dismissal would serve for him, plus the word put around that he was light-fingered; such an accusation would see him in the workhouse, for no one would employ him after a city alderman, a man destined one day to be mayor, had trashed his probity. Such thoughts evaporated, for his white-haired sailor was coming up from below and it was time for business; time to work out, if all was well, a price. That was where Alderman Denby Carruthers was at his happiest; the thought of driving a hard bargain, given the other meaning of the expression on which he had just been cogitating, made him laugh for the first time in days.

In the tangled web that had been created by an illegal act of pressing seamen from the Pelican Tavern there was one other person of consequence in the mix – even if he had not actually been present – and that was Emily Barclay's nephew, Midshipman Toby Burns. He, a weak character, had been coerced by his uncle into lying at a court martial set up to examine the accusation made by John Pearce and his fellow Pelicans, all four of them sent off on a mission to the Bay of Biscay along with anyone else privy to the truth of the matter, leaving depositions detailing the facts of the case of illegal impressment.

Toby Burns claimed in court to have been a member of the party who attacked the Pelicans when in fact he had been all the time aboard HMS *Brilliant*, berthed off Sheerness. His contribution to saving the skin of his uncle by marriage had been to take responsibility for getting the press gang ashore at the wrong part of the Thames riverside, which had provided enough leeway for a deliberately appointed and benign court to acquit.

If the act of committing perjury had been uncomfortable, then the price paid could hardly have been said to be better. Toby Burns now saw himself in the clutches of people determined to do him harm, not least the man who had chosen the officers to sit in judgement at that court martial off Toulon, the same man who made sure that the Pelican depositions went unrecorded. He was the senior officer who had issued orders that sent away the hostile witnesses, those very same Pelicans, as well as any member of *Brilliant*'s crew who could vouchsafe the truth.

Sir William Hotham was a well-connected and very political admiral; he was also the second in command of the Mediterranean Fleet and he had protected Ralph Barclay because he was a client officer, a man who could be trusted to offer support in Hotham's ongoing battle with his superior, Lord Hood. Toby's reward for his lies had been a posting to HMS *Britannia*, Hotham's flagship, where those who shared his rank saw him as much cosseted and granted opportunities to distinguish himself. The midshipman saw matters very differently: to his mind Hotham kept putting him in situations in which he stood a very high risk of being killed or maimed.

These last weeks had been even more uncomfortable as each day he reached into his sea chest to reread the letter that had arrived from London with the fleet's despatches. There, in plain ink, was the upshot of the whole affair, the intimation from a Grey's Inn lawyer, a fellow called Lucknor, that the truth of the whole court-martial charade, as well as his part in it, was known. If the missive did not actually say that – indeed it was couched in a spirit of cool enquiry and requested a response – even a brain as slow as Toby's own could, from the words used, extrapolate the true meaning.

It was nothing more than a threat to dish him, which, if it had merely meant dismissal from the navy he would welcome. But a few seemingly disinterested enquiries of his own as to the penalty for perjury had elicited the probable outcome – it was a hanging offence – information which made him run a hand round his throat and did nothing for his ability to sleep at night; his dreams were nightmares and awake in the dark it was even worse, the whole compounded by the fact that he had no one to confide in, not being gifted with anyone he could really call a friend.

Toby Burns could guess that the man at the centre of his troubles had to be John Pearce; the only other person who knew of his offence, apart from Hotham and Ralph Barclay, was his Aunt Emily and he could not believe that she would sacrifice him and disgrace the family in the process. Yet curse Pearce as he did and frequently, to do so provided no solution to his dilemma – what to say in reply to this Lucknor fellow.

The sight of HMS *Agamemnon*, refitted at Gibraltar and rejoining the fleet after weeks of absence, provided a possible solution. Dick Farmiloe, a fellow mid aboard HMS *Brilliant*, who had truly been at the Pelican Tavern and had been part of that illegal press gang, was serving with Captain Nelson as an acting lieutenant. Could he be asked for advice, given he was a culprit in the original offence and therefore at some risk himself?

The stiffening of those around him was a clear indication that Admiral Hotham had come on deck and Toby Burns likewise became erect while ensuring his hat was straight. Passed a telescope, Hotham raised it languidly to his eye and fixed the approaching sixty-four. If he admired her lines, and many did for she was the fastest ship of the line in the fleet, it was not that which brought forth the subsequent comment but the nature of the man who commanded her, a fellow whom the admiral despised.

'Prepare, gentlemen,' Hotham intoned to no one in particular, 'to be treated to yet another boring account of Captain Nelson's glittering destiny.' The pitch of his voice changed perceptibly, became abrasive. 'One day I look forward to putting the popinjay in his proper place, which for me would be a bumboat. Let him find a burial spot in Westminster Abbey from there, eh?'

Everyone laughed, even if few agreed; the younger men admired Horatio Nelson, as much if not more than the ship he was lucky enough to command. Yet it was the nature of the service that when an admiral made a remark of that kind, then it was politic to seem to be seen to concur. Toby Burns did laugh with true heart, for he approved of the sentiment.

CHAPTER FOUR

On arrival back at the King's Head, Emily Barclay was perplexed to see what appeared to be her trunk and valise outside the front entrance. The latter, a small case being near new and part of her trousseau, it was quite distinctive enough for there to be no mistake. So it was with a degree of deep curiosity that she thanked and dismissed her elderly limner-cum-instructor and watched him as he took off in his rickety single-horse hack, the easel she had used poking up from the rear.

Carrying the work she had done that day, a single canvas, Emily came out of the dipping sunshine into the cool and dark interior, her eyes slowly adjusting to the change of light making it difficult to discern the nature of the two men standing there. That soon eased, allowing her to see the owner of the inn, as well as his concerned face, but her gaze was quickly transferred to the furious and florid countenance of the other fellow. He was a short and rather fat naval officer, bewigged under his tricorn hat and an admiral by the gold frogging that heavily adorned his coat. Added to that, he had a horsewhip coiled in his hand and that was twitching in such a way as to be a matter of some concern.

'Madam!' he cried, lifting the whip and pointing it at her, his eyes sinking to take in the hem of a dress made muddy by traversing the still wet fields. 'Though I doubt the appellation to be the correct one, I demand to know who you are and under what pretext you dare to call yourself the wife of a naval officer, one, I might add, that does not exist.'

The shock of the accusation seemed to pass through her body like that she received when two rubbed pieces of cloth produced an unpleasant effect and even on some occasions a spark. With a tremulous voice she made the only demand she could think of.

'And who, sir, are you?'

'He is Admiral Sir Berkley Sumner,' the owner of the inn responded, wringing his hands and clearly worried. 'A person of consequence in the county.'

'That I am, just as I am here to expose you for what you are, as well as the lying scoundrel whom, I suspect, seeks to dun this poor innkeeper fellow out of his due. I will not use this horsewhip on a woman, God forbid I should stoop so low, but I have it in my hand to chastise the false Lieutenant Raynesford when he dares to appear, and I can tell you he will feel its weight up and down the entire High Street of the town. The reputation of the King's Navy demands it!'

Shocked as she was, Emily had been given those several seconds to think by the length of that tirade. The use of the Raynesford name and the accusation that it was false nailed at least part of the problem. If she knew her situation to be one of deep concern, she also knew that she had no choice but to go on the offensive, mixing truth with some very necessary lies.

'How dare you, sir!'

'What?' the admiral responded, his already ruddy face going puce as he seemed to fill his rotund body with air, in the production of a reply he was given no time to make.

'I am the wife of a serving naval officer, sir, and I expect to be treated with the courtesy that position carries.'

'There is no Lieutenant Raynesford,' the innkeeper said, 'and between you and the man who uses that name you have brought my humble tavern into disgrace. Your names were mentioned in the *Hampshire Chronicle* as being a respectable couple. Now the word is out you ain't and the town's abuzz with it.'

'I do believe my husband paid you a deal of money before he left, enough to cover his absence – enough, indeed, for over a month-long stay.'

'He did, but—'

'Then how can this old fool say he has set out to dun you when I have not been here that long?'

The horsewhip was loosened then, the leather tip falling to the floor. 'Old fool!'

'I cannot think you anything else, sir, since you did not enquire if my husband had put my staying behind here on a bill to be later settled or paid well in advance.'

'Bill be damned.'

'Mind your tongue, sir! I will have you know I am not

accustomed, nor will I tolerate even from my husband, such foul language in my presence.'

That again was true; she had checked Ralph Barclay any number of times when he transgressed and John Pearce had not escaped censure either, though he had laughed off her sense of decorum as if it was nonsense.

'Do not seek to divert me, madam. I contacted the Admiralty seeking to find out who this Raynesford was and the reply came back from the secretary himself that there was no one known to them of that name in the service. It therefore follows the man you call your husband is an impostor, which can have only one reason and if there is no criminality in his dealing with this fellow at my side, I am sure there is some somewhere, either now or in the future.'

'I must ask you to leave, Mrs . . .'

The confusion of the innkeeper's face, added to the continued wringing of his hands, infuriated Emily. The man had been happy enough to take their money without enquiry as to their true status and now he was bleating about his loss of face. No doubt, with the fat little red-faced admiral shouting his mouth off, the whole town was abuzz with the fact that the King's Head was home to a pair of adulterers, as if such a thing was uncommon, when such liaisons sustained half the inns in England. Yet that was a minor consideration: underlying everything was the precariousness of her position, for she had willingly given credence to that impression, willingly engaged in criminal conversation with John Pearce under a false name, and what would be the consequences of such an act? Somehow, in this place she must save face, or at least do enough to ensure her reputation until she could get away.

She had no idea when Pearce would return, so to stay in Lymington, possibly for days if not weeks, as the butt of gossip and finger pointing from the prurient locals, was anathema. However, Emily was not prepared to be tossed out into the street like some common trollop. She and Pearce had lied when they came to this place and for now it was imperative that falsehood be not only maintained but also reinforced, so she manufactured a most imperious tone.

'Nothing, my man, would convince me to stay in your hovel a day longer than I require, but since you have been paid for my accommodation and food you will oblige me by fetching back inside my valise as well as my trunk and, as there is no coach out of Lymington until morning, you will have to put up with my presence for one more night.'

Throughout these irate exchanges her mind had been working on another level, seeking a way to deflect her accuser and she dredged up one card to play that might see this Admiral Sumner off. She knew the nature of the mission that Pearce was carrying out on behalf of the Government, just as she knew it was one shrouded in secrecy, for if he had told her what he was setting out to discover he had also sworn her to keep the information to herself, as well as why.

William Pitt ran a government permanently on the cusp of being outvoted, indeed he depended on the support of his political opponents to stay in office and pursue the war. These were men who would not take kindly to anything smacking of a diversion from what they saw as the main effort and that was an expedition to the Caribbean to take the French sugar islands, this while many of the thinking classes in England harboured a deep suspicion of what was happening in the Vendée due to its openly Papist bent. Thus Pearce's mission had to be kept from scrutiny, the very reason it had been financed by funds hidden from parliamentary examination.

Fixing her countenance in a stern and reproving expression, she turned to Sumner and went on the attack. 'As to you, sir, I think it best you crawl back into whichever hole from which you have emerged, for you are in danger of being exposed as not only a fool but a danger to the nation.'

'What?'

'It did not occur to you to enquire where my husband is or what he is about?'

'Why would it?' Sumner sneered.

'It should have. Do not be surprised, sir, to receive from the Admiralty an admonishment for poking your flabby nose in to matters which do not concern you, for endangering the safety of the nation and for risking the life and reputation of a gallant officer held in high regard by those whose task it is to run the country and prosecute the war with France.'

'What stuff and nonsense is this?'

'I admit my married name is not Raynesford and nor is it that of my husband.'

'Ah-hah, the truth at last.'

It is, Emily thought, but not as you see it, though that allowed her to speak part of what she was saying with utter conviction.

'But you would have been better wondering why a naval officer would choose to employ subterfuge by using a false name rather than jumping to a conclusion that it indicated illegality. My husband is, as of this moment, at sea in command of a King's ship, sir, and I do not know that they are such fools at the Admiralty as to entrust a vessel to an impostor.'

'What ship, by damn?'

'I am not at liberty to tell you that and nor, if my husband were here, could he. Nor would he be able to enlighten you to the nature of the mission in which he is presently engaged, for that, sir, is a secret.'

For the first time Emily could see a crack in the admiral's certainty; if he did not yet look troubled, he looked perplexed.

'Secret?'

'Just that! It is also vital to the security of Britannia, so I suggest it would serve you to depart and put from your mind what it is you have been about, for not to do so could see you in the Tower. The least I can offer you is not to inform the Admiralty of your foolish actions, though I cannot guarantee that my husband, once he has been appraised of your interference in matters which are none of your concern, will not pass on to the powers that be the fact that you have threatened to destroy what it is they are trying to achieve. What the consequences of that will be I cannot tell you, but possible disgrace looms and it will certainly find no favour at the Admiralty.'

Emily could not know how those last few words played on the mind of Sir Berkley Sumner. He was, to those who had known him throughout his naval career, a prize dolt and, in terms of naval competence, a proper danger to those with whom he served. Having got to his captaincy through family connections rather than ability, from there he had, with age and seniority, though without a scintilla of sea time, risen to his admiral's rank. Never likely to be entrusted with a command, Sumner was destined to be and remain a 'yellow admiral', the soubriquet for an officer who might carry the rank but would never raise his flag at sea.

These were opinions of which he was unaware and did not share: Sumner reckoned himself as a genius both in the art of command at sea and the tactics required to achieve a great victory over his nation's enemies, sure that those now leading the fleets were inferior to him in all regards. Thus he bombarded the Admiralty with pleas for a position suited to the talents he held were his and lived in constant fury at the rebuffs he received, however politely they were couched. His face, now showing doubt, told Emily that she had struck home, that Sumner was wondering if he had inadvertently overreached himself.

'The Tower,' he said weakly.

'Perhaps not that, sir, but certainly censure. I decline to mention the fate of Admiral Byng.'

No word could have hit home harder to a vainglorious fool; Byng had been shot by firing squad on his own quarterdeck for his failures off Minorca. But there was the matter of dignity, not to say the need to cover what might prove to have been a mistake.

'Madam, I will not receive censure for doing my duty.'

'I was rather referring to your exceeding it, sir.'

Sumner pulled himself up to his full, if insubstantial

height and again used the horsewhip to point at Emily, jabbing it to make his purpose plain. 'I judge by your manner and facility of tongue that you are a lady of some intelligence. It may be you speak the truth. Have no doubt I will make enquiries regarding that—'

'Do so, Admiral Sumner,' Emily responded, cutting right across him again and forcing onto her face a knowing smile that did not lack a trace of pity; she did not feel as relaxed as she hoped she looked, for in her chest her heart was pounding, as it had been since she had come through the door. 'I see you as a man who cares not one jot for the peril to which he may expose himself and perhaps it will be seen as such. Then again, perhaps it will not. What a sad end it will be to a long and no doubt distinguished career, in the service of His Majesty.'

That got a meaningless grunt, but it also got him brushing past her and out into the street. Emily did not turn to see him go, she looked hard at the innkeeper.

'Be so good as to fetch my luggage and then, when you have done that, make sure that a place is booked for me on the morning coach. I shall, of course, eat in my rooms tonight, and as to payments made and reimbursement, I will leave my husband to deal with that on his return to England. Added to that you will observe the mud on the hem of my dress. I require that to be cleaned.'

The entirely made-up posture held until Emily was safe in her little parlour. Only then did the facade crack and tears begin to wet her pupils as she realised what a close call it had been. She had lied so convincingly and, looking around the rooms in which she and John Pearce had made love against all the laws of the land and holy matrimony, it made her wonder just how much the standards by which she had been raised had been eroded, which was not a comfortable state of mind.

The use of the long oars, even with the tide to help, ensured that progress was slow, so it was late afternoon before Buckler's Hard came into sight. HMS *Larcher* swept round the last bend in the river, a turn of ninety degrees that allowed the wind to play on what little sail Pearce had kept aloft and they assisted the forward movement. This relieved a weary crew to go about the duties required to get the armed cutter to a berth and obliged Pearce to put back on his heavy blue coat, for a boat had set off immediately they were sighted to lead them to the mid-river buoy to which they were to tie up.

There was little to see other than that for which the hamlet had been created by a long-dead Lord Montague; it was a site for shipbuilding set at the base of the New Forest, with enough water to float out empty hulls at high tide and an ample supply of suitable timber, long-matured oaks, near at hand from the forests planted eight hundred years before by William the Conqueror to facilitate his love of hunting. Boats had originally been built on the single hard that stood between two rows of red-brick cottages, these sitting at right angles to the River Beaulieu, literally rising from frame to hull outside the front doors of the resident workers, a practice that lapsed as vessels grew too large in size.

Now twin slipways rose out of the still waters, they containing the vessels presently under construction, one a sleek frigate, the other hull a much more bulky seventy-four. The cottages remained, the homes of the workers and their families, creating a charming aspect given the open ground between them. There were more than a dozen trades accommodated in those cottages and many more workers came in from the surrounding countryside; shipwrights, ironworkers, caulkers, the sawyers with their ten-foot serrated blades used to cut the great planks from solid oak trunks. There were coopers and smiths, plumbers and riggers, all the way down to labourers and oakum boys. Over the intervening distance came the sound of hammers on wood and metal, while smoke rose lazily into the warm evening air from the pitch heaters and forges.

'I got your dunnage ready, sir,' said Michael O'Hagan, very quietly. 'As well as that of the French lady and gent.'

That 'sir' made Pearce smile; if ever there was man not naturally a servant it was his friend and, in truth, it had been no more than a convenience; Michael was to be admired for his loyalty, his strength and his good sense but not his gentility. Pearce's reply, made without turning round, was equally soft, though it was hardly necessary as the commands began to be issued as shouts by the various warrants that would see the armed cutter at anchor.

'You'll be able to go back to calling me John-boy as soon as we're ashore, Michael.'

'Sure, and won't I be grateful for it, for I'm weary of the sound of my grovelling. Mind, I might have occasion to curse you an' all, given you've become too fond of that blue coat of yours, as well as ordering folk about.'

There was no need to turn to note that the remark was intended to be humorous, it was in the deliberately mordant tone. 'Somehow, Michael, I don't think any curses heading my way will be coming from you.'

'There's a rate of trouble awaiting, that's for certain.'

'I'm sure Emily will see sense once matters are explained,' Pearce replied, more from hope than conviction; he was not about to be open on the subject of his doubts even with a close friend.

'Weren't her I was thinkin' of. Your Frenchie might not go quiet.'

'I've already told her that she's . . .'

'Not your squeeze,' Michael said, filling in the gap Pearce had left by not quickly finishing the sentence. 'She might have said that to you, but I see the look in her eye when your attention be elsewhere and you allow her the deck. It is not short of hope.'

'You're mistaken.'

Michael laughed softly. 'Holy Mary, if I were you I'd be looking for an easier life, like puttin' about and seeking out to tackle those French escorts we slipped by a few days past.'

That conversation and the aid of the wind had got them near abreast of the village so that the twin lines of cottages were in full view; so was the lack of anything beyond them, for behind the twin rows of red brick lay a flat landscape bereft of any distinguishing features barring a few fields and endless forest. Both Pearce's passengers were on deck to observe the arrival.

'Monsieur,' called the Count de Puisaye in his own tongue, his face bearing a look of distaste as he gazed at the barren and open countryside now exposed. 'Surely we are not to land here?'

'We will do so,' Pearce replied, speaking in the same language and including an equally distressed Amélie in the statement. 'This is from where we set out and I am obliged to bring the vessel back to this anchorage.'

Obliged, Pearce thought sadly, because of the temporary nature of the command. For all I know, Rackham, the fellow who holds the post permanently, is fully recovered from whatever ailed him and, at this very moment, is gathering his own dunnage to come back aboard, where he can ply his flogging cat and keep going his various peculations, all spotted in the logs Pearce had studied when coming aboard.

'But there is nothing here,' Puisaye cried, employing a sweeping gesture accompanied by the kind of hurt tone, evidence of his personal vanity, which had already irritated his host since their first meeting. It was as if he was expecting a guard of honour as well as a delegation from St James' Palace to be waiting in all their finery, so the reply was short of understanding; in fact it was downright brusque.

'There is a road, monsieur, and one that will take you to where you need to go, just as soon as I can arrange transport.' Then he turned to Michael. 'We will need to take that strongbox ashore as well and find a way to get what's left safe to London.'

'Some of those hard-looking sods that delivered it would be handy. It would make a good day's work for any thief who could get their hands on it.'

'I fear, Michael, the task will fall to you and I.'

'Then happen we'll be travelling with loaded pistols.'

The item referred to had come to them in a sealed

coach with a strong escort, having originally held a sum of some thousand guineas, albeit the coins were from various countries such as doubloons and louis d'or, Dutch guilders, and even the not long minted American dollar. They had been provided in ten evenly filled bags by the Government, or more precisely by the prime minister's right-hand man, Henry Dundas, the purpose to facilitate the rebellion in the Vendée if it was seen fit to disburse it. The strongbox now contained in value near four hundred pounds in gold coins.

Between them Pearce and Michael O'Hagan had carried six of the pouches into the marshes where the rebels resided and they had left the money there for the intended purpose, even if Pearce had serious doubts it would do any good. Given Dundas had said it had come from something called the contingency fund, Pearce reckoned it to be money that had to be kept from public view – such a fund had to have a secret purpose. He could not just hand it over to anyone, which meant the safe option of boating it to Portsmouth and putting it in the care of the Port Admiral was not available. Besides, since it was his personal responsibility, he had signed for it, so there was no choice but to keep the residue under his own care until it could be formally handed back and accounted for.

'Come to think of it, I will have to raid one of the remaining bags to pay for a coach to London for our count as well as the strongbox itself. I'm damned if I'm going to facilitate the journey for either out of my own purse.'

'And who, sir,' Michael asked with a twinkle in his bright blue eyes, 'is going to pay out for the lady?'

'Dundas can pay for her as well,' Pearce snapped, as he turned and entered his tiny cabin, Michael on his heels. 'Now I need to go ashore and bespeak some kind of conveyance big enough to get our charges to Lymington.'

'Are you sure that's were you should take them?'

'I have no choice, Michael,' Pearce responded, as he unlocked the strongbox. 'The coach that will get Puisaye to London goes from there.'

'Sure, John-boy,' Michael hissed, too softly to be overheard, 'you've not thought it through. The coach passes and picks up at a few places on the way, an' if my memory is right some of them ain't much further off than Lymington.'

The response came when Pearce was standing up, a thick canvas bag in his hand, which he was unlacing to open: the prospect of getting Amélie away without Emily ever knowing he had brought her back. 'Now why did I not think of that?'

'Don't you know, sir,' Michael said in a louder voice, as well as one not short on irony, 'that the donning of a blue coat, from what I have been able to see with my own eyes, does little for clear thinking or common sense?'

CHAPTER FIVE

Heading back up the main New Forest road towards his home in Winchester, at a much more leisurely pace than that with which he had made the original journey, Admiral Sir Berkley Sumner was busy composing in his head the letter he would send to the Secretary to the Board of Admiralty. Sir Phillip Stephens was the person to whom he had despatched an enquiry regarding Lieutenant Raynesford, prompted by the appearance of the name in the social column of the *Hampshire Chronicle* as having recently arrived at the King's Head in Lymington.

First he would acknowledge that his curiosity about serving naval officers was an indication of his deep interest in his profession (to others he was a nosy old soak). Then he would show appreciation for the man's acuity, as well as the quite proper discretion he exercised in failing to include him in what was a covert undertaking. He would then tell Sir Phillip of how he had, by pure accident, come across and aided the secret scheme being undertaken by the aforesaid Lieutenant Raynesford, indeed he would make the point that, thanks to his timely input he could modestly suggest that matters were on course for an improved conclusion.

This would back up what would inevitably follow, for he was much given to pestering Sir Phillip and the Board, a repeated request that, given he had proved his worth as a gallant and intelligent officer he be given his due in terms of employment at sea, or if that was not available, a shore command that went with his rank and abilities.

If the *Comte* de Puisaye had been troubled by the sheer lack of anything of prominence in the appearance of Buckler's Hard, the same notion occurred to Jahleel Tolland when he actually got round to examining how he was going to accost John Pearce. He and his brother, when making enquiries, had not attracted more than the slight level of interest accorded to strangers, albeit Franklin's scar being so obviously recent had aroused comment; the same could not be said for a group of eight armed and mounted men riding in to the place at a pace to send up clods of the greensward, and that was not aided by their appearance. They looked like what they were, a band of right hard cases, and in a spot full of toiling labourers they stuck out like a sore thumb.

Seeing they were being eyed by and pointed to by the locals and not with kind expressions, Jahleel ordered a swift about turn before they were a third of the way to the jetty, seeking by his expression to imply that somehow they had taken a wrong route and ended up not where they intended to be. They made their way back to the point at which the road divided and took the turning back towards Lyndhurst, Jahleel calling a halt when they came to a wooded copse about half a mile distant, there to get out of sight and to formulate a new plan of action.

The Tolland gang thus missed an unescorted John Pearce coming ashore to seek a way of transporting his 'guests' out of the area and on to meet the northbound coach at Lyndhurst, not that he was given much more in the way of satisfaction. Buckler's Hard was a place truly at the end of the line – there was no bridge across the river and little beyond it to attract outsiders not connected to the work being carried on or shooting the local wildfowl in the marshlands and forest that extended to the seashore.

The only visitors to the place tended to be naval surveyors or people in some way connected with the acquisition of the ships being built and they made straight for the home of the master builder, which stood some way outside the village on a higher elevation. Anyone else would be a carter delivering those things needed to build the hulls that were not available from the surrounding countryside, and there was a ramshackle inn in which they could stay, a place that also served as an alehouse for the workers who lived and worked on the hard.

Though amply provided with horseflesh and carts, these needed to move the heavier objects such as shaped timbers and forged metalwork from the workshops to the slipways, there was nothing of a more comfortable nature to be had, certainly no covered coaches, and not even a shay for hire. The only conveyance Pearce was offered was an open-topped cart normally used to carry bales of oakum and looking as if it had seen much better days;

two of the wheels appeared set to come adrift as soon as they hit a deep mud patch or, when it was dry, the kind of ruts he had been obliged to negotiate on first coming here.

That he declined for the very simple reason that such a humble conveyance would further serve to upset the *Comte* de Puisaye – and probably Amélie Labordière as well – so it came down to a quartet of the local New Forest ponies, which, if they were animals of no great height, would suffice. He also bespoke a carthorse and panniers to carry the luggage of the ongoing travellers, the whole, including harness and saddles, rented at what Pearce reckoned to be an exorbitant price and that took no account of the deposit the fellow required to ensure his property was returned in prime condition.

Having made his bargain, the stablekeeper, perhaps because he observed how piqued was this client at the cost, became much more sociable, extolling the virtues of his ponies, they being sturdy beasts and very suited to the area in which they lived regardless of season. Bred wild they were captured to either be trained or culled in order that the numbers remained sustainable, the best breeding stock kept and the rest sold on for work in tunnelling and mining where their size and strength was valuable.

'I was a'telling the very same thing to that friend of yours.'

'Friend?'

'Aye, the fellow who came by a few days back asking for you.'

Pearce had never subscribed to the theory that humans had hackles that could rise at a sign of danger, but the way the hair at the base of his neck behaved felt remarkably like that of a dog.

'Looking for me?'

'You is Lieutenant Pearce?' That acknowledged the man continued. 'He was asking when you would be making your berth in the river agin, not that I or any other could say fer certain.'

'Did he give a name?'

That had the stablekeeper sucking his teeth and looking perplexed. 'Don't recall he did, sir.'

Working hard to control his voice, Pearce said, 'Then you'd best tell me what he looked like.'

'A lone, fresh scar on his left cheek, Michael, and when I asked about on the hard he was not alone, and from the description of the two together . . .'

'Mother of God, how did they know where to find you?'

'A question I have been gnawing on since the man mentioned that scar.'

'Not much chance of the two of them being alone?'

Pearce did not respond immediately, he was wondering if discovery of him included knowledge of the whereabouts of Emily; if it did there was not much he could do about it, the only positive thought being that at least she had not booked into the King's Head under the Barclay name, which should protect her.

'None. Eight of them we faced in London and we would have to reckon the same here.'

'Any notion of where they are now?'

Pearce shook his head then sat upright and slowly

looked around the anchorage, a place surrounded by ample woodland – there was a dense oak forest to the west on a slightly higher elevation – and his brow cleared somewhat. He was thinking that there had been no sign of any danger while he was renting those ponies, which led to an obvious conclusion: the Tollands were not in the village. If they had been, and with him alone, what he was doing now would be idle speculation for he would already be in their hands – all it needed was a pistol in the ribs and a demand he do as he was told.

How, then, did they intend to proceed in taking him for he had no doubt that was their aim? If not in the village it could only be on the road that led to both Lyndhurst and, by a detour, the quickest route to Lymington. But to do that they would need a clear sight of his departure, a point he made to the man sitting with him.

'And if they have the ship under observation they will know when we depart.'

'But not how many?'

'The addition of Puisaye and Amélie will not aid us, Michael, quite the reverse.'

'I was thinking the presence of others might give them pause.'

'And what if it does not? Do you recall the words of the older brother when we overheard them talking, that he would have his money or my skin in place of it? That same fate could stretch to anyone who is with me if I'm caught, you included, and I would remind you, we on this ship are the only folk who know of our French pair. Think what it's like out there – miles of deep forest, most of which never feels the feet of man, and ask yourself what our combined fate could be?'

Both men fell silent for a moment as that thought struck home: they could just disappear.

'What about seeking a parley, John-boy and telling them the truth of the matter, that you was robbed as much as were they?'

'They would scarce believe that, given I still cannot credit what I fell for myself.'

No one likes to be reminded that they have been a fool, as had he, and it was near as uncomfortable now as it had been when he first realised just how easily he had fallen for the deception. A sharp fellow who called himself Arthur Winston – not his real name – had dangled before him what looked like a chance to make a great deal of money from the recovery of a contraband cargo, made up of items becoming more expensive by the day as the war failed to progress: bolts of silk and lace, barrels of brandy, fine French wines, perfumes, all the commodities so beloved by those with money to buy.

How much had his own stupidity contributed to his being drawn in to the scheme, how much had it been the prospect of being able to offer comfort to Emily Barclay without the need of anything from her husband rich with prize money? It mattered not; he had recruited his Pelicans then sailed to the Flanders port of Gravelines, seeking to recover 'Winston's' ship and cargo, one for which he claimed to have already put up the money, to free it from a local who had refused to release it without a second massive payment. And he had succeeded, the only trouble being that it had never been 'Winston's' ship or his cargo; it had been the property of the Tollands, professional smugglers who very likely now sat athwart his route out of Buckler's Hard, and if he had scant real acquaintance with them it had been enough to show they were murderous. They were also serious and clearly had connections – had they not pursued him first to Dover, then to London and now, amazingly, to here?

Still convinced that he had carried off a legitimate coup regarding the contraband, Pearce had sailed their ship into St Margaret's Bay just north of Dover and beached it, so that too had been forfeit to the excise. It might be their legal property, but only a fool would reclaim a vessel just taken in the act of smuggling. The cargo? That had disappeared with John Pearce watching and helpless, immobilised by an injured foot, this as the bay filled with men come to make the arrests for which they had been tipped; at least he had been able to get Michael, Rufus and Charlie Taverner away along the tidal shore that led to Deal before they arrived to arrest him.

It was in the nature of things that the two friends reprised the whole affair in detail, being in search of a solution, an exchange that took place at the very prow of the ship and it was one designed not to be overheard because Pearce had made it plain to the rest of the crew that he wanted some private space to talk to his friend-cum-servant. He should have known better; if you could not keep a secret on a ship of the line – it was held as an absolute truth that Jack tar could hear a whisper through six inches of planking – the chances of doing so in a cramped armed cutter were zero. A ship's crew were always agog to know what was being planned; captains made decisions regarding their future, including matters of life and death, without so much as a by your leave and since they cared for it more than any officer it was as well to know what fate awaited them over the metaphorical horizon.

Not that all were privy to what was being discussed; the bosun, known to all as Birdy, slight of frame if well muscled, had slipped into the space below the prow under the bow chaser gun port, open on a warm day to let in to the 'tween deck air enough to dry out the timbers. Birdy learnt enough to make out that if nothing had been said that the crew should be concerned about, what he had overheard meant a threat to their temporary commander and soon, once he had extracted himself from his eavesdropping, that was disseminated.

It would be stretching things to say that the crew of HMS *Larcher* loved John Pearce – few of the lower deck loved any officer and the armed cutter had as well a small number of endemic malcontents who hated him just for his coat. But in the main they had come to esteem him, given the contrast with the real ship's captain, a well-named tyrant. Unlike Rackham, Pearce was honest and fair-minded, given to smiling instead of scowling, polite when called upon to be so instead of in a state of constant ire at slights and failures real or imagined.

He had also shown real flair in a fight, as well as trust in the crew to perform to their best and had said how pleased he was when they did. Sailing through that armada of merchant ships without alerting them or their escorts had been skilful and much appreciated; if he had failed, the best his crew could have hoped for was a French dungeon, with a watery grave a real possibility. Given that their opinion of him stood as it did, one of their number was elected to speak for them all.

'A word, if you please, Captain?'

Half sat on the prow bulkhead and deep in conversation with Michael, Pearce had not noticed the approach, which had been made by a master who in such a small vessel, like the rest of the crew, worked barefoot.

'Mr Dorling.'

Looking up into the man's face, round and clean-skinned, he sensed that Dorling was worried, for his normally smooth forehead was slightly furrowed, while the eyes, small for the size of his head, were narrowed. A fellow who always appeared to Pearce as serious – hardly surprising given his responsibilities at such a young age – his temporary commander felt that underneath lay a personality much more inclined to humour than misery; in another life and at another time Dorling would have been a companion of sharp wit and scant respect.

Given the master did not speak immediately, this allowed Pearce to look beyond him and see that, if they were trying not to look in his direction, the whole crew were somehow attached to this approach, the only disinterested person the Count de Puisaye, who was sitting in a quarterdeck chair plying a makeshift fishing rod; Amélie was in the cabin avoiding the sun, which she was sure would damage her delicate skin.

'It has come to our attention, sir, that you seem in some way troubled. If I were to refer to smugglers I think that would nail the concern.'

Having looked at Dorling as he spoke these opening

words, a sharp shifting of the eyes caught the fact that everyone else on deck, who should have been engaged in the raising of sails for drying, was immobile, which only lasted till they realised he was looking in their direction; the sudden burst of movement was obvious as ropes squealed and canvas flapped.

'Sure you been at the keyhole, have you not?' growled Michael.

Pearce leant backwards and glanced at the open gun port, a clear indication that he too had guessed what had occurred. 'I'm not much given to flogging, but sometimes—'

If he had hoped to cow Dorling he failed; the voice was firm and quick to interrupt, which was ill disciplined in the extreme and very out of character. 'I speak out of respect for you, sir.'

It was O'Hagan who replied, underlining what everyone had believed: whoever the giant Irishman was, and they knew as little of him as their temporary captain, he was no servant. 'And what is it you have to say?'

'Only this, your honour, that if you has a problem then the men aboard would not feel it beyond their duty to help out. From what we know, numbers seem to be the problem an', well, we has that to more'n match, I reckon.'

Pearce had dropped his head before Dorling finished, deeply touched by the sentiment, even if there was still a residue of irritation at the eavesdropping, and the response, when he spoke, went mostly into his chest. 'I'm not sure that would do, Mr Dorling, using men of the King's Navy to settle a private dispute.'

Dorling finally smiled, which wholly improved the look of his features and hinted at the good companion he might be. 'Don't see how you can stop us, sir. All you has to do is allow enough of us ashore, which, I would remind you, can only be done on your say so.'

'And how many do you speak for?'

'To a man, your honour, to a man,' Dorling replied, with real force. He was gilding it, for there were some who maintained it was none of their concern that an officer was in trouble; they could be ignored, there were more than enough willing. 'Christ, even the ship's boys are up for it.'

'Even when they have no idea what they face?'

'Can't be worse than a fleet of Frenchies.'

'It is,' Pearce replied, with much in the way of passion, 'or at least close enough to give pause.'

In the ensuing silence Michael O'Hagan knew that his friend was thinking the thing through, for it was not as simple as either the master or the crew supposed. This was no shore-going barney like you had in a port-side alehouse or gin den, where the worst you would face was a well-aimed fist and maybe being crowned by a chair leg. The Tollands were proper hard bargains and smugglers who carried the weapons they needed to protect themselves and their smuggled goods. They would be armed with swords, at least, and very likely pistols as well and such men were inured to the need to kill when called upon to do so; they could not have survived in their game without it.

'Would you let us talk of this, Mr Dorling?' Michael asked.

'As you wish, Paddy.'

That got a frown. 'I thought it was known that being called Paddy I did not much take to.'

'Sorry.'

Michael grinned. 'Sure, it is the first time you have erred, Mr Dorling. It's the second time that ends in a fuss.'

That had the master looking at O'Hagan's ham-like fists; he knew what a fuss meant. As he made to leave Pearce added, 'I would like this conversation to be completely private.'

'I will make sure it is, sir.'

As he turned and walked away there was a cry from the bulkhead near the wheel, in French, which told them that Puisaye had caught something. His makeshift rod was bent and a couple of hands had, unbidden, gone to help him, given they saw him as an old crock of a fellow, near to being infirm. One grabbed the line and whipped it up and over the side, to show on the end a wriggling trout.

It was a mordant Pearce who said, 'I think I know just how that poor creature feels.'

'We have a good offer, John-boy.'

'Do we, Michael? How can I accept when I have no idea what kind of danger these lads might be exposed to? The Tollands will be well armed and they know how to use their weapons.'

'There are guns aboard the ship.'

'Which could turn Buckler's Hard into a battlefield.'

'They are not in the village, remember.'

'I wonder if we might be able to bluff them by a mere show of strength.'

'I would be more minded to a real one, for bluff only buys time.'

'Which could possibly be achieved without someone being either seriously wounded or killed. If you want to set hares running with magistrates and the like, that would be a good way to do it without any notion of where it might end. I have been had up for too many things in my time, Michael, I have no notion to be arraigned for murder.'

'There is another way, John-boy: we take to a boat and head for another place to land.'

Pearce shook his head slowly. 'Think on how they found us.'

'I can think but I cannot find answer, yet it tells me what has been done once can be done again and since I am by your side I am as much at risk as you. My face is known to them and for all I can tell my name as well. We can run from them now but will that mean running for ever? That is a question to which we have no answer. We have been so very lucky, you and I – even Mrs Barclay – and that must run out sometime.'

'So,' Pearce sighed, which indicated his level of optimism, 'you are saying that it must be faced here and we must find some way of gaining resolution.'

'I am saying you must let the crew aid us. At least with numbers we have a chance.'

That led to a long silence, but Pearce responded finally. 'It might up to a point, Michael, but only up to a point.'

'Frenchie coming,' Michael said quietly.

'Monsieur,' the count demanded. 'When will we depart for London?'

The thud of a boat coming alongside and with no shortage of noise distracted both Pearce and the count. Bellam, the ship's cook, began slinging onto the deck a case of wine, various sacks of fresh victuals, one of which, by its shape and being wrapped in muslin, looked to be a substantial rib of beef that Pearce had asked him to seek out for his last meal aboard, which he intended should be something of a celebration and, to please his guests, one held at a more shore-common hour. The three o'clock naval dining hour they had found as hard to accept as the quality of what they were given to eat.

'We cannot leave today, monsieur, it is too late in the day. Perhaps on the morrow.' The disappointment, if not downright disapproval, was obvious. 'But, for tonight, I promise you a capital dinner, and since you have caught one fish and that will not feed three, I would admonish you to ply your rod again and get us another for it would make a fine opening course.'

'What was all that about?' Bellam asked as he hauled himself aboard.

'Christ knows, mate,' came the reply from Brad Kempshall, the ship's carpenter, dark-haired twin to the blond gunner Sam. 'Lessen you know the lingo you can't tell. But that apart, I would take it as a kindness if, when you was bringing a boat alongside, you showed a bit more care.'

The reply was loud and on such a small deck was taken in by all. 'An' there's me seeking to straighten out the wood you left warped and you plying the trade of Christ's old father hisself. Some folks never give thanks.'

Pearce found himself looking along a deck of laughing tars; he was not laughing, he was trying to work out how to play his hand, which, despite the promise of support, did not seem an exceptionally good one, yet in being barracked by Michael a germ of a solution began to present itself.

CHAPTER SIX

'Light's fading,' wheezed Cole, the man first set to watch HMS *Larcher* and newly returned. 'Added, there's no sign of a boat castin' off. Looks to me as if they was setting out a table on the deck and there's smoke coming from the galley chimney.'

'Damn the sod.'

'We ain't got now't to keep us goin', either, and I'm sharp set.'

'For the love of Christ,' Jahleel spat, 'stop thinkin' on your belly.'

'If'n you can stop it a'rumblin', Jahleel, I'll stop moanin' for sure.' He jerked a thumb to where the hobbled mounts were grazing. 'The only things getting fed are the horses an' that's what we will be on, plain grass.'

'Never mind the rumbling,' Franklin interjected, 'somebody has to go back and make sure Pearce stays aboard.'

'Ain't goin' to come off in the dark, brother,' Jahleel

said, for once without any trace of rancour, looking skyward at what was rapidly turning from light blue to a deeper hue. 'Even if it is a starry night, it is not a road to be travelling by moonlight.'

'A tankard of ale might ease things,' Cole said.

'Now there's a good notion,' Franklin responded with a sneer. 'The only place to get that is in the hard tavern and that is full of the locals. Jahleel's planning to do Pearce in and you want to sit blathering to them and let them see our faces close up.'

'All I is sayin' is I don't fancy sitting out all night with not a drink to pass my lips nor a bite of food to eat.'

Jahleel Tolland laughed, a low chuckle really. 'Should get you in the mood to take it out on Pearce of a mornin', I'd say.'

'Will do an' all,' Cole snarled, 'that is, if you stand back long enough to give a body a chance.'

'Cephas,' Jahleel said to another of the gang, as he pulled out and peered at his Hunter. 'Go keep watch for a bit; I'll send someone to take over after a while.'

'Can we light a fire, at least, Jahleel?'

'It's a warm night and we are sound here, unless you reckon this here forest be full of demons.'

'Why'd you say that?' Cole wailed.

'I know you're a'feard of them, that's why,' Jahleel roared, 'an' if they's ever comin' for you Cole, this night is as good as any. Bless me, did I see yonder tree move a bit closer?'

A chorus of ghoulish wails from all of the gang followed that, which had Cole covering his ears; he was man who believed very strongly in evil spirits. But Cole got his way; enough dry kindling was found to get a blaze going, bits of broken-off and seasoned branches, of which the forest was well supplied, only dampened on the bark by the recent rain, turning that into a warming fire that each man was reluctant to leave when it came to their turn to take over the watch on the armed cutter.

A small table had been set up on the tiny quarterdeck, with lanterns rigged above to provide light when the last of the sun disappeared, a more comfortable way to dine than they had enjoyed at sea, sitting on the casement lockers in the ship's cramped cabin, yet it was far from a relaxed occasion despite the improved quality of the food. Pearce gnawed on what he had planned while the Count de Puisaye was once more in the kind of expansive and confident mood regarding the future of his country, claims that grated on his host's nerves, given it was so divorced from reality.

The citizen armies that had defeated the likes of the Duke of Brunswick and forced the coalition raised against the revolution to retreat, and had, from what he knew, made life a misery for the British Army's action in Flanders, would be swept aside by the ragtag peasants of the Vendée, for they had their faith as well as God on their side. A great host would be gathered on the march to Paris as people rose up in their thousands to sweep aside the apostates who had so ruined proud France. For John Pearce the only way to avoid his direct gaze, demanding agreement to these preposterous claims, was to hide behind the rim of his tankard and pretend to drink deeply.

Amélie was silent throughout and Pearce wondered if it was because of her fellow countryman's hyperbole of if she had an inkling of what was going to happen on the morrow, which seemed to add a deepness and unhappiness to the looks she threw in his direction, not dissimilar to those mention by Michael O'Hagan. If he had seen them, Pearce had worked hard to avoid them, yet he knew they were present. He had been deliberately indifferent to her over the preceding days for the very good reason that any show of sympathy could have untoward consequences, not that his attempts to get to sleep were unsullied by temptation; he could hear her movements, and worse for slumber he could remember the pleasure of their previous couplings.

At least the food was good: fresh trout – for Puisaye, with much assistance, had been successful twice more; the beef was pink and the vegetables were fresh from a cook who, at anchor on a calm river and with no discernible wind, reckoned there was scant reason to boil the meat and instead oversaw it being properly roasted; likewise the carrots and greens were crisp rather than soft, the potatoes allowed to roast in the juices alongside the beef. Proud of his efforts, the fellow hovered until he was complimented for his efforts.

'It is so good, Mr Bellam, it could match any meal I had in Paris.'

As soon as the words were out of his mouth, Pearce was aware that if he had drunk little, it was enough to loosen his guard; a mention of the French capital was not a good idea in the present company, the truth of that immediately apparent when the count asked for a translation. Much as he tried to weave a tale round it, the name of the city still hung in the air, causing Amélie to respond.

'Do we not have many fond memories, Jean, of our time together in Paris?'

This being almost the first time she had spoken without she was responding to a question from Puisaye, Pearce found he needed his tankard again, this time to avoid her eyes, which had about them a pleading look. That could not stay at his lips for ever and when it was downed he had to reply.

'That is in the past, Amélie.'

'And what is to be my future?'

Pearce was not only cursing the question but the fact that it had been posed in the presence of Puisaye – the few exchanges he had allowed outside normal conversation had been done out of earshot of the only other French speaker aboard; not now, and it was as plain by his expression that the count was just as curious as Amélie, which was damned annoying.

'You are a charge upon my conscience.'

'What a strange expression, Jean.'

It is, he thought, but I am not going to say I will take care of you, for that is an expression too loaded to employ.

'I cannot give you what you lost, but . . .' The tankard came up again to be drained, for he did not know how to conclude the sentence.

It was telling the way her hand went to her cheek, as if she was underlining that her beauty, with which he had been so struck on first meeting her, was no longer as it had once been; Amélie had suffered in her flight from a life of luxury to a Vendée swamp, but it was more than that, for she had also aged. So had he, but time had been unkind to a woman who was already many years older when they had first met, her worldly knowledge being, to an inexperienced youth, a great part of her attraction.

'No one can give me back what is gone.'

'Your husband—'

The interjection was sharp. 'I was not referring to Armand.'

'He died in a noble cause,' said the count in his customary sententious way.

'Odd,' Amélie replied, a sour note in her voice, 'that all causes are termed noble, monsieur. I have heard Jacobins use the same expression and I am sure it is one used by that ogre Robespierre and his Committee of Public Safety.'

'You cannot doubt that the cause we represent is anything other than just!'

Amélie dropped her head and spoke the single word, '*Non.*' It implied the exact opposite, inferred that such sentiments were for fools, and if Puisaye had possessed half a brain – a department in which he was seriously lacking – he would have spotted it. His next words underlined that.

'In the future you will recover that which was both yours and that which belonged to your late husband. France will once again have a king and will once again have our prelates and priests, as well as a docile and contented peasantry. I have no doubt of my ability to convince the Government of England—'

'Great Britain,' Pearce interjected, losing patience with this posturing. 'England is only part of the country of which you speak.'

Puisaye waved that away as if it was no account, which annoyed Pearce even more; if he was far from even slightly rabid in the cause of Caledonia, he still came from Scottish stock. Failing to mention that country or Wales was a habit hard enough to bear in the English and not to be borne at all in a foreigner.

'As I was saying, when I have outlined to them what can be achieved with support, I am sure that they will despatch powerful forces to the Vendée. Then it is we who will employ the guillotine to rid our beautiful land of the scum who have despoiled it.'

'You have yet to answer my question, Jean.'

'I . . .'

'You are committed elsewhere.'

'I am not sure the lady of whom you speak would understand.'

'What is to understand? We were lovers – that has cooled but we can still be friends.'

How could he say that such a thing could not be, that this was stuffy England not lax Paris, to even attempt it might destroy the thing he sought most at this moment in his life? He was sure that even to mention Amélie to Emily – God they share a name, which he had not realised previously – would cause complications over which he would have no control. The chance to speak the truth was there for him to take advantage of; prevarication won hands down.

'Let us leave that aside for now,' Pearce finally responded, picking up the full bottle that had replaced the one just emptied. 'More wine?'

HMS *Queen Charlotte* had raised Penlee Point and with much banging of signal guns from the flagship the Channel Fleet entered Plymouth Sound. Those vessels most in need of repair were sent upriver to the dockyard, the rest anchoring as commanded by the flagship. As soon as they were secured and the necessary reports and logs were delivered to *Queen Charlotte* the ship visiting began and along with that invitations to dine.

Ralph Barclay was forced to decline that he should be called upon to move – he pleaded his wound – and so missed the first round of dinners, instead receiving aboard HMS *Semele* the following day a pair of officer acquaintances who esteemed him as a colleague and had been made aware of his infirmity. Whistles blew and marines saluted as they came aboard; Albemarle Bertie from HMS *Thunderer* and Anthony Molloy of HMS *Caesar*, accompanied by their premiers, the table made up to full with the addition of Ralph Barclay's own remaining lieutenants and a spotty midshipman.

He was in possession of ample stores, having been a recipient already in this war of a decent amount of prize money, and he had been granted ample time to send ashore for the very best local produce. Thus Ralph Barclay was able to set a good table and ply his guests with wine of a high quality. Throughout the meal the battle in which they had so recently been engaged was re-fought in a manner that allowed it to move from the experience of each of the commanders individually to a collective appreciation of the whole.

With the guests as cheered by victory as their host it did not take long, and this was the nature of the service, for Lord Howe's actions in the battle to come under a less than flattering scrutiny. Had he pressed home the attack with sufficient vigour? Could more have been done to confound the enemy? Why had the fleet not pursued the fleeing French to seek to take more prizes, given the damage to many of their ships was greater than that of the British Fleet? On the whole it was agreed any captain present – indeed most of the lieutenants, they were informed – could have done better.

'He's far too old for the task,' opined Bertie, his round, childlike face being shaken to underline the folly of giving command to a man of such advanced years. 'Word is he left the deck before the action was over. Past his three score years and ten, and as for Curtis, well he's an old woman, to my mind.'

There was a moment of silence as that thought was ruminated upon; as Captain of Fleet, in essence the executive officer and advisor to the commanding admiral, Sir Roger Curtis would have had a great say in what actions had been undertaken and he would have taken over direction of the battle when Howe retired to his cabin. His abilities were equally traduced.

'Then there is the grain convoy,' Ralph Barclay said, this to fellow officers who looked mystified at the reference, causing their host to add, with a degree of caution, 'You surely recall that the purpose of the fleet being at sea was to intercept that convoy, which we signally failed to do.'

'Never saw the damned thing,' Molloy responded.

This was said in a tone more forthright than he had employed in discussing the battle, an action from which HMS *Caesar* had emerged unscathed, having not been in a position to close with the enemy. His peers had nodded sagely as he explained why that should be, accepting that regardless of Howe's orders to do so, the state of his ship and the nature of the wind had made such a thing impossible.

'Precisely,' Ralph Barclay said, slapping the tabletop and fixing his guests with a knowing look. He reminded them of the first sighted frigate and what had followed as they, indeed the whole Channel Fleet, had pursued it. 'I have an inkling that we might have been deliberately drawn off by that fellow. Led us straight to his main fleet, did he not, and quite possibly away from the grain convoy.'

Nods were all his fellow captains would allow themselves as they recalled what their host was saying was true and what it might portend; France was rumoured to be on the verge of starvation after yet another poor harvest and if that came to pass the revolutionary government was bound to fall. The convoy in question, up to, it was said, a couple of hundred deep-hulled merchantmen, had set sail from the United States weeks before with enough grain aboard to alleviate the problem of famine, which, in essence meant the continuation of the war.

Ralph Barclay carried on talking, the note in his voice emboldened by a decent amount of claret. 'Might have been better to have ignored that frigate and gone in search of the convoy. Happen Black Dick Howe will get a rap on the knuckles instead of the praise and the dukedom he expects.'

'You might have the right of it, Barclay,' Albemarle Bertie insisted, 'but you'll have the devil of a job persuading anyone now of such a view. Hindsight rarely does the trick in such matters.'

'Not so, Bertie, given I took the precaution of noting that possibility in my log at the time. We are talking of foresight not hindsight.'

'How much do you reckon on the prize money, Barclay?' Molloy asked, looking bored with what was being discussed.

That changed the subject swiftly and it was generally agreed that the sum to be distributed for what had been taken, this calculated by men who knew their stuff, could not be much less than a quarter of a million pounds sterling, which had the junior officers trying to silently calculate what it meant for them on fiddling fingers hidden under the table.

Bertie raised his glass at the sum mentioned. 'Then I say, damn the grain convoy, let's drink to that.'

'Hear him,' chorused the assembled lieutenants and the solitary mid, as hands appeared to lift and empty their wine.

The meal on the deck had a dual purpose; if HMS *Larcher* was being watched – in truth, John Pearce – then he being in plain sight was highly desirable, ten times more so as the light began to fade and the rigged lanterns made it easy to concentrate on the trio sitting at the table. What would not cause comment was a couple of boats going from ship to shore picking up stores – fresh bread and newly baked biscuit, as well as vegetables that even as temporary captain Pearce had an obligation to purchase by a warrant drawn on the Navy Office. It would have taken a sharp eye to discern that each time one returned laden it had two fewer men aboard than had set out. That allowed for the gathering of a small party to go out and ensure, first, that the Tollands were not as Pearce suspected in the village, but encamped somewhere off the road he must take out.

Dorling and another hand had taken the jolly boat downriver, rods out and seemingly fishing, to seek out the second part of Pearce's plan and that had not happened until the master had assured his captain that he was prepared to be on the wrong side of the law in carrying out what was proposed, the crew likewise, though, in truth, the risks for the future and any censure all lay with Pearce. He and Puisaye were consuming some of Rackham's supplies of port, Amélie having retired, when Dorling returned to say he had found what was required.

'Then, once the lanterns are doused I will make a show of bedding down for the night. Let us hope that whoever is watching has no trouble keeping their eyes open.'

'As long as they see you at first light, sir, they will be confident.'

The last word produced a frown; he might have thought the whole matter through but John Pearce was very far from sanguine about everything going to plan, even when Dorling knelt to tell him all was in place on the shore.

CHAPTER SEVEN

Sleeping through noise at sea was necessary: the wind whistling through the rigging, the creak of moving timbers. On a ship sat in a quiet tidal waterway it should have been different, with only an anchor watch set and no requirement change every four hours or to be up at first light. Yet the ship's hour bell still tolled and that by habit caused a single eye to open. Then came the dawn birdsong, the odd cawing seagull included, but these were not the only things to disturb a fitful night's sleep as, once more huddled on deck in his boat cloak, John Pearce gnawed on all the problems that beset his life and not just his fears for the coming day, the whole compounded by the buzzing in his ears of insects made more numerous by the recent rain, which provided many shallow puddles in which to breed.

Intent on feeding off his blood they had been inside his boat cloak leaving behind itches that demanded to be scratched, but really it was the early dawn that made sleep impossible. Forced to be up with the lark and uncaring about being observed from the shore, Pearce stripped off and dived naked into the chill water of the river. Michael O'Hagan, through habit, was also awake and by the ship's side to haul him out, a towel at the ready added to an expression that told the swimmer he was mad to so expose himself. Dressed before the hands were piped to breakfast Pearce was, in all respects, ready for whatever the day might bring.

'Mr Dorling, is all prepared?'

'As much as it can be, sir; all we need now are your passengers.'

Pearce was eager to depart, but he was required to wait while Amélie used his cabin to carry out a lengthy and elaborate toilette, which had her one-time lover pacing the deck with impatience and asking Michael more than once if they might ever get ashore this day or any other. Not that matters would have been hastened by more alacrity on her part – *le Comte* de Puisaye likewise devoted much attention to both dressing and applying fresh powder to the wig he had not worn since coming aboard. He then produced from his travelling chest a fine crimson velvet jacket as well as a pristine white stock, breeches and stockings, to set off his silver-buckled and freshly blackened shoes, that before he began to festoon himself with various orders studded with jewels.

'Monsieur, that coat is inappropriate,' Pearce barked, then forced to produce an excuse that had nothing to do with facing armed and dangerous smugglers he added, 'we are travelling on horseback over dusty tracks, indeed there may still be mud.'

'Nevertheless, Captain, who knows what we will

encounter on the way?' There was a terrible temptation then to tell him. 'I would not have your countryman think me anything other than that which I am.'

Pearce had to bite his tongue a second time then, to stop himself from saying, 'A pompous old dolt.'

Like the count Amélie Labordière had dressed as if she was going to a levee, in a gown of silk set with patterns of sequins, albeit she had covered her garments with a cloak. She had also taken much trouble with both powder and rouge, which went a long way to restoring her to an image of the beauty he remembered. That she knew it to be so was in the cast of her eye and the slight smile as she nodded to John Pearce, which had him turn away to meet the amused gaze of Michael O'Hagan.

He was carrying short pieces of rope, at the ends of which he had expertly fashioned a sort of cradle, this to carry the remainder of the Dundas gold, that not being something he could leave behind. The strongbox was too big and would have required a carthorse of its own so Michael had suggested a repeat of what they had done to transport it in the Vendée, only this time it would be carried in individual sacks which could be slung over the carthorse's flanks and not their shoulders, he having sworn he still bore the marks of the weight.

Pearce fished for the key to the great padlock, which had never left his coat pocket, and made his way into the cabin, there to extract from the strongbox the four weighty bags, these secured in Michael's contraption once his friend had extracted from one what he thought he would require to facilitate the journey, a sum in fact in excess of the suspected requirements, given there was no knowing how the day would turn out.

'Don't go back in the water with that in your purse,' Michael joked, seeing how much he had taken, 'or you'll sink to the bottom.'

'Might be a blessing for all concerned.'

'I have not packed your pistols and they are loaded and primed.'

There was a moment then when the two locked eyes, for in planning his scheme, Pearce had been insistent that no risks be taken that might see anyone killed. But Michael held his gaze and Pearce knew he would not budge, so he shrugged and threw the padlock and key into the open box, wondering what the man he had temporarily replaced would make of its presence when he came aboard.

'Keep them out of sight.'

'Place smells a mite better than normal,' Michael said, a twinkle in his eye, as he sought to kill off the crabbed mood. 'A lady's perfume is better than vinegar any day.'

Pearce was not in the mood to be ribbed. 'If you are going to keep this joshing up I can see where those pistols you loaded might come in handy.'

He grabbed his logs and returned to the deck. The boat was over the side waiting for them and Pearce was touched to see that the oarsmen had taken as much care in preparation for his departure as their French passengers had for their own; whether it was play-acting or genuine he did not know, but they were wearing their best shore-going rig, the long pigtails were greased and ribbon-festooned, each oarsman sitting stony-faced and looking forward as if they were crewing an admiral's barge.

Nor did they deviate from that as Pearce made a short speech of thanks to those lined up on deck, shaking hands with the warrants before going over the side, boat cloak over his arm, to the high-pitched whistle of the bosun's pipe. With chests occupying space and the sheer bulk of O'Hagan there was scant room to sit and misfortune had him pressed against Amélie on the same narrow thwart; with the sun now well up on a warm morning he could smell both the familiar perfume, the same as had infused his cabin, as well as the musk of her body, both of which played upon his memory. Added to that was the heat of her skin as their flesh inadvertently made contact, at which point he was made aware by his own bodily changes just how far he was from being immune to her charms; in short, his folded cloak, over which he had laid his sword, was a blessing.

The occasion of the party coming ashore was unusual enough to have a few idlers gather to watch their landing, which took all of two minutes from ship's side to the jetty, the sight of a finely dressed pair of French aristocrats certainly being far from normal in such a backwater. Curiosity turned to amusement as the mounts were brought forward, animals that so contrasted with the sartorial elegance on show – one, the carthorse, with a set of leather harness with which to strap on luggage.

Puisaye had about him an expression of aristocratic sangfroid even when faced with a fourteen-hand pony; he was not going to demean himself by showing the local peasants that this was anything other than normal and he got aboard his animal and sat on it as if it was the finest steed in creation, his nose high and eyes fixed forward as if he was about to lead an armed host into battle. Amélie, even on such a short-legged mount, had to be aided by Pearce, which produced more unwelcome intimacy.

Michael, once mounted, a satchel containing the encased brace of pistols over his shoulder, looked as if he could walk and ride the animal simultaneously; Pearce, albeit his legs were shorter, was not far off the same and thinking the sword he was wearing a damned nuisance. Loading complete they trotted out of Buckler's Hard, pursued by the local urchins making ribald comments about which arses were the fattest, equine or human.

'Shall I dismount and clip a couple of these cullies, John-boy?'

'Leave them be, friend, for if you don't look like a fool, I'm damn sure I do.'

'They're coming, Jahleel. I watched them land then mount and now they just left the cottages behind, our blue coat up front.'

'"They", Cephas?'

'Aye, four in all,' the smuggler replied. 'You recall that big bugger we traded blows with in London? Well he's along bringing up the rear an' towing a packhorse, but there's two right strange coves in't middle, a woman in a cloak and a man dressed like a nob on the way to a ball, powdered wig an' all. Whole party's aboard ponies too small for proper ridin', so we can take 'em as easy as kiss my hand.'

'Four makes matters altered,' Franklin said, as he primed and loaded his pistol, left till late because of the dampness of the forest. 'I was set for two to deal with.'

'Not to me, brother, if others are along where they've no right to be, that will be their misfortune. Now, let's get mounted and be at 'em.'

'Jahleel, think on it, for the love of Christ! Four folk and as described by Cephas won't have departed Buckler's Hard unseen. They might have made a right show and if that be the case they will be talked about all over the county in time. They go missing and there will be a hue and cry for certain.'

The lack of a response showed that Franklin had struck home and not just with his sibling.

'Go too far and you'll risk the rope for us all.'

Jahleel aimed his pistol at one of the trees and squinted down the barrel, which had the virtue of allowing him to avoid his brother's eye. 'He's not goin' to slip me again, Franklin; I said it an' I meant it, and if worst comes to worst, by the time their loss is noticed we will be long gone.'

Now it was the younger brother's turn to point up his scar, this done with his fingertips. 'I has even more cause to want revenge than you, Jahleel, but what is it we really want?'

'Blood – Pearce's blood.'

'No, we want that for sure, but just as much to know what happened to our cargo and the money it raised, sold on. Happen he was only a small part of it and if his blood would be a bonus, which I grant you, we'd be better served finding out the names of those who had the means to get our stuff ashore and profit by it.'

'We ain't got time for this,' Jahleel insisted, as two of the gang, sent to fetch the already saddled horses began to make their way back.

'They's movin', but dead slow,' Cephas intoned.

'So it makes no odds if they go by us,' Franklin added. 'We're well mounted and can catch them easy.'

'Get on those horses now – I ain't letting him pass an' I seem to recall what I says goes.'

'No killing,' Franklin insisted.

Jahleel stuck his weapon in his belt and grabbed the reins of his horse. 'Happen it might not be our choice, brother.'

Having been in the copse all night and most of the morning, even moving around, the wildlife had almost accepted their presence and it never occurred to men who were of the sea and not of the land that it could be otherwise. But the movement of eight horses and their riders changed that and the first pigeon broke noisily from the thick-leafed branches, an act which spooked the others. Within seconds the sky above the trees was full of flapping wings and they startled the other birds, the sight of which made Pearce feel much better. He knew that the Tollands were in that copse and he had been relying on them acting before he got abreast of it, for if they did not, things would be much harder.

If he could have heard Jahleel Tolland cursing he might have had a proper laugh; it was, of course, the fault of others not him, but he knew that very likely surprise was gone and he spurred his mount out onto the roadway without any attempt at subtlety, the rest behind him.

Pearce had already spoken in French to give instructions that his charges should stay still, brusquely dismissing the count's attempt to enquire as to why that should be, a question that became superfluous as the road ahead was filled across its width by eight properly mounted, grim-looking men all with pistols in their hands.

'Hold, Pearce,' Jahleel yelled, 'it time you paid for your folly.'

Michael, at the back, had taken out the pistols from the wooden case, that thrown to the ground, eased back and locked the hammers, before kneeing his pony to get it to move forward until he was abreast of Pearce and could hand one over, an act remarked on by Tolland.

'It will be two pistols agin eight and no time I reckon to reload.'

'Monsieur?' the count demanded. 'What is this about?'

Pearce was brusque in the way he told the count that he had no time to explain, accompanied by the sound of Jahleel Tolland's voice again floating through the warm morning air. 'You can come on or flee, Pearce, it be up to you, but it will, in the end, make no odds.'

'What is it you want?'

That got a loud snort; it had to be to cover the distance that separated them. 'Now't much: a sound ship, a valuable cargo and, as a bonus, some of your skin, and I reckon you would do all a favour if you send off the lady and gent and allow us to have a little talk with you and your hulking mate.'

'I doubt it would do any good if I told you we made not a brass farthing from the whole escapade, that I was dunned as much as were you?'

'None at all,' Jahleel shouted, 'for we would not credit it. You'se a thieving bastard an' that be that.'

'Does the name Arthur Winston mean anything to you?'

'Never heard of him,' Jahleel spat, clearly thinking what Pearce was up to. 'Now stop playing for time, that is if you don't want your lady and the gent in velvet to share your fate. Get rid of them now.'

Pearce had never thought they knew the man who called himself Arthur Winston but it was something he felt he needed confirmed; Tolland's dismissive tone implied that he had spoken the truth. As he trotted back to take station alongside Puisaye he was smiling, for he was indeed playing for time and he gave a long explanation of their predicament to both the count and Amélie.

'Monsieur, I will not explain why these men have come to seek me out, enough to tell you they mean me harm.' Amélie, close enough to hear the words, responded with such a sharp intake of breath that he addressed his next words to her. 'But I beg you not to worry, matters are in hand. Might I ask you, as I approach these men, to move over to one side of the road and get close to the trees.' Seeing the count's mouth open he added sharply, 'And please do not ask me why.'

Then he spun his pony again and, slowly, pulled out his sword, rested it on his shoulder and kicked his mount into a trot.

'He's going to do a death or glory charge,' suggested Franklin. 'He wants us to kill him.'

'Then shoot his pony,' growled Jahleel.

If they wondered what Pearce was about they were too busy looking at his face to concern themselves overmuch. Halting some twenty feet away he smiled at both brothers and said. 'Gentlemen, I ask you to cast an eye over your shoulder.'

'Oldest trick in the game,' Jahleel snarled, unaware that Cole had done just that.

'Best have a look-see, Jahleel.'

'Don't be a fool . . .'

The elder Tolland had only turned to look at Cole, but he got no further, for there, in the very corner of his vision, lined up on the road, stood a party of a dozen sailors, each with a musket up and aimed at their backs. When he looked for Pearce he was no longer there; he and Michael were heading for the trees and out of the line of fire, at the same time opening enough distance to render the Tolland pistols close to ineffective.

'Hell and damnation!'

'Don't you go getting a twitch,' called Matthew Dorling, at Jahleel Tolland's cry. 'In fact, don't so much as do other than let those pistols drop to the road.'

'You reckon to do murder?' Franklin called, hoping to bluff a way of escape.

'We reckon to match what you was about, yes. We'll down you if you want, but at this range, I reckon a musket ball will tear a right hole in your flesh, enough to maim if not kill.'

'I should do as he says,' Pearce called, as he and Michael O'Hagan emerged from the copse in which the Tolland gang had been camped, to take up station halfway between his tars and the gang, but to the side to remain out of the line of fire. 'Drop the pistols, then the swords.'

'You have not the heart to kill, Pearce.'

'No, but I have the heart to put a couple of balls into your knees so that none of you will ever walk again.'

'Sure,' Michael cawed, 'I am not soft. One right in your eye will do for me.'

'It won't end here, Pearce, so happen you best let your Paddy do his worst.'

'Mother of God, the man doesn't know how close to the wind he's sailing.'

'You can, of course, send for a Justice of the Peace and

perhaps explain that you are not highwaymen. I wonder if he would believe you when you are up against the word of a King's Officer, half the crew of one of his vessels, not to mention two total and foreign strangers. I think you know the penalty for highway robbery. Make quite a spectacle, and bring a huge crowd, eight men swinging at once.'

Dorling had brought his men forward in a line, so close that the musket barrels were now close to being pressed into the backs of the gang.

'Drop the weapons. Now!'

'You saying you won't hand us in?'

'To the Justice, no.'

'Murder us?'

'You can choose that course if you wish.'

'Jahleel, for the love of Christ.'

'Best listen to Cole, brother,' Franklin hissed. 'We've been right humbugged but at least we'll live to fight another day.'

Jahleel Tolland slowly let fall the hammer on his pistol and one of the sailors leapt forward to grab it from his hand, an act repeated until they were all unarmed and their weapons, swords and knives included, were gathered and made safe. Then they were obliged to dismount and once on the ground their horses were taken to be tied to the trees. The men of HMS *Larcher*, not without the odd sly and painful poke, expertly tied their hands, the whole eight then lashed to make it easy to walk in line.

'Mr Dorling, perhaps you would show our captives something, that little notion you whispered to me last night.'

'Line them up,' the master shouted, 'an' get your muskets, all of you.'

Weapons that had been laid aside were fetched, those who had stood armed and ready joining in to stand ten feet away from the Tolland gang, each musket raised and aimed, eye along the barrel, at a man's heart.

'I reckoned not to believe you,' Jahleel rasped.

'You'll hang of this, Pearce,' Franklin shouted, but if it was laced with anger there was high dose of fear included.

'Sir,' Cephas cried, 'we was only doing—'

He got no further; Jahleel headbutted him, which would have sent him reeling if he had not been tied. 'Don't beg, never beg.'

'I want you to know what kind of man I am,' Pearce replied. 'Steady yourself, lads, take good aim and now . . .' He held the suspense, saw many eyes close, but not those of Jahleel; he spat on the ground to let his executioner know what he thought of him. 'Fire.'

'Holy mother of Christ,' the one called Cole yelled, his open mouth showing his lack of teeth.

A dozen triggers were pulled, a dozen cocked hammers struck the flints to produce the necessary spark but there was no flash in the pan – the only sound was a dull click, and then the crew began to laugh. One of the gang fainted and had, like the still groggy Cephas, to be held up by the ropes that tied him. Two, judging by the pools that began to form at their feet, had soiled themselves and one was weeping. But there was one pair of eyes fixed on those of John Pearce that told him that the next part of his plan was as essential as what had just taken place.

CHAPTER EIGHT

There were matters to sort out, not least that the count and Amélie should be allowed to choose a horse to replace their ponies; they, like the carthorse, would be taken back to Buckler's Hard. Michael O'Hagan was going to be their escort to Lyndhurst, his task to get both on to the coach to Winchester, where, after a night's stay they could catch the flyer to London. The Irishman would then make his way to Lymington to where Pearce would go after and if his scheme was complete.

The old man continued to press for a more detailed explanation than Pearce was inclined to give; the men now sitting in a circle on the ground were people who meant him harm for things that had happened in the past and these were matters about which he was prepared to divulge the facts. He had underestimated the count's persistence and eventually, to fob him off, he hinted at there being a lady involved. That to a Frenchman made perfect sense; such a pity that Amélie overheard it, thus further diminishing him in her eyes; from being that young and eager lover in Paris he had, no doubt, descended to being seen as something of a satyr.

There was another argument with O'Hagan, who hated to see good money wasted. 'You can't just let the spare mounts go, John-boy, five good horses, not to mention the saddlery and harness.'

'They won't starve, Michael, we are surrounded by some of the best pasture in Britain, neither will they be lonely given the place is full of mare ponies. Who knows, they might improve the stock and, in time, some of the forest verderers will rope them in.'

'They would fetch a goodly sum of money.'

'They would also attract attention, Michael, for you will only be mounted on three. Why would such a small party have so many spare horses? No, we will let half of them go, take a fourth for the chests and if you can sell them in Lyndhurst, do so, but I have my doubts that anything equine has much value around here. In which case stable them until we can pick them up when we make our way back to London. We'll get a better price for them somewhere on that road, I'm sure, and besides, they can be got rid of one at a time, which will arouse less comment. Now I have to tell our French friends what I have in mind for them, so fetch me that bag of coins we raided earlier.'

'The others?'

'Will go with me.'

That took time and it was obvious neither of his one-time passengers was entirely happy at the proposed arrangement, that was until Pearce produced that which he had held back, a half-full purse of gold. If Puisaye did not know how much it contained he could feel its weight and that mollified him somewhat, his only objection that without John Pearce he would struggle to make his case to the British Government.

'Monsieur, I will be in London in three days at the most. Please take the coach and make for Nerot's Hotel, where my name will aid you to get rooms. I will come to Nerot's as soon as I can and from there we will send word to Whitehall.' Then he turned to Amélie. 'I will also, from there, make contact with the French émigrés already in London, in the hope that one of them will find both you and the count a more permanent residence.'

'I have no desire to be a burden, Jean, on your conscience or your purse.' That made Pearce smart; he was having his own words thrown back in his face. 'I have my jewels to sell to support myself.'

'I do not say,' he responded coldly, 'that you will not have to consider such a sale, but not yet, not until I have seen you comfortably settled. Now, Monsieur the Count has the means to keep you until then, so if you do not mind I have matters to attend to which cannot be delayed.'

Michael had to be provided for as well, which Pearce did from his own purse, more than enough to get him to Lymington, and he took off him the satchel Michael had so that he could carry his pistols, recovered case included, and the remains of the government gold. While they were mounting up to depart, Pearce had the smugglers' saddlebags taken round so they could extract any personal items, he joking that unlike them he was not a thief and that what they took out could be rolled into their riding dusters, these tied into bundles for them by the *Larcher*'s crew. As that was happening, with much unobserved rummaging from Jahleel Tolland, he was saying a final farewell to his friend, now mounted.

'I take it, John-boy, that none of what has occurred here is to be told to Mrs Barclay?'

'God no, and forgive me if I remind you not to call her by that name. Remember its Raynesford in these parts.'

Emily Barclay knew that, waiting outside for the midday coach to make a short and prearranged stop at the King's Head – the morning one had been full – she was the object of much interest from the local population. Many women had found an excuse to promenade up and down, for her imminent departure had been passed down the parochial rumour-fed grapevine. All seemed to be in pairs, this no doubt so they could whisper to each other under their parasols and compare impressions, not one of which would be flattering.

There were a fair number of menfolk too, the idle of course, who might have been loitering anyway, but not just them. Better dressed and more well-fed creatures seemed to have found a reason to traverse Quay Street, which they did alone and, if they glanced in her direction and she caught their eye, Emily saw in that a message wholly different from that of their womenfolk – nothing short of a desire that, in better circumstances, they might have become acquainted.

Partly to damn the whole charade, she had dressed well in a gown that showed a decent amount of décolleté and done her hair so it was a crown above her head, that flattering her long and slender neck. She had also eschewed the wearing of a bonnet so that anyone who wished to gaze on her very obvious beauty could do so, that not being the reason Emily had dressed in that manner; like many very attractive women she did not see herself in that way, which would have meant indulging in the sin of vanity. Her motive was to face down their ill-informed criticism and to send the message that, for her, their opinion, especially that of the ladies of the town, carried no weight whatsoever.

There was also the fact that those well-heeled male admirers who had looked in her direction – many if not all of whom would have been hard-pressed to give a valid reason for their perambulations – would be marked, and she was in no doubt they would pay a price in local tittle-tattle for showing any interest in a person perceived as a fallen woman. Lymington, if smaller, was little different from her hometown of Frome; these were the provincial mores that were followed there and they would likewise pertain here.

The curious seemed to congregate as the four-horse coach made its way up the incline that formed the road to the harbour, its iron hoops rattling on the cobbles and the driver calling loudly to his team to put in more effort, till finally it stopped outside the front entrance. For a moment Emily thought she was going to be obliged to load her own luggage, so tardy was the man on the box to get down – no one from the inn itself was to hand – but having fixed him with a cold stare, he responded with a grunt and leapt down to do his duty.

'An' where would you be headed, lady?'

'Does it not suffice that I am leaving Lymington?'

'Curious, that's all.'

As, thought Emily, is everyone else; the whole town is dying to know where I am going, no doubt with a mind to writing if they have a close-by relative or friend to warn of what now resided in their vicinity. This was what John Pearce did not appreciate, that the act of living openly with another man out of wedlock was far from as simple as he supposed. Still, it could have been worse: she had once seen someone named as a strumpet pelted with sods of mud when being driven ignominiously out of Frome; it was to her shame now, as she took a seat in the coach, that she, a fourteen-year-old, had heartily approved of both the censure and the method of demonstrating it.

There were three other passengers in the coach and they had obviously been advised of her character; none would catch her eye.

With Michael gone in one direction and the Buckler's Hard equines in another, the time came for Pearce to gather his charges and get them moving, which took them into the forest and down a sloping track to the riverbank. Enquiries as to where they were being taken were ignored, as they joined two eight-oared ship's boats waiting in a small inlet, brought there by eight more sailors. Untied, the captives were split into two parties of four, were ushered aboard and once their restraints had been lashed to the thwarts on which they would sit, their escorts followed to take up the oars.

'What's the game, Pearce?' Franklin Tolland asked

as the two boats were pushed off, the oars beginning a rhythmic dipping that took them quickly downriver.

'Peace and quiet, the latter of which you would be best served to follow, lest you want to be gagged. That goes for all of you. Stay silent and breathe easy or take a gag and struggle to get in air.'

Pearce would have loved to talk, to seek to tell them the whole story of his foolishness, to prove to them that he as a source of any information was a waste of effort. He probably would still not be believed and, besides, he had no desire to diminish himself in the presence of even such a benign group of tars that manned his boat. Not that his offence was extant: he had paid his price for the crime of smuggling, or rather Charlie Taverner and Rufus Dommet had done so by volunteering for the navy to get any sanction against him set aside. Smugglers, which they claimed and were believed to be, were highly prized aboard a warship, given they were already competent sailors who required no training in any aspect of sailing a ship or keeping it in good repair.

It had been a well-practised gambit for *contrabandiers* over the years to avoid being jailed or strung up for their nefarious trade: sacrifice a couple of their least competent men to the King's Navy and magistrates would set aside their convictions and see them wiped from the record. It never seemed to occur to those freeing their villains that they immediately went back to their old trade; replacing lost hands was never a problem in east-coast and Channel towns where smuggling was a near industry.

The boats moved at a steady enough pace on fresh water and a falling tide but that became less so as they exited the estuary and pulled out on to the Solent, where if there was not much of a sea it was enough to making rowing twice as hard. Pearce went down to four oars at a time and settled for the slower pace that imposed; if he wanted the business finished he had no mind that the crew of HMS *Larcher* should suffer for it.

In a busy shipping lane they occasionally came under scrutiny, in one instance close enough to a frigate for Pearce's blue coat to tell them that here were a pair of navy boats. Also the dishevelled state of their passengers, being in riding clothes clearly not tars like the men on the oars, was noticeable. The hail from the quarterdeck for information got no more than a wave; he was not about to shout out where he was going and given the frigate was heading out to sea they passed each other by in such a short space of time to not allow for repeated request.

'No need to be shy, Pearce,' Jahleel Tolland said, speaking for the first time since he had been forced aboard and lashed down. 'Don't take a sharp mind to work out what you're about, given the heading.'

'It won't last, Pearce,' Franklin spat. 'I for one will come after you till death takes my breath and there will be no more mercy in my thinking.'

'I never thought there was much anyway, and I would say this is a poor place to be sending out threats, that is unless you can swim.'

'Idle that,' Jahleel crowed. 'You ain't got the stomach to see a man die an' your hand in it.'

'So you keep telling me, which sits odd with the fellow you think I am. No, even if I can imagine what extremes you might have gone to question me, I cannot just do murder, nor condemn you to the hangman's noose. All I can assure you is a degree of discomfort that will be a daily burden on your black heart, for I have served before the mast in a King's ship.'

'You, now't but a hand.'

'More than just that, I hope, but none of your concern. Now be silent or face the gag.'

It was a long row, four on four, rarely out sight of the shore, until they raised the classical frontage of the Haslar seamen's hospital and Pearce got all the oars working. There was no mistaking the vessel he wanted, given it had three short stumps on its deck instead of tall masts. An old 100-gun ship it was now a hulk anchored offshore, the proximity to Haslar more to convenience the medical coves that needed to visit with frequency than anyone aboard.

As a vessel anchored head and stern and one that never moved, the receiving hulk HMS *York* was surrounded by its own filth – waste from both cooking, cleaning and the heads – dependent on the tide to remove the effluent, and that only ever wholly successful when there was a bit of a blow. Thus the smell easily overwhelmed the briny odour of clear water and had even Pearce's oarsmen looking uncomfortable as they swept round the stern to pull close to a gangway that led up to the barred entry port to the main deck.

If Jahleel Tolland had worked out the destination long past, half his gang had not and the sight and smell set them cursing and wailing, noises which Pearce made no attempt to stop; he had never taken pressed men aboard a vessel such as this but he had good grounds to feel that that was how they commonly behaved. Ordering the boats to be tied off he made his way up the gangway and spoke to the marine sentinel, who unlocked the gate and ushered him in. There was no ceremony here, no bosun's whistles or guard lined up, even if an admiral came calling; this was the pit of hell and indifference as far as the navy was concerned.

Nor was it a posting to attract the better class of officer, and the man in command, a Lieutenant Moyle, though he had granted himself some comfort in what had once been the captain's cabin, was very much not out of the top drawer. There were, to Pearce's mind, an excess of mirrors in the space but Moyle had a settle on which he could conduct business and a comfortable chair for his visitors or guests, for the pay and perks were good. It was a command that went to someone well connected or perhaps a fellow owed a favour by some superior officer.

His face was wide and his skin showed a trace of a bloodline not wholly British, perhaps with a Caribbean influence, for all that his eyes were blue, only truly visible when he took them from their common drooping state to wide open and that came about at any mention of money. Not that the subject came up first, for Pearce, while he was willing that the Tolland gang should be pressed and trigger a bounty, also had certain favours he wished to request, all designed to fit a policy yet to be forwarded.

'Prime hands, you say.'

'They are that, Mr Moyle, and it would not surprise me to find that they were engaged in the smuggling trade.'

'Then doubly welcome, sir. Would you care to make that assessment official?'

'No, but perhaps you could question them and ascertain the nature of their occupation.'

'There's credit to be had, Mr Pearce, for fetching in such men, and not just from the navy. The Government might issue you a reward.'

'Then, sir, let it be yours, for I am sure it will enhance your situation many times more than it will do so for my own.' That was when Pearce had to pause and look Moyle right in the eye, aware that such a statement of generosity had shocked the fellow. 'And for that perhaps you could do me a service in return?'

Moyle did not respond right away and the slight smile that came upon his face was far from reassuring; he looked to be a man too calculating to trust. 'And what would that be?'

'It is my intention to write to a certain post captain who has aboard his vessel two men I consider followers of mine.'

'You fear he will not release them?'

Now it was Pearce's turn to produce a wry smile. 'I fear we are not what you could call friends. I had in mind to offer him in their place twice the number and if they were prime hands, which I fully suspect these fellows I have fetched along to be, it would be an odd commanding officer who would hold out against such an offer.'

'You said eight volunteers in all.'

Pearce had to stop himself then; the navy called everyone they pressed a volunteer but it was pure smoke.

'Yes. I am aware that when a demand comes in for hands, a man in your position is not always able to oblige a fellow officer, even as much as you may desire to do so.

I am very afraid that if these eight are sent together to one ship then that may be introducing onto the lower decks a nuisance capable of causing much dissent.'

Moyle knew what that meant: mutiny.

'So in order that such a thing should be guarded against, that is if you are unable to hold them and meet my previous request, the eight men should be split into two fours and sent to different vessels, with the added fact that two of them are brothers and should be separated. You cannot mistake them: one you will see as a natural leader—'

'He will not be that aboard my ship, sir,' Moyle barked, 'and if he tends to that, be so good as to point him out and I will see he receives special treatment to cool his spirit.'

'I believe his given name to be Jahleel and I do think a little extra discipline might do him good. The other brother is younger and seeks to appear more cultured. He has a scar on his cheek and is easy to mark.

'Be assured we shall take some rough sand to buff off his refinement.'

'Then I am content.'

'You are due a bounty, Mr Pearce,' Moyle said, standing from the settle and walking to his deck, pausing on the way to catch his image in one of the many mirrors, which hinted to Pearce at an excess of vanity. 'I will be happy to write the warrant that allows you to draw it from the Navy Board at your convenience.'

'Mr Moyle, I discussed with those hands I have the honour to command and we felt that since taking these men up was in the nature of being fortuitous it was felt that any bounty should go to the Greenwich Chest.' Pearce produced a false laugh. 'For none of us knows when we might be in need of a pension and with Haslar hard by it is also, in wartime, a place any one of us could end up with a wound.'

'That, sir, is very noble, indeed!' Moyle exclaimed, yet the look of cunning that crept into those narrowed eyes implied the opposite: that only a fool turns down a bounty. 'Charitable indeed.'

'Also,' Pearce said, knowing he was at the crux, 'it may well incline you towards my earlier request.'

That made Moyle sit down in his desk chair, very slowly, and it was clear his mind was working at pace and when he spoke he was obviously playing for time to continue whatever train of thought he was on. 'Your earlier request?'

'Yes, it is one that concerns me as you may have noticed. No officer likes to see his personal followers under the command of another and the officer in question is . . . how should I say . . . strict.'

'Of course.'

That was followed by several seconds of silence, in which all that could be heard was the creaking of the old hulk as it rose and fell on the swell. Then Moyle spoke, in a voice meant to be friendly, which it was not, unlike the calculation, which was clear.

'It occurs to me, sir, that if I enter these fellows as soon as they come aboard, I cannot keep them from any draft that is called for from a vessel short of hands and needing to get to sea, and that happens very frequently since every captain is short of hands.'

'To do so would risk your position, sir.'

'Sir, it would destroy it.'

'I am aware of what is at stake.'

'I have it!' Moyle cried, leaving Pearce sure he was about to articulate a thought he had arrived at long before. 'The trick is not to enter them right off, but to leave it to me to register them as volunteers when I hear from you regarding your followers.'

'Sir, that is nothing short of brilliant, but can you carry it off?'

Moyle's voice dropped, taking on an air of imparting a confidence. 'I am very much my own master here, sir. The men I command fear me, as is only right, for I can ship them off to sea as easy as any of the men we hold. And as for higher authority, well, I never see them for one month to the next. I will hold these men in an unlogged capacity and await your instructions. How would that suit?'

'It would suit me fine.'

The brow furrowed, again Pearce thought a bit theatrically.

'One problem does present itself. When the time comes to enlist them I will have to do so under my own name.'

'Yes.'

'I am happy of course to do so.'

Happy, Pearce thought, to take the bounty yourself or assign it to some relative or friend for a commission: neither the Greenwich Chest nor Haslar would see a penny.

'Sir,' Pearce cried, standing up. 'It is rare to have dealings with such an honest, and may I say perspicacious fellow. I give you my hand.'

'And I, sir, am glad to take it.' The grasp was firm, but Moyle would not look him in the eye lest it reveal his avarice. 'Now, lead me to your volunteers, so I may see them aboard, checked for vermin and settled in cells.'

CHAPTER NINE

Ship visiting was not a prerogative much extended to midshipmen, added to which HMS *Agamemnon*, for the officers of Hotham's flagship, was a destination it would be unwise to frequent, given the admiral's known dislike of Commodore Nelson. Toby Burns suffered a few frustrating days in which he could see but not touch deliverance; like many people who form a notion untested against reality, the idea that Richard Farmiloe was his route to salvation grew from a possibility to an absolute certainty. In the end it was the reverse; Nelson came visiting and brought with him his acting lieutenant, more as a courtesy to the lad than necessity – when it came to the conference being held to discuss the attack on Calvi, as far as the navy was concerned it was captains and above only.

Given his acting rank, Farmiloe was invited to the wardroom, likewise barred to mids, and Toby had to wait until his erstwhile saviour had been wined and picked clean of news from home – so much more available in Gibraltar – mostly about the progress of the war. The twin and mutually exclusive desires of his fellow lieutenants would be exposed: the men who occupied that section of the ship wished for the nation to be triumphant but they also hoped that if victory came it would not be too soon to allow them the chance of advancement and, of course, prize money. Eventually Farmiloe came up for air and Toby could accost him.

'Gosh, Dick, it's so good to see you.'

The effusiveness of that greeting threw Farmiloe somewhat, for if he had known Toby Burns since the outbreak of war he did not consider him to be a close friend, even if, both aboard HMS *Brilliant* and at the recent siege of Bastia, he had intervened to provide cover for his manifest shortcomings. At the latter they had manned a forward battery together, trading shots with a too close enemy, the recollection of which added another stream of terror to the Burns nightmares, not least that he should have been in receipt of a wound like the man originally given command.

'How is Lieutenant Andrews?'

'Fully recovered, Toby, which I daresay you could tell by the mere use of a long glass to rake our quarterdeck.' The head gesture to *Agamemnon*, berthed within plain view, underlined the point. 'How do you fare with all your afflictions?'

That made serious the Burns countenance; his health and well-being a matter of prime concern. Yet it also presented him with an opportunity to take matters all the way back to Sheerness.

'I am in topping form, Dick, almost since the first time we met.' The Burns face took on a wistful look now. 'Do you recall that day when you first came aboard my uncle's frigate?'

'Hard to do so here, Toby, in "brilliant" sunshine.'

Farmiloe waited for the pun on the ship's name to strike; he waited in vain, for his companion was more concerned with the low cloud and scudding rains of the Medway, immediately recalled and described. 'And that was before the mids turned to unpleasant duties.'

Farmiloe laughed. 'I seem to recall that we new mids found any duty we were asked to perform congenial.'

'Some more than others, Dick. Do you recall, for instance, the night you went out pressing seamen?'

The change in Farmiloe's posture, the stiffening, was palpable. 'Not fondly.'

'You regret it?'

'I do, not that I hold any responsibility for the act, that falls to your Uncle Ralph.'

'Who faced a court martial for it.'

'And was acquitted, I seem to recall.'

There was a note in Farmiloe's voice, faint but detectable, of something like disapproval, or was it latent amazement? He had been sent off to the Bay of Biscay with John Pearce and his Pelicans, under the command of Henry Digby, a former lieutenant aboard HMS *Brilliant*, in short all the people who could have blown the testimony given at the court martial out of the water.

'Dick, I think I need to confide in you, but before I do, I would ask that you peruse this letter I received from

London, I think from a lawyer fellow acting on behalf of John Pearce.'

'Named Lucknor?'

'How do you know that?'

'I had a letter too, asking me about that night.'

'They seek to embroil you?'

'No. It merely asked for information and made it perfectly plain that I was in no danger, given my rank.'

'Mine is, I think, less kindly meant. Will you read it?'

There was clear reluctance; Dick Farmiloe had been part of the gang doing the misdeed on that night and it had until recently been long buried at the back of his mind. He had not enjoyed having it dragged up by Lucknor's letter. It took no genius to deduce who the lawyer was after and on whose behalf he was working. Added to that, and despite what the lawyer had intimated, if Ralph Barclay came a cropper others would get caught up in the backwash and he might be one of them.

'Who do you think is behind it, Toby?'

'Why, John Pearce of course, he means to dish my uncle come hell or high water.'

'I reckon the same, but I apologised to Pearce for my part and I am glad I did so, for he turned out to be a very decent fellow and damned brave at that.'

'Apologised?'

That was said so Toby Burns could cover for the hearing of an opinion at total odds with his own; Pearce decent and brave? The man was a menace. He did however press the letter on Farmiloe, who took it very reluctantly and read it very slowly. When Burns thought he had finished, the point at which his eyes flicked back to the top of the page, it was time to speak.

'Dick, I have something to tell you and, in part, it is a confession of my stupidity.'

The letter was waved. 'I have no desire to be involved in this.'

'But you are my friend, not in as deep as me, but involved nonetheless.'

Sensing Farmiloe trying to digest and rationalise that, Toby started speaking quickly, outlining how Hotham had arranged matters to ensure an acquittal.

'Anyone who knew anything germane was sent away – you and Digby, for instance. The depositions that the Pelicans made and signed, Pearce included, written out by Hotham's second clerk, were never introduced into the hearing. My uncle lied, so did his clerk Gherson and me – well, I was pressed by family obligation to come to the aid of Captain Barclay.'

That, 'family obligation', sounded so much better than the truth; Toby Burns had done as he was asked for a number of mixed emotions: downright terror of that uncle by marriage and what he could do as a post captain to a lowly midshipman. Added to that was a compete absence of backbone compounded by a visceral hatred of John Pearce. Toby Burns, very early on in HMS *Brilliant*'s commission, had received accolades for an act of conspicuous bravery; the man who truly deserved the plaudits was none other than the same John Pearce, acts which had earned him and his friends a reluctant discharge from Barclay, nothing short of a release from the navy.

Added to that was the fear that retribution would be visited upon him for obeying another instruction from his uncle; that should they, in the act of taking home a prize ship, encounter in soundings any vessel looking for hands, then the fact that the Pelicans had been released from the navy on the grounds of being landsmen need not be made plain. Toby Burns had remained silent when he could have spoken to save them from being pressed for a second time and, on many an occasion, he had uncomfortably reprised the threat that Pearce had made: that one day he would be made to pay.

'And that letter indicates what I was called upon to say.'

'Why were you called as a witness?' Farmiloe demanded. 'You never left the ship that night.'

'No, but my uncle, as far as the hearing was concerned, had me in place of you. He persuaded me to say that I made a mistake and landed the press gang in the wrong part of the river, in the Liberties of the Savoy rather than just upriver of Blackfriars Bridge where anyone we found could have been taken legally. In short, the impressment became illegal by my faulty direction rather than any action by my Uncle Ralph.'

'And they believed this?'

'Dick, it was rigged from the start. Who do you think chose the captains to sit in judgement, the same man who suppressed those depositions?'

'Hotham?'

Toby held a finger to his lips; that was not a name to mention out loud on the man's own flagship, given the subject. 'Trouble is, somehow my part in the farrago has become known. The fellow who signed that might only hint at seeking information, but the questions he poses leaves me in no doubt of what he is fishing for.'

'Evidence against your uncle?'

'Damn my uncle, Dick,' Burns quietly wailed, 'he's out to get me. I lied to the court, and is it a defence to say I was coerced?'

'You want my advice?'

'Do you know that you can hang for perjury and I was under oath?'

'Do you?'

'Yes.'

'Then tell the truth now.' Seeing the shock on Toby's face, Farmiloe spoke at a more rapid speed than hitherto. 'Reply to this fellow as I did, tell him everything, the truth unvarnished, as I did and I am sure that such an admission will sit well with any court assembled to judge the case.'

'Court? You think there will be one?'

A piping voice floated from the quarterdeck. 'Mr Farmiloe, is that young Burns I see you with?'

'It is, sir.'

Nelson lifted his hat. 'Good day to you, Mr Burns, I hope I find you well.'

'You do, sir,' Burns replied, cursing the man for his intervention at this time; there was, however, the requirement of a reply. 'And you, sir, how are you?'

'Plagued as ever, Mr Burns. Farmiloe there will tell you, if there is an affliction in the air, and as you know that is full of such things, it finds Nelson first and most viciously. I swear I am naught but a medical bellwether for those with whom I serve.'

'Until a cannon goes off in anger,' Farmiloe whispered, a fond and, to Toby's mind, a mistaken note of affection in his voice. 'Then the cure is instant.'

'I fear I must tear you apart, my young friends. Mr Farmiloe, it is time you called in my barge.'

That Richard Farmiloe then bent his head to talk earnestly to Toby Burns had every other officer on the quarterdeck of HMS *Britannia* – and the conference just concluded, there were many post captains – either nonplussed, or, in one or two cases, seething with fury. Commodore Nelson had issued a precise instruction to one of his officers, a very junior one by his appearance, who then saw fit to take his time in obeying; the only person not in the least put out was Nelson himself, which only underlined to many his main failing: he might be a tiger in a fight, but he was a booby when it came to discipline!

'Write that letter, Toby, tell all and condemn yourself if need be, but do not spare anyone else either, whatever their rank.' That was plain enough: if it meant dishing Hotham along with Ralph Barclay he should do so. 'This is bound to come out if Pearce is pursuing matters and the only hope you have for your own neck is a confession.'

'Damn Pearce,' Toby said, tears pricking his eyes.

'Damn your uncle if you must, but not John Pearce, for I am sure if he were here he would forgive you.'

No he would not, Toby thought, as his hand was grasped and shaken. Why is it that I am the only one who can see Pearce for the poltroon he is? As he was ruminating on that and his own endangered future, Dick Farmiloe was shouting that the commodore's barge should make for the entry port. Soon, with much whistling and stamping of marines, the ship began to empty of all these captains and their attendants but what emerged as gossip was not anything to cheer a midshipman who wished to avoid danger; the siege of Calvi was about to begin, indeed it would proceed as soon as Lord Hood signalled it should proceed.

Alongside fellow passengers who could not even talk to each other, lest it inadvertently include her, Emily Barclay was free to peer through the gap left in the coach door blind and take stock of the sunlit New Forest, a place to her of some attraction. Having made her statement about leaving, it had soon occurred to her that she had very few choices of where to go. The idea of going back to Frome was anathema, not least because it would require her to share her marital home with Ralph Barclay's twittering sisters, all spinsters and destined to remain so. To them their brother was the very soul of probity, brave beyond peradventure and close to saintliness in his personal habits. To tell them the truth, that he was a bully as well as an endemically dishonest satyr, would bring Emily satisfaction but it would not be believed.

Nor could she return to her old family home, for to do so would send a message to the whole town that the marriage of one of their most potent citizens was not as it should be. Never mind the rumour mill, her parents would be aghast that their comfortable life would be threatened by her actions. They would not see her case even if it were explained; selfishness and the fear of gossip would combine to bring upon her pressure to make amends with her husband, something she knew she could never do.

Nor did she have friends outside of her hometown and all of her relations lived in close proximity; from there, upon marriage, she had gone aboard her husband's frigate and if she had met other naval wives none were more than an acquaintance. How distant that seemed and not only because of the dismal February-March weather. Unlike now, there had been no money to spare then – Ralph Barclay had been on half pay for five whole years and was plagued before departure and after the wedding with impatient creditors. Keeping his wife on the ship saved him the cost of leaving her at home where she would require to run the house and incur expense; his sisters were enough of a charge upon his purse without he should add to it.

If her new husband was not passionate there had been romance in that one act, for it had only come to her afterwards that it was brought on by dearth. When first mooted it had sounded different, for Emily was told very quickly by others that for a serving naval officer to have his wife aboard was against all the rules of the service and here was her new spouse flouting them for, she supposed, proximity to her. She had found out the true reason when, in the company of other wives, she had gone shopping in the Medway for the kind of stores a naval captain needed to hold up his head afloat. Ralph Barclay had gone wild when he saw what she had spent and most of her purchases had been returned forthwith.

Would John Pearce get the note she had left, or would that innkeeper fail to hand it over on his return? Even then he should go to where she was now headed, for he had kept rooms at Nerot's Hotel and that was, at least, a place where she was known and could book into under her own name. Pearce had taken a room for her there after that unfortunate fracas with a group of men she had come to understand were smugglers. Even if he failed to get the note, given he must report back to the Government, he would come there regardless.

Pulling into Lyndhurst, Emily guessed that they would stop at the local inn for a fresh team of horses, then wondered if the passengers would change, glad that two of them appeared fidgety enough to indicate that they might alight here, that more obvious as the coachman called down to say they were approaching the Stag and that they should get ready. There was the usual creaking and sudden darkness as they swung under the arch that led to the stables and she too made ready to alight, in her case to take some refreshment and stretch her legs. Such things were the commonality of travel; the surprise was that when the coachman jumped down and opened the door, the first person Emily saw, standing with two well-dressed people, one male the other female, was Michael O'Hagan.

'Michael,' she called, leaning out of the door. 'Is John here too?'

Under his breath, as he turned, O'Hagan was cursing a God in whom he wholeheartedly believed but knew to be fickle. 'And Jesus,' he hissed to himself as he hurried to the coach door, 'Not only what is she doing here, but how do I greet her?'

'No, John-boy is on an errand.'

'But he is back from France, he must be if you are here.'

'Yes, we berthed yesterday.'

The brow furrowed as Emily demanded, 'And why did he not come to Lymington?'

'He had some pressing matters to attend to, like those folk you see me with. They are envoys from where we went to, come to talk to the Government, I believe, and I am to get them aboard this Winchester coach and off to London an' may the Good Lord aid them when they get there, for there is not a word of English in either of them.'

'Then I must help them, for I speak French and I too am on my way to London.'

That she thought the Irishman confused became obvious as he threw his eyes skywards. It was not that simple question that troubled him but many others, not least the notion of a pair of women John Pearce was determined should never meet sharing near two whole days of intimate coach travel.

'But were you not to wait in Lymington?'

Emily dropped her head to hide a slight blush. 'Circumstances forced a change of plan. Now best you introduce me to these people.'

'Which I will do Mrs . . . Holy Mary, what do I call you?'

'Emily will do, Michael; after all, we have seen too much together to be anything other than good friends.'

'Sure, I thank you kindly for the sentiment, but I am going to have to introduce you and I was told by John-boy to use the name Raynesford.'

'I am back to being Mrs Barclay,' she replied rather testily.

'Strikes me, Mrs Barclay, that you would be better alighting here and going back to where John-boy expects to meet you.'

'Do not ask me to explain, Michael, but that is not possible.'

'I am to go there so I could escort you.'

'No! I will make my way to Nerot's and have left a note saying so. Are you all right Michael, you look pale?'

'Perfectly so, Mrs Barclay,' he lied, for he was feeling that if he had been standing on an insecure trapdoor it had just opened to cast him into a pit of all the snakes the saints had rid his homeland of.

'Introductions.'

'Happen, since you have their tongue, you'd be best seeing that yourself, for I am bound to falter over their names, them bein' hard to pronounce.'

'Then hand me down.'

Which he did, to lead her over to the count and Amélie, the former getting a half curtsy, the latter receiving a warm smile and a welcome to *Angleterre*. At least, Michael thought, with some relief, Emily Barclay does not recognise the Labordière name. He was not to travel with them, so if the dung did fly inside the coach he would be well out of it.

'I am going to take our guests into the inn for refreshments, Michael, would you care to join us?'

'No time, Mrs Barclay, I've got to see to certain matters that I am charged to perform for John-boy.'

'Jean-boy? *Une appellation, très jolie, n'est-ce pas?*

Amélie Labordière, having said this with a warm smile, got a curious response from Emily Barclay, given it hinted at an intimacy that should not have been formed in what could only have been a few days' acquaintance. Michael watched them as they went indoors, thinking that when his friend next met Emily Barclay, there was going to be hell to pay and no pitch hot.

Sir Phillip Stephens was wondering if that bane of his life, Admiral Sir Berkley Sumners, had gone off his head, for the letter he had sent in this time made no sense at all. What was the old fool talking about with secret missions and his aiding them to fruition? And who was this Lieutenant Raynesford whom he had already told the sod was an officer who did not exist? There was a suspicion that Sumners was just making waves where none were present, but the undertone of his letter was that there was some chicanery afoot somewhere – either this Raynesford was a projector seeking to make some underhand money; the other thought, that perhaps he was a French spy, had Sir Phillip calling in a clerk.

'I need to send a note to Mr Dundas.'

CHAPTER TEN

Freed of the Tolland gang, the eight-oared cutters were much lighter, but against that the tide was still rising, which would make it a doubly long haul back to Lymington, the next destination; from there the ship's boats could be taken back the relatively short distance to Buckler's Hard at a time of year when, thankfully, there was no shortage of daylight. The option of waiting in either Gosport or Portsmouth did not appeal, so Pearce aimed for the boatbuilding seaside town of Cowes, which had the advantage, even so close to Spithead, of not being naval in any way; the only military presence resided in the forts built by Henry the Eighth to repel a French invasion and they were manned by soldiers.

Snug in the River Medina they could tie up at one of the many jetties and proceed to a tavern to eat fresh food, albeit the instruction was to go easy in the article of drink, and it was there that John Pearce heard first of the great victory being claimed by the Channel Fleet, of which the place was abuzz, not that anyone expressed surprise; Britannia ruled the waves and if the French had ever beaten a British fleet – and it had to be admitted that had happened – then it could only be by the employment of low and despicable cunning.

Not only had the King's favourite admiral, Black Dick Howe, trounced the French battle fleet, but he had sunk – it depended on who was declaiming – anything from a hundred to five hundred merchant ships bringing grain from the Americas. Seeing one of his oarsmen about to respond and put the boaster right, Pearce intervened and ordered him to be silent. His mission had been a secret one and even here it had to remain that. The subject did not arise again until much later, when on a falling tide they were rowing south-west towards the Lymington Estuary and one of his crew raised the question.

'Savin' your presence, sir, how can that be, for we saw those very ships an' too close for comfort?'

'Simple, is it not? Rumour runs ahead of truth every time. For all we know Admiral Lord Howe has suffered a reverse and is at this very moment sitting in a boat this size wondering what happened to his ship.'

The reaction to that was amusing, so much so that Pearce had to control his features; if the people of Britain held that their ships and men were inherently superior to the French, that was as nothing to the opinion of the men employed to sail them, which never ceased to amaze the man on the tiller. He did not know if any aboard HMS *Larcher* had been pressed, it was not an enquiry any officer made, but he did know that for every willing volunteer going to sea they were far outnumbered by those who chose to serve as an alternative to a miserable existence ashore, which could extend to downright starvation. It had always annoyed his father that such people carried within them a patriotic attachment to a form of government that served them so ill.

'But we must assume,' Pearce added, to restore his own standing as much as anything, 'that our men had trounced the sods good and proper.'

'Hear him,' came the chorus, even from those whose breath must be constrained by the need to row.

'You're sure of this, Gherson?' Ralph Barclay demanded, as he sought to digest the information that his clerk had brought back from *Queen Charlotte*, where he had gone to deliver the ship's logs and accounts.

'One of Lord Howe's fellows chose to confide in me, sir, I daresay in respect to the freemasonry of our occupation. The despatch to the Admiralty was dictated by Sir Roger Curtis in the presence of Lord Howe and it questioned the actions of several of the ship's captains as to their participation, or not, in the battle. Many, it was claimed, were tardy when it came to obeying what were clear orders. Others were praised for their application and they have been recommended for special favour.'

'Any names given?'

'Captain Molloy was particularly censured for inaction it seems, but he was not alone. The general tone of Sir Roger's communication was that too many officers dithered instead of acting promptly.'

'I meant me,' Barclay snapped, 'as you damn well know.'

'Your name was not mentioned, sir,' Gherson replied, leaving his employer in limbo.

Sitting on the cushioned casement at the rear of his cabin, injured and bandaged leg stretched out, Ralph Barclay was back in that action, examining his own behaviour and wondering if it could be interpreted as sluggish? He recalled that the flagship had ordered him to close with the enemy several times before he actually did so, but he was sure he could justify those actions on the grounds of a crew not fully worked up, with the added problem that being so close to *Queen Charlotte* as she engaged – *Semele* was the next vessel astern – he knew, as she put down her helm to close, he stood a chance of being a victim of her shot as much as the enemy; thus he had held off until that threat had diminished.

Yet he had fought hard once he met his opposite number, having let the one he was ordered to engage go by. That had come about because he had really been given no choice as their forward rigging became entangled. Only superior gunnery, the rate of fire of his cannon, had saved HMS *Semele* from a severe mauling. After a long pounding it was *Vengeur* that had suffered and, added to that, damn it, he had taken a serious wound.

'I daresay a good dinner and a few bottles of claret could tell us more.'

That got Gherson a very cold stare; he no more trusted his clerk than the man trusted him, not that Ralph Barclay was much given to reposing faith in anyone. If he did not quite see himself as alone against a hostile world he did know that there were forces extant who seemed to have it as their aim to do him down and it had been like that since his first day of service as a midshipman. It had come home to Ralph Barclay very early in his naval career that no man got anywhere lest he had on his side someone with more weight. Thus he had always attached himself to men with power, first senior lieutenants, later captains and finally admirals, the most potent of whom had been Lord Rodney, a man who knew his responsibilities to his followers: he saw to it that if there was a plum going it went to them.

Rodney's death had been a setback compounded by the elevation of Lord Hood to the Board of Admiralty. Hood had little regard for Rodney and he had no inclination to promote those who had depended on a deceased superior, which had left Ralph Barclay, a very outspoken and loyal follower, on the beach for five whole years until the outbreak of the war, and even when he had been employed it had not matched his place on the captain's list. The likes of Nelson, one of Hood's favourites, got a ship of the line; he had been given a frigate and one that only just made its rating as a post captain's command.

'Do you wish for me to arrange to meet with the said clerk, sir?'

That brought Barclay back to the present and his original thought that Gherson probably already knew the answer to the proposed question and was just seeking to dun him for a good meal ashore. Not that he felt he had much alternative but to agree: slippery Gherson, who now had on his absurdly handsome face that knowing smile which so irritated his employer, would never let on lest he was indulged.

'Very well, but before you go I want you to read back

to me that repeat letter I composed to my wife. I want to make sure it leaves her in no doubt of her choices now that circumstances have altered, then it can be sent.' The voice changed, becoming harsh. 'Which are to return to the marital home or damn well starve.'

How do I tell him, Gherson was thinking, that he is in no position to make demands? In his mind he imagined Emily Barclay reading such a letter, which would be passed on by a solicitor called Studdert she had engaged. It was not so very different from those that had preceded it except it did allude quite openly to her having nothing now with which to threaten him, which she would almost certainly know to be false. He had arranged for the solicitor's offices to be burgled by a low character called Codge but they had not found the copy of the court martial record, leaving the only possible alternative that Emily Barclay had retrieved it before the break-in.

She would thus be well aware that she had no need to pay any heed to his instructions, so much so that she had refused to even reply to the previous communication he had sent before HMS *Semele* sailed to join the Channel Fleet. Was now the time to be open and save his employer from making a fool of himself, to tell him the robbery had gone wrong? Never one to leap before it became imperative, Gherson held his tongue and went to Barclay's desk, there to retrieve and read out what had been dictated, aware of the change in his employer's demeanour each time he espoused the more threatening passages.

The knock at the door led to a command from Barclay to wait until Gherson had finished. The cry that the visitor could enter brought in a midshipman with a message from the officer of the watch to the effect that there was boat alongside with an invitation from Captain Molloy to dine, the name making Barclay frown and raising an amused Gherson eyebrow.

'My compliments to Captain Molloy and I fear my injury prevents me from acceptance.'

'Aye, aye, sir,' said the mid prior to his exit, which left the two men looking at each other, for both knew that had he so wished, Barclay was healed enough to cross to another ship and back without danger to his wound. But Molloy was under a cloud, the flagship clerk had named him, so he was not a safe person to associate with, regardless of long acquaintance.

It was impossible to invest Calvi purely from the sea; the castle which guarded the bay sat on a high and rocky promontory right above the only deep-water channel into the harbour, while the rest of the wide cove was cursed with extended shallows that precluded a ship of any draught from taking up a position to bombard the town from anything like a reasonable distance, which was in itself dangerous against shore-based fire. Likewise the coast to the east was low-lying, and while eminently suitable for landing by boats, did not put the attacker in any position to use their own artillery to subdue the defences, which would have to be completed before any actual assault could take place and even then that would be bloody.

Thus, after much discussion, it had been decided to land at a bay a little down the west coast then seek to take the high ground above the town itself, which would at least give the guns parity with the defenders, the caveat to that being the need to get the cannon off the warships and ashore, then up the steep escarpments to where the battery positions would be constructed, something the defenders might well think impossible. For all the jocularity and keen anticipation of the forthcoming battle, there was an undertow of hidden concern throughout the fleet. They would be landing on a hostile shore from boats – never easy, and if the garrison of Calvi was limited and insufficient to hold the beach they were still numerous enough to inflict heavy casualties prior to withdrawal.

Thus, with the fleet hove to and Lord Hood's permission to proceed, there was a final conference aboard HMS *Victory*, anchored off San Fiorenzo, really an excuse for a capital dinner at which the commanding admiral could praise those like Nelson whom he admired and do his very best to make sure that all knew it was not an emotion he extended to his second in command. If he and Hotham were naval rivals that extended to their politics, for Hood was a Tory and Hotham a Whig. Hood's problem was Prime Minister William Pitt's lack of a binding majority; while he could master the domestic agenda he needed the support of what were called the Portland Whigs to successfully prosecute the war. Hotham was of that faction and in constant communication with the Duke of Portland, and every letter did nothing to praise the abilities of his commanding officer, not that such an opinion was a secret.

All around the fleet, flagship included, those who could write home were composing their final letters, the ones that would be sent to their loved ones should they expire in the coming action. In reality naval letters read like a chronicle; they were often written with no knowledge of when they would be sent, for even in such a well-ordered fleet as Lord Hood's they would wait for the arrival of a packet bearing despatches and letters from home. So they tended towards a lengthy tale and most were only adding to what they had already composed and were penning sentiments that, regardless of the truth, sought to reassure their relatives of their happiness and good cheer, while inserting what should happen if anything should befall them.

Toby Burns was bent over his own letter, but it was not to his family. These were communications he found hard to compose, not being as willing as his peers to disguise his loathing of a service that had him existing on a diet of foul food, often near to rotten in the cask, in the company of people with whom he shared at best mutual disinterest, and under the command of men whose soul aim was to make his life a misery. Occasionally he summoned up the will to lie, but always he really wanted to write home to say that his only wish was to get out of the navy and back to a school he had, at one time, desired to get away from with equal passion.

Writing in reply to Lucknor was not easy and he had to remind himself that paper on which to do it was not in great supply, so he ended up with a set of corrected scrawls that would have taxed one of those coves that sought to decipher ancient languages. Toby did not want to blame himself in any way, yet even he could see that to plead outright coercion would not wash on the page, for it smacked of a weakness of personality that he did not recognise and was certainly not prepared to commit to paper even if it was designed to make him look innocent. Once again family obligation came to his rescue, and taking a fresh sheet he composed the best of what he had penned and scored out before sanding the letter, folding it and applying sealing wax, then penning the address.

'Damn me, Burns,' cawed one of his fellow midshipmen as he waved it to ensure the wax had dried, 'I reckon the time you've been at it you have told your life story.'

'At least, Myers,' Toby responded, standing and crouching, for the deck beams were low, 'I have a story to tell.'

He was out of the berth when he heard Myers answer to that. 'Am I alone in despising that admiral's bumboy?'

That led to a chorus of negatives, which infuriated him; why could they not see he had no desire to be cosseted by Admiral Hotham, no wish to be constantly put in jeopardy, which those with whom he shared his quarters mistakenly saw as an opportunity to distinguish himself? He would have gladly given those opportunities over to them, for in each one he had been granted the possibility of not surviving had been present, higher in his imagination than true, perhaps, but there nevertheless. Then there was his reputation as a hero, gained on the back of John Pearce off the Brittany coast. That it was false mattered less than the yearning he had to be shot of it, for that made everyone expect him to show reckless courage.

The letter went to the second of the admiral's two clerks, as did all those being composed, to wait for the next packet or a sloop being sent off to Gibraltar with despatches. Not an overly nosy individual the fellow nevertheless looked idly at the superscription, which was so unusual that he stared at it for some time. What was a toad like Burns doing writing a letter to the Inns of Court? The curiosity was mentioned to the senior clerk, Mr Toomey, who had been with the admiral for years and was something of a confidant – no letter went off to the Duke of Portland that he had not had dictated to, and approved by, him – so that when a seething Admiral Sir William Hotham returned from his uncomfortable dinner aboard HMS *Victory* this was mentioned, in turn, to him.

Those who knew Hotham were given to remark on what seemed to be his endemic indolence. Had he been informed of that, the man in question would have pointed out that haste in making decisions was inclined to lead to crass errors of judgement; he was a fellow who liked to weigh matters before pronouncing on them and this was no exception, even if he could immediately discern what it might portend.

'Are we at liberty to . . . ?' Hotham said eventually, not, as he often did, managing to finish the sentence. It made no odds – he was with a man who could read his mind.

'We have a responsibility, sir,' Toomey replied, 'that no communication should be permitted that would diminish the effectiveness of His Majesty's vessel of war on active service.'

If that was imparted with confidence it was all show; there was no right by anyone to interfere with the private communications of correspondents writing home.

'And the letter is available to us?' Toomey nodded, as Hotham, for once, was able to quickly construct a suitable conclusion. 'Then I fear young Mr Burns may be in some difficulties, Mr Toomey.'

'Very possibly, sir,' came the smooth reply.

'I do wish he had possessed the faith to trust to me for advice.'

'It had always been my position, sir, that lawyers are best avoided.'

'He is too young to be making judgements that he might not appreciate the consequences of, don't you think?'

'Therefore it would be best if we know the contents of his letter, either to advise him if it is serious, or to merely forward it on if it is harmless.'

'The seal?' Hotham asked, only to receive in response a look that enquired if he was being serious. 'Best fetch the damn thing, then.'

Toomey reached into his pocket. 'I took the liberty of bringing it with me, sir. With your permission I require a candle and a knife.'

Having landed at Lymington, Pearce could not say goodbye to his oarsmen without he gave them something for their trouble – if it had been a private matter they had come to his aid so willingly; and then there was the rest of the crew to consider, which led to him dipping into Michael's satchel and pushing aside his pistol case to extract a bit more of the money given to him by Dundas.

'Can I say, sir, on behalf of the crew, it has been a pleasure to serve under you.'

'Thank you, Mr Dorling, it has been equally agreeable to see what a fine body of men Mr Rackham has under his command.'

The mention of their permanent captain's name produced a commonality of responses, many frowns, a few hissed curses and one man spitting over the side, which had the effect of making Pearce feel cheap rather than glad; it was as if he was courting flattery and that was an activity he despised in others.

'You had best be off, Mr Dorling, for there is not much daylight left. Convey my regards to Mr Bird, the Kempshall twins and, of course, Mr Bellam, the cook. Who knows, one day we may meet again.'

'For which I can say they would hope, your honour.'

He stood on the quay and watched the boat row away, staying there, much as he was eager to be off, until they were out of sight and then, with a lightness in his step he knew to be keen anticipation, made his way up from the harbour to the King's Head Inn, aware that he had a physical as well as an emotional yearning for the presence of Emily Barclay. Indeed he was singing to himself as he entered the doorway to be confronted by an innkeeper who took one look at him and disappeared into the back of his establishment. Following him opened up the taproom and sitting there nursing a tankard was Michael O'Hagan. He stood up when he saw Pearce, but he did not smile and the way he said 'John-boy' while crossing himself did nothing to provide reassurance.

'What in the name of creation has happened?'

If, as he asked that, John Pearce had feared the worst, it came as no comfort to him to be told the truth. No, Emily was not harmed in any way, but at this very moment, if she did not know already, she was about to discover the one thing her lover had sought to keep from her.

'Is it too late to procure a pair of horses?'

By lantern light, Sir William Hotham, for the tenth time, was reading Toby Burns' letter to Lucknor and wondering how to deal with it. The boy had gone from being a necessary asset to get Barclay off the hook – though being a bit of a nuisance by his needy presence – to a downright threat to his position, for if he had sought to limit the damage to his own reputation in his composition he had certainly done nothing to diminish the ordure he was prepared to heap on both his uncle and Hotham himself. What had been a very necessary construct to save a gallant officer from a pernicious accusation laid by a gimcrack officer was made by the young toad's hand into a most damning conspiracy to utterly pervert the course of justice.

To confront him was not a consideration, though Hotham was sure he could browbeat the lad into continued silence. The problem was that in the future some other person might lean on him just as hard to repeat these exaggerations he had just penned, and who knew where that would lead if there was no one around to impose restraint? All being well – sea state and weather – the assault on the beach south of Calvi would be going ahead on the morrow at dawn, so he rang a bell for Toomey.

'Mr Toomey, when the orders were written for the morning, as regards our boats, where did you place Mr Burns?'

'Why sir, right at the point, hopefully in the first boat to beach. That is the position where he can garner most honour. Have you not always shown him much favour in that regard?'

'I have, many times, much to the annoyance of those with whom he shares his berth.' Looking at the letter, now on the table, Hotham growled. 'Still, he deserves no less!'

'It's not too late to make a change, sir.

'No, Toomey, leave the orders as they are.'

CHAPTER ELEVEN

Emily Barclay read French reasonably well but had rarely spoken to a native with any degree of application until she had been resident in Toulon, first with her husband as prisoner of war, then in day-to-day contact with the locals as she helped out in the shore hospital set up by her good friend and surgeon Heinrich Lutyens. Being a nurse had provided both a distraction and a reason not to reside and sleep aboard HMS *Brilliant*; indeed it had given her an excuse to initiate a separation from Ralph Barclay that she hoped would not set tongues wagging. In that Emily was being naive; when it came to gossip a fleet at sea could match a clutch of fishwives on any given day.

She had learnt the language under the tutelage of the governess from one of the local manor houses, who saw that having other girls in her class could provide a foil to aid her own charges. Seen very much as an aristocratic refinement she had attended twice-weekly sessions with a group of other aspirant girls and for the same reason:

to be bilingual was to enhance the prospects of making a good marriage. The struggle to separate the divergences that existed had not been comprehensively mastered, not least the way gender was employed when referring to specific objects – but more tellingly was the need to employ the correct verb endings, and if that had been refined in Toulon, it had not been wholly conquered.

So when she began a conversation with the count and Amélie Labordière, first inside the Stag Inn at Lyndhurst, then ensconced in the coach when they departed, being drawn by fresh horses, her conversation was not entirely fluent and if she managed to make herself understood it was not without repetition allied to some confusion on the faces of those with whom she was seeking to communicate. Then came another problem: her ear was not attuned to what was being said in reply, it consisting of sounds so unfamiliar and addressed to her in an accent with which she struggled to cope, for it was nothing like that of the Mediterranean French naval port.

The Parisian accent was very different and originally her governess had learnt her French in London from a fellow Briton, so that, as well as any refinement that was Provençal in accent, rendered the conversation, if it could be called that, stilted in the extreme. This left Emily wishing she had the fluency brought on by living as a native Parisian that had been enjoyed by John Pearce. The expression '*lentement, s'il vous plaît*' was frequently employed to slow what was a too rapid exposition from two companions; one reserved, the other extremely voluble.

The Count de Puisaye was eager that this *femme*

anglaise should know just how much the Revolution had impinged on him personally: the loss of his several houses as well as his estates, and naturally the rents and revenues thereof, the whole taken over by a rabble of *sans culottes* who would reduce them to a desert. The count had barely escaped with his life, but soon all would be restored to him when the British Government saw the sense of sending him back to the Vendée with the means to put the trouserless peasants back in their place. Even if Emily could only really pick up one word in three, it was noticeable from the odd barely suppressed yawn and expression of boredom that Madame Labordière found this exposition and complaint tiresome and it was with a sense of escaping what was turning into a tirade that she sought to engage more her fellow female.

'And how, Madame,' Emily asked, her voice paced and deliberate, 'did you come to be rescued and brought to England by the Royal Navy?'

Pearce had found horses in Lymington and they rode out as the sun was setting in a clear sky that would soon produce, once it had risen from its cheese-coloured position on the near horizon, a clear moon aided by strong starlight by which to proceed. He left behind him a very chastened innkeeper who had taken his tirade regarding Emily without a murmur; Pearce only realised why when they were well gone – he had forgotten to demand reimbursement for the days of non-occupation. The fellow might look cowed but he was much in profit, so being insulted was worth it.

Michael had, as requested, left horses stabled in

Lyndhurst, saddles and harness included, that he could claim as his own, so there was no sparing the ones he had rented from Lymington; they were driven hard so that he could get to a change before the Lyndhurst stables closed for the night, which they would do early in a quiet country town. In his imagination Pearce reprised any number of conversations that might be taking place, none of them inducing much in the way of comfort; perhaps Amélie would smoke who she was travelling with and show discretion, but if the way she had behaved aboard HMS *Larcher* was any guide, that came under the heading of pigs might fly.

Likewise the notion that Emily would, on discovering that she was bouncing along a turnpike road with his ex-mistress, accept that the whole *affaire* was over, bordered on risible; if it was, why had he brought her to England? Many scenarios presented themselves and that continued after Lyndhurst when the pace, of necessity, had to be more measured; these horses had to get them all the way to Winchester, a distance of over twenty miles. It was a tempo that allowed him to share his worries with his friend and riding companion, not that he got much in the way of sympathy.

'How can you say I brought the whole thing on my own head, Michael?'

'For no other reason, John-boy, than it be the plain truth. Sure, I will admit you're a victim of your own soft heart, but Mary, Mother of God, it has done naught but get you into trouble since the day we met.'

The reply had a definite note of pique. 'It has led me to get you out of a few scrapes.'

'It got me into more.'

'It's all the fault of those damned Tollands. If I had not had to deal with them I could perhaps have avoided such a meeting.'

'Well, you are shot of those sods now.'

'Not entirely, but they will serve in the navy for the duration of this war, which will keep them from bothering us.'

'Did you not feel shame, pressing men after what we have been through?'

'Not a jot – they were murderous villains who deserve a flogging captain and I hope they get one. Besides, I have yet to tell you of the arrangements I have made with the fellow in command of the receiving hulk.'

As they rode, Pearce talked of his hopes in that area, which had the advantage of keeping his mind off more pressing concerns, making no attempt to sound anything other than a fellow proud of his own scheming.

'So with luck we might see ourselves joined up again with Charlie and Rufus very soon.'

In the waters off Gosport, on a creaking HMS *York,* Lieutenant John Moyle, his duties complete for the day, was considering, over an evening snack of cheese on toast washed down with some strong Gascony wine, how to play a very different game. That fellow Pearce had tried to be cunning, yet in truth he had been too open, for he had indicated to Moyle that at least two of the men he had taken up were not run-of-the-mill fellows. If he wished them to be separated that meant they were trouble together, and if they were a smuggling gang that told a mind not short of calculation that they might well be the leaders. It was not a question posed that was likely to produce a straight answer, but there were ways to ask that would get to the truth and perhaps, if his nose was leading him in the right direction, even more profit than he had got from his dealing with Pearce.

He had watched them as they were brought aboard and stripped for examination, prodded and poked for disabilities and their orifices checked for signs of disease. It had not been hard to spot the men about whom Pearce spoke, the one with the scar too obvious. Yet it was the other who was of the most interest, for where others had complained he had remained silent and that told Moyle he was likely the fellow to deal with. Slowly, as he munched on his supper, Moyle framed his questions as well as the possible answers, then called to the man who guarded the door to his cabin to tell one of gaolers to proceed below to the very lowest deck and fetch up for him the fellow brought in this very day called Jahleel Tolland, adding a description, given he had not been listed as being aboard and had as yet no number. By the time the summons was answered – he could hear the clanking of the leg irons and chains – he had finished his food and a servant had cleared it away, but the bottle, not yet empty, was left on his table.

'Leave us,' he said to the man who had brought Tolland up from below, an individual in a short blue coat with brass buttons gone green from the rank atmosphere and white ducks that had been clean once but were grimy now. Then he added, as soon as that was obeyed and the cabin door closed, 'Would you care to sit?'

Jahleel Tolland raised his chained hands and replied in his rasping voice, 'I'd care more to have these struck off.'

Moyle smiled, which would have looked pleasant if his eyes had not narrowed at the same time. 'The wish of every prisoner, everywhere.'

'I'm not a prisoner, nor am I a volunteer to the King's Navy, which is what I reckon you have in mind for me and my company.'

'Company? That is a strange expression. Are they not mates, friends, companions?' Moyle picked up the bottle, filled his tankard, then added, 'I suggest you sit and perhaps drink some of this wine.'

Jahleel Tolland had come up from below expecting to be humiliated, on the grounds that John Pearce would have left instructions that it should be so, taking him down a peg prior to this fellow sending him to serve before the mast: there he would be, till he could find his feet, at the mercy of anyone with a rope starter. This was not like that, and if the elder Tolland was a ruffian he was no fool. He had been obliged many times in his life to deal with folk who made him appear saintly by comparison, for smuggling was a business full of violence. But it was also one in which subtlety was as necessary as a pistol and one where the need to pick up on the least hint was required for success and profit.

'I would be wanting to know if there's a price for that wine?'

Moyle smiled again. 'There is, Tolland, a price for everything.'

Tolland clanked forward and sat down, picking up the tankard. 'Then I do not mind if I partake of some, happen enough to cover what was in the purse your men filched from me when we were stripped of our clothing.'

'That is a serious allegation,' Moyle replied.

In reality the lieutenant was cursing himself for it had not occurred to him that, coming aboard as they had, these fellows might have possessions of value still upon them, the sort of things normally stolen by the press gangs long before they ever made the hulk. He sat rigid until the glass was drained, saying nothing but watching unblinking, like a cat examines an unsuspecting bird. Finished, his prisoner was in no hurry to speak either, which left the pair in mutual examination, seeking to discern from eye contact alone what could only be explained in words.

'I am told you are a smuggler?'

'By a liar, so why believe him?'

'Do I take kindly a fellow naval officer being so traduced?'

'You should have put that question to John Pearce, not I, for he's your smuggler.'

'And you?'

'A man seeking a bounty by bringing him in, which failed, for we did not know that he had a whole crew from a King's ship to prevent his being taken up.'

Moyle leant forward, his elbows on the table. 'If we are to understand each other, then I require the truth, not some made made-up tale.'

'Are we to understand each other?'

'The possibility exists, Tolland, but first I need to know to the very last detail what I am dealing with.'

What followed was another double stare, but it could

only have one outcome: Jahleel Tolland had the choice of telling the truth or being taken back to his stinking cell not much above the bilge. After a few seconds he nodded and began talking to a man who had the ability to listen without in any way showing on his face either surprise or understanding. It was lengthy and the glass was refilled to wet Tolland's throat, but eventually all was explained from the very first sight of the Tolland ship sailing out of Gravelines with Pearce at the helm, to how they had come to be sent aboard HMS *York*.

'You got to admire this Pearce, have you not?'

'You can if you wish, that I will forgo.'

'I have to tell you Pearce has made the strangest request, one that has seen him "forgo" a decent bounty.' Now it was Moyle's turn to explain, which he did in short, sharp sentences, but never once letting his eyes leave his visitor's face. 'So, Tolland, what do you make of that?'

'Is it your intention to meet his wishes?'

'I must, but I have room to manoeuvre, do I not?'

The question was left hanging in the air, not that there was any doubt as to what it was. 'A better offer might change matters?'

'As of this moment none of you have been entered as having been brought aboard. I have to tell you that not to meet Pearce's primary concern is something I suspect might backfire, but that only applies to half of your . . . what did you call them? Company.'

'You could be brought to let half of us go.'

'I could be brought to let go anyone who could prove to me he was a gentleman, indeed I would be obliged by law to do so. It is not often that a press gang takes in a forty-shilling freeholder but it has been known to happen. But I must have a care, for there has never been a case where a press gang has taken up four of such fellows.'

'Two?'

'Highly unusual, but possible,' Moyle replied.

Tolland picked up the empty tankard. 'And then there is the price?'

'Of course, but the other question is can you meet it?'

'I would need to know what is being asked for.'

Moyle nodded, then shouted out for a gaoler, his lips compressed in a more cynical expression. 'However, I do think a night with the rats will make you more amenable when it is discussed.' The door opened and the man who had brought Tolland up from below appeared. 'Take him back down, and tell my servant on the way to fetch another bottle of wine.'

'Aye, aye, sir.'

The destination of the Lyndhurst coach was another inn called the Wykham Arms, which, like all of Winchester was in total darkness by the time the two weary horsemen rolled up. They were required to bang hard to rouse out what passed for a night porter, in truth a fellow who, judging by his rank breath, drank too much and looked very unthreatening albeit he had a cudgel in his hand. That, originally raised in a defensive manner, dropped as he lifted his eyes to take in the height of one of the men he might be obliged to thwack – Michael O'Hagan made it look as if he would hardly reach, for the porter was short in the leg, so he undid the chain and let them into the hallway.

'The Lyndhurst coach came earlier?' That got a nod and a foul exhalation. 'Were there aboard two French folk and an English lady?'

'There were, took their bags in myself.'

'How did they seem, I mean in each other's company?'

'Weren't attending to that.'

'Did they dine together?'

'Can't rightly say, don't take much to foreign folk who don't know a coin is due for porterage and I has other work to do, any road.'

'Would that be the supping of ale?' Michael asked.

Courage came from somewhere, probably what he had consumed throughout the day. 'None of your damn business, Paddy.'

That got the fellow a grab at the front of his grubby shirt and a lift that had his feet off the floor until Pearce admonished his friend to put him down. As soon as he was released and breathing normally Pearce asked for a room they could share. For all he was in fear of the giant before him, that did not extend to rousing out the innkeeper or his wife, so both new arrivals had to settle for a bench in the taproom with Pearce moaning that he seemed to spend all his nights now on hard board instead of a comfortable cot. That fell on deaf ears; Michael O'Hagan was already snoring as through the window by John Pearce's head came the first whistle of the dawn chorus.

Toby Burns had not slept at all, but at least in that, on this occasion, he was not alone. Brave as they sounded, every fellow going ashore was prey to nerves and it was a relief to man the ship's boats and, when daylight came, head for the troop transports to load on the bullocks who would carry out the main assault. On a shore in plain view it was obvious that the French garrison had a clear idea of where to mount a defence: files of blue-coated soldiers could be seen deploying and some of them digging, their backs to the slight dune that kept storm tides at bay.

On board HMS *Britannia* the marine officers had paraded their men, for it was the Lobsters who would mount the initial landing given they were more nimble, on a swell, at getting in and out of cutters and the like and quickly engaging. In reality it was because, inured to life at sea, they were less likely to be seasick, which the soldiers would most certainly be, for the swell in a ship's boat cannot compare to that of a large capacious transport.

'You have done this before, Mr Burns, I am informed.'

Staring glumly at the shoreline through the open entry port and lost in a reverie of a life so much less dangerous, Toby started at being so addressed. Walker, the man who had posed the question, a captain of marines, had arrogance written all over him, nose high, chin in and a look in his eye that implied he was of superior mien. The captain had served on the ship all the time that Toby had been aboard, yet these were the first words he had ever addressed to the midshipman, no doubt a lowly creature in his elevated eyes. The thought of his previous experience in carrying out a by-boat assault was not a fond one and his reply was almost savage enough to be disrespectful.

'I was, sir, at San Fiorenzo, and the man who

commanded my boat took a ball in the leg.' He had no idea what had happened to that naval lieutenant but he felt it deserved embellishment. 'I do believe it led to an amputation.'

'It will be hot work right enough,' the captain replied with studied calm, which had Toby cursing the man under his breath; this was not work, it was slaughter.

'Hotspur's on deck,' came a whispered alert, which referred to Hotham, whose wholly inappropriate soubriquet that was, ironic rather than complimentary. 'An' heading your way.'

The marine officer had gone rigid and Toby too was obliged to stand upright, to turn and to raise his hat. 'Well, Mr Burns, here you have another chance to distinguish yourself.'

'For which I am truly grateful, sir,' he replied. 'I was just explaining to Captain Walker how I lost my officer the last time and perhaps he would not be pleased to know that in a previous action above Bastia the fellow in command of the marine detachment was taken by a ball in the chest when we attacked a French redoubt. Come to think of it, the lieutenant who commanded our battery at the actual siege was wounded too.'

Hotham was not alone in glaring at him, for the implication was plain; Walker was too, for no man likes to be told that he is going to action in close proximity to the kind of Jonah that draws enemy fire, which was what Burns was telling him. It took some effort on the part of the admiral to recover a degree of composure.

'Then, Mr Burns, it is time that matters were altered and I am sure even if Captain Walker leads you into the thickest part of the action, you will both have tales to tell your grandchildren.' He addressed Walker directly. 'Not that he lacks for those, for did you know, captain, that this lad here was wounded at Toulon and, on his first voyage, stole back a merchant vessel that had been taken by the enemy.'

'I had heard the tale, sir.'

'"Tale", Mr Walker? I rate it more than that.'

'Time to get my men into the boats, sir.'

'Carry on, Mr Walker, and since young Burns here is something of a talisman to the fleet, I suggest you gift to him the prow of your cutter. It will inspire those who follow to see an acknowledged hero standing to lead the assault.'

CHAPTER TWELVE

The boat took time to load and when complete it was crowded like every other in the initial assault. The number of marines that shared their thwarts cramped the rowers, with their muskets upright between their legs and bayonets glistening in the morning sunlight, the only difference being that the Lobsters faced forward while the oarsmen had their back to the shore. As they set off from the side of HMS *Britannia*, they were joined by marine detachments from the remainder of the fleet. Many of them in reality were soldiers who had been drafted into naval service to raise the numbers, but that notwithstanding – the two services heartily disliked each other – they received a collective cheer of encouragement from every main deck.

As it died away, Hotham's voice could be heard in what was, for a man of his elevated rank, a rather undignified display of being partisan, given nearly all of his flagship lieutenants and midshipmen were engaged in getting the fighting men ashore and the more senior they were, the more they resented the apparent favour being shown to one of their number.

'Good luck to you all, and I know, Mr Burns, you will not fail to show an example.'

Under so many eyes and sat on the tiller, despite Hotham's suggestion of the prow, there was little choice for Toby; he took hold of the berthing line and, wrapping it round his wrist, he stood, feet as far apart as he could, using his attachment to the body of the boat to stay upright and still able to steer, gazing into the stoical faces of those men it was his duty to command and seeing there no joy. The notion of shouting slogans of bravery, which should have accompanied such a gesture, was beyond him and Captain Walker, sat in the prow with his back to him, showed an indifference to the idea that he might do so.

The warships and transports were obliged to anchor far offshore in order to ensure a good depth of water under their keel, given the very rocky outcrops, and also they were subject to wind and the state of the tide, not much of a rise and fall in the Mediterranean but sufficient to create eddies and flows as well as choppy waves. It needed a tight grip on the line to hold his place and that lasted as they passed the bomb ketches, further inshore and firmly anchored in the soft sand of the bay, the mortars primed and ready to play upon the hastily slung up French defences.

For these fellows, given the range of their weapons left them normally too close to the defence for any comfort, it was in the nature of an exercise; the enemy had nothing with which to retaliate and that lent to their cheers as the stream of boats began to pass a less than welcome bent that implied rather you than us. Toby could see the lips of the sailors move and the marines' as well, most likely, all cursing the idle buggers in whispers and asides.

From such an elevated position and with the eyesight of his years, the youngster had a good view of the beach. He could observe that pieces of driftwood had been used to create ramparts against musket fire and in some cases sacks had been used to build up more. In his mind's eye he could only too easily imagine rushing up the tilting sand, his feet dragging and slowing him down, as several Frenchmen took aim at his heart, which had him struggling, so vivid was the vision, to hold on to his bowels.

Soon they were over the shallow waters that ran all the way to the beach, able to see the rippled bottom and to make out the swaying seaweed where it covered the bed. Also, if indistinctly, he could see the enemy, not just their uniforms but individual faces, as well as the cocksure walking to and fro of parading officers, no doubt telling their recumbent men that this was the day they would achieve glory. Down at the water's edge a single fellow stood, wearing a tricolour sash, a plumed hat and with gold frogging to his jacket that denoted superior rank. He had a small eyeglass raised and was sweeping the line of boats. Having held his position for some time he suddenly dropped the glass and slammed it closed, then turned and walked back up to join the rest of his men, which brought forth the first words from Captain Walker that he had uttered since casting off from the flagship.

'We will be in musket range soon, my lads, so make yourself small. Mr Burns, I would suggest that the position you have adopted is an unwise one and you will oblige me by not only sitting down but doing your best to use the men before you as protection against a ball.'

'But the admiral, sir—'

He got no further and the reply, in tone, was icy. 'Sir William is master on his own deck, and so it should be. But I am the ranking officer in this boat and what I wish supersedes the desires of admirals, however hungry they are for the glory of those they cherish.'

That shocked Toby; even if it was a thought many held it was not one to articulate in public and Walker turned to drive home his point. 'Get down, sir, this instant, for there will be enough futile injury on that strand of beach without we add to it by braggadocio.'

Toby obliged, easing himself down to look into a stony-faced superior, who merely gave a sharp nod, as Walker, still facing the stern, issued his orders to all.

'You, Mr Burns, will take equal cognisance of what I am saying. On the tiller you will oblige me by grounding at an angle of forty-five degrees and on my command, which will be given when we have alignment with our confrères in the other boats. My fellows, you will stand and deliver one volley of musketry. As for you tars, you may cower in the bottom if you so desire but do not get in the way. My Lobsters will then disembark on the seaward side, for the water will scarce cover their ankles.' His voice now rose and it was harsh. 'No man is to get onto the dry sand and expose themselves until I give the order and I'll break at the wheel any sod who disobeys.'

He had to pause then, the bomb ketches had opened up, sending huge balls arching towards the shore, there to land and send up great plumes of sand close to the water's edge that seemed to rest in the air before settling slowly down in the form of a cloud.

'Useless,' Walker spat. 'More of a danger to us than John Crapaud, but it is not too much to ask that perhaps they will up their range and keep down French heads. Now, we are coming in long range, so prepare to receive fire.'

Toby Burns was slightly taken aback; if Walker had previously addressed no words to him, seeming arrogant and taciturn, he was certainly employing enough now, while what he explained was in itself remarkable. Officers, both naval and doubly so marines, rarely explained anything to their men; they just drilled them and expected them to follow orders when engaged. Yet here was this fellow outlining in detail what he wanted to do, while seeking to keep them from unnecessary harm.

'Mr Burns, the men rowing at the point of disembarkation become yours to lead, the boat yours to command. Once we have ceased to use it as cover and have begun our advance it will be entirely at your discretion as to whether the oarsmen take part in seeking to secure the beach or return to bring in reinforcements. You do not have to seek my permission on how to proceed.'

'Sir.'

The voice softened, as Walker added, 'Orders which should have been issued to you by your superiors – I take it they were not?'

'No, sir.'

'Well, you have them now, so act as you see fit – and,

Mr Burns, a piece of advice: valour does not come from what others wish of you but what you do yourself and unbidden.'

Toby would have replied if he had not been forced to duck into his own body as the first musket balls fizzed into the water alongside, the captain still talking.

'Steady lads, it's all chance at this range, so pray to God that he wants you spared. Now hang onto something as we strike the sand.'

Toby, looking left and right, could see others in line and seemingly setting their pace by Walker, who had just asked the oarsmen, politely, for extra effort, a request to which they responded by bending their backs. If the boat picked up a bit of speed it was, in open water, hard to tell, but the marine captain seemed satisfied and within what seemed like seconds, and still a goodly distance from the waterline, the keel grounded, bringing the cutter to a shuddering halt, at which point Walker did stand, to order his men up with him. They obeyed and with a sluggishness that amazed Toby – it was as if no one was shooting at them – they lowered their muskets as if they were in no danger, took aim and fired off a very disciplined volley at their officer's command.

'Wet your feet, lads.'

The boat dipped heavily to one side as they leapt into the water, which in truth came up to their knees, setting about the ritual of reloading as soon as they were steady on their feet. Toby, cowering down now that he was fully exposed, found the voice of Captain Walker close to his ear, as were the cracks of passing shot aimed in their direction.

'It never will do to have the men you lead in ignorance of what we are about, Mr Burns.'

'Ready, sir,' called his corporal, which had Walker ordering another volley, this as mortar balls flew over their head to land three-quarters of the way up the beach, the onshore breeze carrying the sand over the enemy defences to hide any success the marine fire might have achieved.

'Damn me,' Walker hooted, 'we are going to drive them away with the discomfort of sand down their necks.'

'Will we drive them off, sir?'

'Oh yes. Our aim is to clear the beach, not die trying to take it, though I daresay some fools, even if they know that, will earn themselves a Corsican headstone for their stupidity. The French cannot hold, they lack the numbers, and nor have they fetched out field artillery to impede us, not that we are sure they possess any. They will seek to hold us up, to make the landing as bloody as they can, then, when the situation ceases to be tenable, they will withdraw back to their citadel and outer forts where, in time, unless a relief force comes from the mainland to drive us away, we will accept their surrender.'

'They should surrender now,' Toby spat.

'Nonsense, lad, even the French are careful of their honour.'

'Main body coming in, sir,' shouted someone from along the beach, by his tone another officer, which drew all eyes to a mass of boats heading for a point where the beach ended and the hills began, mostly men in red, but also several boats full of men in white, French Royalists come to do battle with their fellow countryman.

'The Bullocks are heading for the northern section,'

Walker continued, 'and once the Johnny in command of our enemies sees that they are about to succeed in securing it he will blow for the retreat to avoid being cut off from an easy withdrawal. At that point, and not before, my men and I will advance.'

'Reinforcements, sir?'

'Judging by the rate of fire I doubt we'll need any. You'll be fetching cannon ashore soon and my poor lads will be obliged to haul the damn things up that great hill you see to the north. Once over that we will then be set to filling bags for battery ramparts and a good month of looking down on our foes.'

If Walker thought it was close to a finish it could not be discerned by silence; balls cracked overhead, others thudded into the side of the cutter to embed themselves in the strakes and every so often, regardless of using the boats as cover, somewhere along the waterline a marine would spin away having been hit in the upper part of his body or his head by a lucky shot. The mortars kept up their bombardment, mostly useless on such soft ground that just sucked the balls in to dissipate the effect. The odd one did land where it was needed, the screams of those it had hit rolling down to the shoreline, until from their left came the sound of cheering as the army units came ashore to rush those who lay before them.

When, as predicted, the bugle sounded the retreat, Walker ordered his men out of cover and, after one volley and in extended order, they began to advance, this as flags waved out to sea to bring an end to the bombardment. But the French were not routed, they retired in good order, able to turn and subject those pursuing them to volley fire every so often, some of those missing and sending up founts of sand near the boats.

'Man the oars,' Toby croaked, his throat feeling as dry as sandpaper.

'We'll need bodies over the side to get us off,' a voice called. It was, no doubt, that of the senior hand aboard, keen to remind a young gentleman – useless as a breed in most sailors' eyes – of what he should have thought of for himself. That they did not respect him was in the next words addressed. 'An' since you ain't rowing, Mr Burns . . .'

There was no choice but to expose himself and as he leapt over the side two others followed, putting their shoulders to the prow and driving the cutter back till it floated. One man to his right, from being bent over suddenly became upright, then arched backwards, this before he fell forward with a moan, his hands clutching at a rowlock, the midshipman transfixed by the sight as the same gruff voice called out.

'Get Tosh inboard, for the love of Christ.' Hands dragged at the wounded man and the second sailor who had helped to free the boat secured his legs and heaved, the inert body crumpling into the bottom followed by a less than respectful shout. 'Get aboard, young sir.'

At that very moment, holes appeared in the wet sand by his boots and Toby could not move; his legs were useless even as he mentally ordered them to comply. Was it collective or did that leading hand give another command. Whatever, the oars were dipped and the boat was moving, a voice floating back to the ears of the rock-still midshipman.

'Got to get him to the surgeon, quick.'

It took several seconds for Toby to realise that the distance between boat and shore was now too great to cover, to realise that he was stuck ashore in what was still a battle for possession of the beach. Running out of the shallows he threw himself down in the sand, praying to God to be spared.

'What are you about, Mr Burns?' called Captain Walker. 'Can you not observe that the enemy are now in full flight?'

The first boats bringing in the heavy cannon, their wooden and wheeled trunnions, as well as powder and shot, provided Toby Burns with a way back to HMS *Britannia* and he left a beach now full of men, strangers to him, constructing tripods to get them ashore with ropes and pulleys, and slatted roadways to get them across the soft sand to the base of the hills. He had declined Walker's invitation to join in the advance of the marines, shepherding the French back into their pen as he called it, on the grounds that it had to be dangerous, only to find when he came back aboard he was being praised, not too fulsomely, for staying ashore when he could have departed.

The boat crew, or whoever had taken charge of them and had elected to leave him behind, did not tell anyone in authority that the Midshipman Burns had been abandoned, that they had sought succour for a wounded sailor above both his needs and his position of command. Instead they had reported Mr Burns as insisting on remaining where there was fighting, which left the youth

– who could have seen the grating rigged for what they had done – in no position to dish them, without likewise doing the same to himself. Later a hand, taking advantage of the lack of anyone else close by, spoke behind Toby's back, to point out that it would do him no harm to drop by the sickbay and look in on the fellow who had taken a ball in his back.

'Name's Feathers, an' he's in a bad way. Might never have the use of his legs again, young sir, which you has to say is a foul jest played by a spiteful God, seeing it did not need a ball in the spine to brace your'n's rigid.'

Toby turned to remonstrate only to find himself looking at the back of a checked shirt rapidly moving away and beyond him the quarterdeck, where stood the officer of the watch and, unfortunately, Sir William Hotham, who was glaring at him. All Toby could do was touch his hat, note the flash of very apparent disgust and wonder what it was he had done to deserve it from a man who had so recently given all the impression of smiling upon him, Toby being unaware of how much of the admiral's time had been taken up thinking of a way to deal with the problem he presented.

'You see, Sir William, if you read this Lucknor fellow's letter, it is plain that he has never corresponded with Burns prior to this.'

'I do not see how that changes matters, Toomey.'

The admiral's senior clerk had on many occasions been obliged to suppress his frustrations, working as he did for a man who too often seemed incapable of seeing the obvious, and that had to be kept from his tone of voice as well, for Hotham was just as prickly of his honour.

'He has no knowledge of the lad's hand, sir, so if he was to receive another letter, penned by me in the same style but with a vastly different list of responses, how is he to know it is not genuine?'

'What if your letter and Burns are together in one place, eh?'

'The chances of that are slim, sir. This Lucknor is in London, Burns out here with us.'

'But it is possible, for that lawyer is not airing a grievance of his own, he is acting on behalf of a client.'

Toomey knew the import of that, for he had in his possession the depositions made by that fellow Pearce and the trio of sailors who were attached to him. Given they and Burns served in the same navy, who knows what might happen. Matters were bad enough and if forgery was added to his suspect court martial it could become an even steeper slope to perdition. Hotham merely wanted to suppress what Toby Burns had written – to not forward his reply – but there was strong argument against that. The affair could not just be left to stew for, if he was not a lawyer himself, he suspected that this fellow Lucknor, in the absence of a response, would write again, and how could they be sure of the same level of interception a second time? This, slowly and tactfully, he explained to his superior.

'You said, sir, I admit in some passion, that you were damned if you could keep Burns within sight.'

'I want to swat the treacherous little toad every time I clap eyes on him and, damn me, I might lose myself one day and do it in front of the ship's officers.'

'So it is your intention to have him shift to another berth?'

'It is, and damn soon, but not before he has had a few weeks of service before the guns of Calvi. I intend to send him to the siege batteries where he can share whatever risks that popinjay Nelson affords himself. Given his stupidity that will be right with the foremost guns.'

There was no need for Hotham to elaborate on that; Burns would be put in a position of maximum danger as he had in the beach landing. That this was an act of pure vindictiveness did not trouble Toomey, his task was to serve his master and keep his own position, which was about to be much enhanced. Lord Hood could not remain in command for much longer and his admiral was in line and had the political backing to succeed him. That would take Toomey to the pinnacle of his trade; to be the senior clerk to a commanding admiral was a position from which a man could make a fortune and such a notion was just as appealing to him as the actual role was to Hotham.

'Then that gives me time, sir, to put my mind to a solution.'

'More than your mind, Toomey, I want your heart and soul engaged in this.'

The solution was not long in being presented. Toomey would write a letter of his own to Lucknor and, as he pointed out, any further immediate attempt to contact Burns would come to the flagship and could thus be intercepted, which would be rendered especially safe if the youngster was shifted to another vessel, preferably one where the captain had a strong attachment to Hotham and one who could be primed, with a made-up tale, that any correspondence that Burns undertook should be passed first to HMS *Britannia*.

'Shifting mids is not easy, Toomey, a captain likes his own choices aboard ship.'

'I am aware of that Sir William, and I point out to you that Lord Hood has called for an examination after the fall of Calvi so that the high number of midshipmen acting as lieutenants should have a chance to attain the actual rank.'

'You're not suggesting that I put up Burns?'

'I am, sir.'

'Won't work, dammit, I doubt the little bugger would pass.'

'He would if he knew what the questions were going to be and had the answers. After all, I daresay if you offered to relieve Lord Hood of the burden of arranging the examination, to which I think given his great responsibilities he would accede, the choice of captains to sit on the judging panel would be yours.'

Hotham was now toying with a nut and a pair of crackers, though one showed no sign of being placed in proximity to the other and as usual he was applying his less than rapid mental processes to the suggestion. If it was not a commonplace for an admiral to stuff the board about to test the skill of a relative it was not unknown and a hint to those sitting, no less than it had been at Barclay's court martial, that a certain result was required, was one that would be taken on board. The only difficulty came from those same captains having sons or nephews of their own; the day would come when a favour granted would be one called in.

'And what then?'

'Then he could be placed aboard another ship as the most junior lieutenant, out of your sight but still under your supervision, given there are no plans to change the make-up of the fleet.'

'That will not pertain for ever.'

'I am proposing an immediate solution to an immediate problem. No one can know the future, but if we can kill off enquires now, that argues we may choke off the whole affair.'

A gleam came into Hotham's eye then, for he thought Burns would make a poor, indeed a terrible deck officer – the boy had no spunk in him – that would expose him to the wrath of his captain, especially if another hint from him indicated that would be permissible. What he would really like was for the sod to stuff a cannonball down his breeches and jump over the side on a dark night and at that moment he was fancying a fellow could be driven to that.

'That seems to me,' Toomey pressed, 'to be the only alternative to keeping him on the flagship. After all, we cannot send him home.'

Another long pause ensued and Toomey knew not to press; Hotham had no ideas of his own and also little choice but to accept those put to him and that eventually penetrated his thinking.

'No. Write your letter and send it off.'

'Sir.'

'And send Burns to me so I can give him news of his new appointment and his future prospects.'

CHAPTER THIRTEEN

Pearce had become accustomed to sleep being short but the same could not be said for spending the night on bare boards and his bench seemed harder than deck planking. He awoke stiff and in an ill temper, caused as much because of what he might have to face as his limbs, well aware that he felt grubby and needed, before he faced anyone, a wash and more particularly a proper shave. The inn was up and buzzing with activity, preparing for the day and at last he and Michael could retire to a room where hot water was provided, not that O'Hagan was interested: he dropped his boots on the floor and lay down to continue his slumbers, despite the loud ringing of the bells from the nearby cathedral.

A man was sent up to take Pearce's uniform coat; that to be sponged and pressed, his stock washed and ironed dry, while, razor in hand over a bowl of steaming water, looking into a less than clear mirror, he rehearsed again and again the lines he had worked to death on the way to Winchester, continually aiming to hit the right tone. It had to be firm but apologetic that no warning of what had occurred could be made. Breakfast came as well – he was assured that the other guests had yet to appear or request refreshments – added to the information that there were no places on the London Flyer until the next day; whatever was about to happen would take place here in the Wykham Arms.

After a knock, the door opened and the serving man returned with his clothing, which he handed over with a look at O'Hagan, awake but still recumbent, that promised hellfire for his being fully clothed while laying on the establishments linen. All he got in response was an exaggerated wink and the remark that, sure, soft bedding beats a hammock any day and if he had a wench handy his pleasure would be complete.

'Saving your presence, but you asked to be informed if the other guests were up and about. I am to say the ladies have called for hot water.'

'There's no justice in the world, John-boy, here's you with two paramours hard by and me bereft.'

If they, as a pair, did not already stand very high in the regard of the staff of the Wykham – no doubt the night man had described their arrival – that remark and its implications, judging by the expression on the servitor's face, took it to a new low. He exited murmuring about the world going to the dogs, with Pearce calling after him to fetch two hearty breakfasts and quickly, as well as an inkwell and paper, the latter immediately.

'I have no mind to face anyone on an empty stomach.'

'Am I allowed to be an observer, John-boy?'

'No you are not. This is serious, Michael, and the last thing I need in the background is you grinning and leering at me.'

That was what Pearce got now. 'Then you will give Mrs Barclay my compliments.'

'Would you not be better seeing if the horses are being well looked after?'

'Why, brother, are we planning a quick getaway?' O'Hagan started to laugh, his body heaving. 'Sure that would be a sight, the hero John Pearce in flight from a couple of women.'

Another knock, another glare at the bed, but the means to communicate was handed over, with Pearce carrying it to the dresser and immediately sitting down to write.

'Instead of vexing me, Michael, you would do me a service if you were to ask for a private room in which I can speak to Emily. There will be one on the ground floor, I'm sure.'

Michael dragged himself up, pulled on his boots and headed for the door. 'And here was me thinking my days of being a servant were at an end.'

The note Pearce wrote was short, simply saying that he was staying in the same inn and that he desired a word in private. The temptation to add 'to avoid a scene' he considered but put aside; Emily, if she knew the connection to Amélie Labordière, would smoke his reasons without them being spelt out. Michael returned to say the room had been reserved and where it was, just off the hallway, and that Pearce appended, as well as a time he hoped she would accept. Breakfast arrived next and the pair sat down to a couple of beefsteaks washed down with strong local cider. The plates were clean and the cider jug empty when Emily's reply came that she was at his convenience.

'At my convenience,' Pearce moaned, for it was so very formal. 'This is going to be worse than even I imagined.'

'Hell hath no fury, I am told, like a woman scorned,' Michael said, getting to his feet. 'And now, if you will forgive, I must go about my occasions, as polite folk say.'

'I have another letter to write, to Dundas, telling him I am returned and who with.'

Michael's eyes were twinkling. 'Your one-time mistress, John-boy?'

'Damn you, no, the Count de Puisaye.'

'Sure, I cannot help but think your man would prefer the former.'

Aboard HMS *York* Lieutenant Moyle was likewise examining his empty breakfast plate, washed down in his case by a bottle of claret, and ruminating on the state of his existence, which seemed as messy as the remains of the fowl he had just consumed. Like all young men he had entered the navy full of ambition and had, in his first midshipman's berth, dreamt of the glory of command in battle, of a great victory that would set him up with his richly deserved estate and carriage and four with which to go about and impress. How different it had been in reality! A struggle to maintain even employment as a midshipman, then once that had been achieved a scraped pass in the lieutenant's examination followed by years of pleading for a place afloat and, on landing one, being shown to be barely competent in the necessities of his profession.

He still occasionally shuddered to recall the very obvious mistakes he had made, added to the realisation that he was not cut out to be a seaman. It was a distant relative and MP, much badgered and eventually worn down, who had secured for him this posting, which if it was a lowly one was at least secure as long as he did not foul his own anchor. But it was also, most assuredly, not a platform to better things; to be promoted to captain, to be made post from his present position was too fanciful for words, so it was incumbent upon him to make the best he could out of what was a dead-end position.

'Tolland, sir,' said the guard, a different fellow from the previous night, through the open door.

'Let him enter and close the door behind him.' The guard obliged and Jahleel Tolland clanked forward as he had before, to stand just inside the closed door, his eyes on the breakfast remains with Moyle jesting as he observed the direction of the look. 'I daresay you did not eat as well as I.'

'You knows I did not,' Tolland growled. 'I had gruel not fit for pigswill.'

Among Moyle's less attractive traits, and he would have been pushed to admit it as true, he seeing himself as an upright soul, was his tendency to bully and the tone of the prisoner's voice irritated him enough to bring what was never far from the surface to the fore. When the nature of his task and his lack of prospects took him into a depression, which it did on many occasions, there was the saving grace of always having other people to physically take it out on.

'I could have you flogged at a whim, cur, and be

assured it is not a task I delegate to others. It is my own arm I employ and my own retribution I satisfy.'

'I daresay you provide what you can,' Tolland replied, working hard to look contrite, for there was a game to be played and an angry hulk commander was not helpful.

'I do,' Moyle purred, 'and I am seen as generous.'

Outside the door, the guard who had fetched Tolland from below raised his eyes to the deck beams above his head in disbelief; with the exchange loud enough, he could hear clearly what was being said and his reaction would have been greeted by his fellow guards as correct. Moyle was a lying, thieving bastard who stole what rations he could, a tyrant and an oppressor of those beneath him, as well as an arse-licker to anyone who had the means to allow him to further line his pockets. The last thing the guard heard was that Tolland should sit down; with the two now close the talk was too indistinct to make sense.

'I sense you have come to a proper appreciation of your situation?'

'Hard not to,' Tolland responded, holding up manacled hands that showed evidence of being bitten more than once.

'Ah yes. The ship's cats do their best, but with rodents so numerous it would take a blaze to shift them.'

'Moving up a deck would suffice some.'

'So it would, Tolland, but I am sure you have not come to see me seeking only a bit of deck elevation.'

'I want to know what would it take to get my brother and I free?'

'Not a great deal – someone to attest in writing, of

course, and it would need to be a person very respectable, that you are not seamen and are, in fact, gentlemen.'

'And how would this person of standing be made aware of where we are?'

'You would have to communicate with them by letter. I take it you can write?'

'My brother has a fair hand, yet he lacks the means to do what you say, for he too had his purse swiped by your men.'

'True,' Moyle replied, with a grim smile, 'but I do not lack the means.'

Dealing with a plague of rats did not preclude thinking and Jahleel Tolland had been gifted many waking hours to do that. He had guessed that this Lieutenant Moyle had in mind to set them free and for a price, only neither of them knew what that should be. Moyle was keen to extract the maximum he could, without any knowledge of what kind of funds the Tollands had access to; Jahleel had the opposite aim, to get off this ship for as little disbursement as he could.

He had hidden the money he carried in his saddlebags in a pocket on the inside of his riding boots, unobserved by Pearce and his sailors who were not, in any case, looking to steal. That was now hidden in the filthy straw on which he and his gang had been obliged to sleep; even if rats might leave the odd mark of their teeth they could not eat gold. Having palmed a couple of guineas on being called to come to the great cabin, he moved his hand across the tabletop and left them in plain view. Eyes drawn to them, Moyle moved slowly to pick them up.

'There has to be more than this?'

'For paper and an inkwell?'

'For the right to walk free.'

'All eight?'

'Two, no more.'

If Jahleel Tolland thought about that at all, it was not for long; his other men would just have to take their chances. 'Happen the man I write to could satisfy your needs and mine but I would need to know how much that would be. I can scarce ask if I do not know.'

Moyle sat back, still playing with the coins. 'I would need ten times this and more. Judas priced Jesus at thirty pieces of silver. I am sure you value your head higher than that.'

If Jahleel Tolland was thinking, I've got you cheap you grasping sod, there was no sign of it on his face. If anything he looked worried, as if what was being requested was too steep. He had that sum hidden in the straw, but he knew this Lieutenant John Moyle was not a man to trust. He could just take what Jahleel had, then laugh in his face; better a couple of night's fighting off rats than that.

'I'd say he might go to that, but there's only one way to be certain.'

'A letter?' Tolland nodded as Moyle flipped the coins. 'Let us say this pair of beauties will cover pen and ink, shall we?'

'Does it cover a higher deck too?'

'Perhaps when your letter is written and I have seen what it says and to whom it is addressed. After all, I must make sure you do not try to dish me by some code I cannot comprehend.'

'My brother will write in front of you.'

'He will have to,' Moyle laughed.

'When?'

'The guard that takes you down can bring him up.'

'After we's had a word, so he knows what needs sayin'.'

Moyle nodded, loudly ordered Tolland taken down, then went to admire his image in one of the many mirrors that dotted the bulkheads of his cabin, thinking that if he was not as much a sailor as many of his contemporaries, he was very much their match in the means to extract profit from a situation.

Pearce was standing by an unlit fireplace when Emily entered the private room, his elbow on the mantle. He had been staring at a very poor reproduction of the kind of painting done by the leading London artists – in this case no doubt executed by a travelling limner and copyist – of men mounted on horses, their pack of hounds chasing a fox across, he assumed, the Hampshire landscape, and thinking how often in his life he had been the prey and not the hunter. Turning as the door opened, what he observed, a tight-lipped Emily Barclay, did nothing to make him feel less so and that was compounded when he walked towards her, holding out hands she declined to take, with a sharp shake of the head.

'Emily, I . . .'

The head dropped so he could not see her eyes. 'Do you not think, John, that explanations are superfluous? I assume that you have arranged the meeting for that purpose?'

'It is all coincidence, happenstance. I found Amélie to be in distressed circumstances and felt obliged to help her.'

'While providing for yourself an outlet for . . .' That obviously conjured up a word for Emily she could not use. 'How very convenient that must have seemed.'

'It was not convenient, in fact it was damned . . .' Pearce threw up his hands, for to use such language with Emily was to destroy his case on its own. 'Forgive my blaspheming but can you not see that I am being judged in a light that is unfair?'

'It is not a pleasure,' Emily whispered, 'when you think you have secured someone's heart, to find you are required to share it.'

'You cannot think I would do that. Is your opinion of me so low that you can even consider such a thing?'

'You have needs, have you not?'

'I am a man, I grant you.'

'Which I seem to recall you expressed in embarrassing circumstances in Leghorn. It did not seem to affect you at all that you were the butt of the laughter of the fleet, running through the streets, pursued by an irate husband, in nothing but your smalls.'

'That was before you and I discovered our mutual regard. I cannot be blamed for red-blood prior to—'

'To what, John, my disgrace first and humiliation second?'

Her shoulders started to heave, not much but it was easy to discern her distress. Slowly, and with no pressure, he put his hands on them. 'I pledged myself to you and I do so again now.'

'So Madame Labordière means nothing to you?'

'I cannot say nothing,' he replied moving one hand to lift her chin, 'but in comparison to my feelings for you . . .' Emily allowed her head to be lifted, and as it was, the shaking of her shoulder turned from suppressed to violent and as soon as he could clearly see her face, John Pearce exclaimed, and not with joy, 'Emily, are you laughing?'

Her hand went to her mouth. 'Forgive me, I cannot help it, and only the Good Lord knows how I kept it hidden for this length of time. You looked like a lost child when I came through that door.'

John Pearce swept past her and flung open the very same door. Michael O'Hagan was standing in plain view, as so were the Count de Puisaye and Amélie, they looking at him with some curiosity.

'Michael,' Pearce barked. 'Is your hand in this?'

'Mother of God, I did you a favour, for I could not imagine the poor fist you would have made of matters had I not explained them first. Now gather yourself, for Mrs Barclay has arranged to take these poor travellers on a tour of the city and they are anxious to be on their way.'

John Pearce felt his arm taken by Emily Barclay, his mood unsure. Was he angry or glad? – it was hard to tell.

'I'm told the cathedral is especially fine, John, and as we walk we must indeed talk, for while you have been away, I cannot say that I have been comfortable regarding our future.'

'You and Amélie?'

'Have become, on a very short acquaintance, very firm friends. After all, what a boon it is to be able to talk with someone who knows all your faults and is prepared to list them, albeit I sometimes struggle with the French.'

'What faults?'

Emily smiled sweetly, then sighed. 'It is a blessing we have the whole day to discuss them.'

'I suppose you have taken the count to your bosom as well.'

The reply was an emphatic 'No'.

That was a condition the fellow in question did nothing to alleviate as he disparaged that which he was shown: Winchester Cathedral was fine, if cramped compared to Notre Dame, Chartres, Reims or the great double basilica of Bourges, proper edifices built to the glory of God, of which he was sure this English church was just a pale copy erected by poorly trained masons. Not a religious man at all and certainly disinclined to defend the unnecessary property of what he knew to be a bloated established church, John Pearce was thinking that the guillotine was too good for the old fool.

Franklin Tolland wrote his letter still chained, which did nothing to aid the fluency of the quill; indeed he could bareley recognise his own hand, a point Moyle dismissed as he picked up the sanded page and read it, nodding as he saw that the sum of forty guineas was required for release, close to a year's income for a gentleman. Added to that which he had been gifted by Pearce that would add up to a tidy sum that he could invest in government Consols, as he did with anything he could get from his benighted office.

One day he would have enough to relinquish HMS *York*, enough to add to his half pay as an unemployed lieutenant, the means to purchase a cottage and a bit of land that he would see worked to his advantage, and then there was also the possibility of a woman with whom to share it. The name of the addressee he noted, to be written down later. This Denby Carruthers fellow was surely well heeled and might, at some future date, be a source of more funds.

'I will have you and your brother moved up a deck, away from the most pernicious rodents.'

'No,' Franklin barked, 'you must move us all or the others will become suspicious that we mean to ditch them.'

Moyle was halfway across his deck before Franklin finished. 'Do not use that tone of voice with me, lest you want a scar on your other cheek to balance up your looks. And for your tone you can stay where you are!'

'The letter?'

'Will be sent, never fear, but I wonder if your friend will want you and the vermin you will fetch along?' The look that crossed Franklin Tolland's face then gave Moyle the impression that this Carruthers fellow might not – that indeed he might not get what he now considered his due. 'Pray he does, cur, for I have it in me to make what you have now seem like paradise.'

CHAPTER FOURTEEN

A flurry of communications arrived in London in a very short time. Ralph Barclay's demand that his wife return to her married state the first, and this from the solicitor to whom it was originally addressed but unopened and forwarded to her last known address at Nerot's Hotel to await her anticipated return. There was one from Mr Studdert too, still trying to recover from a burglary in which every document he had stored in his strongroom had been stolen, which meant that wills had to be rewritten, copies of deeds and all sorts of other papers acquired, the sheer time taken merely to contact his clients and inform them leaving him a weary man. Added to that, to reassure his clients, Mrs Barclay included, and for future security, a cellar was being dug out under his office floor, which a steel trapdoor would cover, for he was not about to risk a repetition of the previous loss.

Pearce had written to Nerot's, bespeaking rooms for his whole party and, of course, to Henry Dundas,

William Pitt's right-hand man, though the letter was delayed in actual delivery due to it having to be paid for – in all departments of the state there was a reluctance to accept private letters for that reason; government correspondence was carried out on pre-franked sheets and only a certain level of government employee could sanction a delivery sixpence. It did eventually end up on the right desk and was then shown to a minister too busy to sort out his own mail.

'Send to Nerot's,' Dundas, said. 'I shall see Pearce and this . . .' that required another perusal '. . . *Comte* de Puisaye tomorrow evening; Pearce first, then the Frenchman.' The clerk responded with a quizzical expression, which had Dundas waving the communication. 'This does not fill me with the feeling that we have on our hands something of which we can take advantage, but I need to get chapter and verse from the man who has seen the situation on the ground.'

The letter from HMS *York* was the one to produce a string of curses, given Alderman Denby Carruthers had invested a great deal of money already in buying a ship with which the Tollands could resume smuggling; had he not done so he seriously questioned whether he would accede to their request. But having got in so deep, there was no choice but to sell the ship at a loss – everyone would know how short his ownership had been and would suspect he had discovered some flaw in the vessel he was trying to pass it on.

'Portsmouth, sir?'

'Yes, Lavery, or to be more precise, Gosport, which is across the water. You are to take with you this sum of money and pass it on to a Lieutenant Moyle, but only on his granting to you a pair of gentlemen wrongly taken up for the navy and to whom I owe a favour.'

'Might I enquire what kind of favour, sir?'

'No you cannot!' Carruthers barked. 'I have noted lately in you, Lavery, a tendency to ask questions that are outside your remit as my clerk.'

Being far from the first flush of youth and with a pallid countenance made more pronounced by his bulbous, purple nose, Isaac Lavery did crestfallen well. 'I seek only to be of full use to you, sir.'

'I will decide what use you are to be and, while we are at it, I would ask you to stop running errands for my wife without informing me of where they take you.'

'I felt it my duty to oblige her.'

That got the man who had replaced Cornelius Gherson a cold look, for his master was wondering if the old booby really thought he could fool the man for whom he worked; Lavery was betraying him and was being used by Catherine Carruthers to find her one time paramour, with whom, no doubt, she would take up again if he were found. Odd that Denby Carruthers knew exactly where Gherson was, what he did and for whom. Captain Barclay was a client of his brother-in-law, a partner in the Prize Agency practice of Ommanney & Druce. There was temptation to enclose a sealed note to the Tollands asking them to see to Lavery and dump his cadaver somewhere on the way back, but on reflection it was not yet time to settle matters and, in truth, he did not know them well enough to be sure they would do his bidding.

'In future, if my wife asks you to do something, you will come to me, tell me the task, and I will either approve its execution or not.'

On the way to Portsmouth in the public coach, Lavery passed a private one moving in the opposite direction, a conveyance hired by John Pearce on government money to get him and his party to London. While there was a general air of calm aboard – the count continued to drone on about his glittering prospects – all travelling had their concerns, not least the man who had hired it and the woman he loved, for even if she had not referred to it since that private meeting, and being in company on their walk round Winchester, it was obvious that they would at some time have to talk and decide their future, shared or not.

The only one who gave the impression of having no worries was Michael O'Hagan, though that was far from true; the last time he had been on the way to London, on foot with Charlie Taverner and Rufus Dommet, they had come across a poster telling the world that a fellow fitting his description, and he was quite singular in that, was wanted for theft and assault. Having no idea how close he was to the part of the country where that had been displayed he felt it wise to stay out of sight.

'You're not getting down, Michael?' Pearce asked, as they stopped for a change of horses, the three others already gone into the parlour of the busy coaching inn.

'Sure, I'm comfortable here, John-boy.'

'Damned if I know how, brother – my posterior aches.'

'You've not enough flesh on your arse and too much in your head.'

'A drink, food?' Pearce enquired, grinning.

'Can wait.'

'Michael, I cannot believe that of you. I have never known you turn down a tankard of ale.'

'Happen I'm goin' temperance.'

'And the moon is cheese.'

'Might be a tadge dangerous, John-boy, me being easy to recognise and in a part of the world where folks could be looking for me. Folks lookin' to take up bounties are the types to frequent coaching inns.'

'Sorry, never occurred to me.'

Michael had recounted the adventure in getting from Portsmouth to London overland when they had met at the Pelican, and Pearce had heard with his own ears, from an impress gang, what had happened when the Irishman had nearly been taken up by a couple of low-life crimps on the Sussex shore. He had seen to them good an' proper, but that had led to the poster offering a reward of twenty shillings for his arrest.

'So send someone out with a tankard and some bread and a bit of that moon.'

Pearce left Michael in the coach, to find when they all came out to get aboard again, on a warm sunny day, the blinds were pulled down. He was obliged to take back to the inn the tankard and plate his friend had used, and inside Michael stayed until they were safe in Nerot's Hotel.

Afforded a chance to be alone with Emily at last, Pearce went to her room and knocked – opened, he was not cheered by her attitude. 'John, this is not fitting.'

'It will have to do, Emily, so am I allowed to enter or shall we talk of matters personal with me in the hallway where the Lord knows who will overhear me?'

The look of determination on his face left her in no doubt he was not to be deterred and she stepped aside to let him pass, where he went to the unlit fireplace, turned and faced her. Pearce nearly faltered then; even in her distress she was so damned beautiful, the auburn hair framing flawless skin, saving a few entrancing freckles, and those green eyes that could flash so enticingly when she was angry. At the moment they were expressionless, which had to be deliberate.

'I cannot believe, Emily, that you are suggesting our attachment to each other should cease.'

Her reaction was odd; it was as if that had never occurred to her. Seeming deflated she sat down in an armchair. 'John, I do not know what I am suggesting for I am at a loss to know what to do. I have not had a chance to relate to you what happened in Lymington while you were gone and why I left prior to your return. I was about to do so in Winchester, but you did not allow me time and the rest of the day was spent with our French companions.'

'Then tell me now.' Which she did, leaving Pearce dumbfounded. 'I have no knowledge of this admiral of whom you speak and nor can I fathom how he knew you and I had lodged at the King's Head.'

'He did know because our arrival and names were printed in a local newspaper, and that indicates what things will be like in the future: we constantly on guard lest our unmarried state be revealed to everyone around us.'

'Then let us not lie about it.'

'What are you saying? That wherever we go I should expose myself to scandal?'

'Only here, in a nation so prurient that such a thing is considered worth remarking on.'

'Unlike France?'

'Not so! London is full of folk having affairs and it is common knowledge that the King's own sons are amongst the most active in that regard. Damn it, the Prince of Wales is openly living with a Catholic and rumours abound that they are secretly married. William, the so-called Sailor Prince, shares a home with a woman who has borne him half a dozen children.'

'And this you approve of?'

'Actually, yes, much as I see them as wastrels and a burden on the common man, let them do as they wish.'

'And that is what you would want for us?'

'I want for us to be together.'

'And I cannot see how that can be possible without my having to defend myself each and every day from the like of Sir Berkley Sumner and his horsewhip.'

'Should I ever encounter him he will regret carrying one.'

As her head dropped he moved swiftly, in what was not a large room, and he was forceful, pulling Emily Barclay to her feet and kissing her. She sought to resist at first, seeking to push him away, yet that effort faded and her body, while not going limp, ceased to be rigid. Pearce was on fire and he knew that he had it in his power to proceed as he desired, that Emily would not, could not put up any resistance. He was edging her towards the bed when the knock at the door broke the mood, not aided by his exclamation of 'damnation'.

They had to break contact, she had to go to open the door and there stood Didcot, the hotel servant who had been both a bane and a boon to John Pearce since the first occasion on which he took up residence.

'Letters for you, Madame, two of 'em, which was left at the desk and should have been given over when you arrived, though you would wonder at some folk not doing their job proper.' The open door also revealed John Pearce and that brought to the old fellow's eye a salacious look, for he had watched this pair sparring before; he knew what Pearce was after just as he guessed what he was not getting. 'Saving your presence, Lieutenant Pearce, will you be taking supper in your room?'

The servant's gleam sharpened when Emily, having looked at the addressee on the first one, showed the unopened letter to Pearce, for he had given both a good look over before delivery and he had a nose for these things: Captain Ralph Barclay RN. HMS *Semele*; Plymouth Roads, was whom it came from, no doubt a husband often away at sea. These two were thinking on the old diddle-me-de he had no doubt, which was one to tuck away, for there was money to be made from both silence and letting on if it came to ought, given one had to be from her husband and the other had come from a lawyer.

'No!' Pearce said coldly. 'Shut the door, Emily.'

'Emily is it he calls her now?' Didcot said to himself as he lurched down the corridor. 'It were Mrs Barclay in public afore. Happen they're more hugger than I thought.'

Inside the room Emily had cracked the seal on her husband's letter, unfolded it, and as she read it her eyes widened. Finished it was handed to John Pearce who spotted very quickly what had caused her to react, a passage saying that she was no longer in a position to do him harm, this while she read the letter from Studdert.

'What can he mean by that?' Pearce asked. 'That you have nothing more with which to threaten him?'

Emily passed him the second letter, her eyes wide with what Pearce took to be wonder or surprise; it was only when he read it he knew it to be another reaction entirely, for the solicitor had only written to confirm that Emily had removed from him the single set of papers she had left in his care and there were no others, his apologies for any inconvenience, but he required to be sure in case copies must be acquired; he did not read on about the precautions being taken.

'Burgled?' Pearce said.

'And everything in his strongroom taken to the last will and testament.'

'Match it with that remark in your husband's letter.'

'Coincidence?' Emily asked.

'Too much of one. It seems there are no lengths to which your husband will not go.'

'What am I to do?

That was asked in a spirit of enquiry, not with any sense of fear or despondency.

'I think it is time you made your husband aware that not only will you refuse to return to the marital state, but that you have other plans, and if he chooses to keep pursuing you, you will embarrass him further.'

'You and I?'

Pearce nodded.

'I might as well tell the world – place an announcement in *The Times*.'

'Emily, we cannot keep hidden what we have.'

'Have?'

'Do you not trust my advice?'

'I don't know who or what to trust.'

'I would start with your instincts, but, just in case, I have invited Heinrich Lutyens to dine with us this evening. I know you value his judgement and I ask that you allow him to exercise it.'

'Would you abide by it if it were negative?'

'No. Now come here and let us take up where we left off before that old goat Didcot knocked on the door.'

Isaac Lavery was seasick in the wherry that took him from Portsmouth to the receiving hulk and given he lacked colour anyway that gave him a greenish hue. His stomach was still troubled as he enquired at the gate after Lieutenant Moyle, giving his own name but not the purpose. Nor, once he was admitted, was his state improved by being on a larger vessel, for if HMS *York* did not move much, she did react to the incoming swell to tug at her anchors. Entering the great cabin he found Moyle adjusting his stock in one of the many mirrors, an act which imposed a period of silence until he was fully satisfied.

'Are you the person to whom the letter was addressed?'

'No, sir, I am his clerk.'

Moyle turned and pulled a face. 'A fellow of means, then?'

'Mr Carruthers is a man of business and a competent one.'

'Rich?'

Lavery did not care much for his employer; the man was a bully to him and treated his lovely young wife shamefully, so much so that she sought comfort with him, conversational comfort to be sure, nothing untoward. Yet Lavery had hopes that his ministrations of sympathy might proceed to something more tactile, for if, when Catherine Carruthers looked at him, she saw that bulbous nose on a lined face, enclosed by those big stuck-out ears, added to the age bags under watery eyes, he, if he cast a glance into one of the cabin mirrors, saw a fellow not so very long past his prime. But regard for the wife did not mean he was about to betray a trust with a total stranger, moreover a man to whom he had been instructed to pass what amounted to a ransom.

'It would not be my position to answer such a question, sir.'

'You have what was requested?'

'Do you, sir, have the gentlemen in question?'

'Gentlemen,' Moyle hooted. 'I would not be after calling them that and nor will you when you see what the rats have done to them.' The humour vanished and Moyle looked at Lavery hard. 'Show me the payment.'

Feeling decidedly queasy, and in any case not a brave man, Lavery nevertheless managed to hold the glare. 'I believe in such matters it is common that both sides show their assets at the same time.'

'You're a clever bugger, are you?'

'I doubt I am one and certain I am not the other.'

'Guard!' Moyle yelled, happy that it made Lavery jump. The door was opened and the order given to fetch up the Tollands from below, as the lieutenant added, 'Two smugglers for you to take away with you.'

Lavery had to bite his tongue then, for the word 'smugglers' nearly had him blurt out that they could not be anything other than gentlemen. He was aware that not everything Denby Carruthers did was above board; he, like his city contemporaries, often sailed close to the wind to ensure a profit. Downright illegality had never occurred to him but if he was getting smugglers out of trouble, why would that be? If the information did not settle Lavery's stomach, it did make him feel better; at last he might have something concrete on his employer.

When they appeared Moyle could not be faulted for his description, for they had been provided with no means to shave or stay remotely clean and they smelt high, like a pair of workhouse wastrels, even to a man well used to the dung-filled streets of London. Lavery still refused Moyle his money until the chains were struck off, at which point he handed over that and the letter claiming a high enough status to allow for their release, this necessary to cover Moyle against any retribution. With no ceremony the three left the hulk and took to the waiting wherry, which cast off immediately.

'Didn't see fit to come to our aid hisself, then?' Jahleel asked.

Lavery just leant over the side and tried to vomit from a stomach that had been voided on the way out.

* * *

'My dear, Emily, there is no such thing as untrammelled happiness, there are only degrees. Some days the world looks bright, the others it looks dark and forbidding and our souls are no different from one to the other.'

Heinrich Lutyens raised his head as he finished that peroration on the nature of existence, and if seriousness of countenance could be a mark of conviction her friend had certainly told the truth. His upturned nose was raised and his fish-like eyes, if they were incapable of flashing, had a brightness to them that accentuated the translucent nature of his skin. Having finished dinner they had taken to a couch in the foyer, away from prying ears, where they could talk of what she needed to do in the future.

'That, Heinrich, does not answer my question.'

'Do you believe that you will be judged by God?'

'I do.'

'John does not.'

'That does not make him right.'

'Can you envisage a just God that would punish a poor soul for allowing love to triumph over a miserable duty?'

'It is not necessary for the Lord to be merciful.'

'Then you must decide to torture yourself in this life or the next.'

'Which would you choose?'

'Science demands that facts take precedence over faith. But it is not for me to choose, or, my dear, even to advise. It is such a pity we are at war with France, for if we were not I would recommend crossing the Channel to allow yourself time to think.'

'Run away,' Emily sighed. 'Leave everything behind.'

'I seem to recall you telling me that everything did not amount to much.'

Both looked up as John Pearce approached, waving yet another letter. 'From Dundas, I am to see him on the morrow.'

'And then, John?' Lutyens asked.

Pearce looked hard at Emily then. 'The freedom to choose what I do, when I do it and with whom.'

CHAPTER FIFTEEN

The Count de Puisaye, an object of much amusement to both the staff and most of the guests, stood in the foyer of Nerot's, once more bedecked with jewels on velvet, his wig re-powdered, and quite heavily, so that when he moved he left behind a slight puff of white dust. He had also acquired a long cane, which he leant on in a bored posture, acting as if he desired to embody the monarchical regime of which he had been a part, now coming up to five years in the historical dungheap. That was where John Pearce found him, having returned to fetch both the count and the satchel containing the residue of the government gold, which had spent the night locked in the hotel safe.

He had spent a trying morning doing the rounds of the groups of French émigrés, previous escapees from the Revolution, seeking some with whom Amélie Labordière could take up residence. That sorted out he had then gone on to visit his prize agent, Alexander Davidson, and Lucknor, the lawyer who had written to Toby Burns, neither visit producing much in the way of satisfaction: nothing had come back from the Mediterranean and all his prize cases were still mired in dispute, while the whole trade was agog with what would come from the victory of the Channel Fleet.

This got Davidson an irascible lecture on the fact that Lord Howe had totally missed what Pearce now knew he was supposed to be after, that damned grain convoy, but he returned to a more important matter fairly swiftly: Charlie Taverner and Rufus Dommet. Davidson was charged to establish the whereabouts of HMS *Semele* and get a letter off to Ralph Barclay, with an offer from him of four prime hands from HMS *York* to replace the two men to be released back to that hulk under Davidson's surety. His name was not used, but he had no doubt Barclay would smoke the source of the request, which left open any hopes of a swift and positive result and did nothing for his mood.

His temper was not aided by the fact that he was still suffering from the frustration of having spent the previous night alone, this due to the fact that there was no way Emily was going to consider letting him stay in her room when she was registered under her married name, which came as a great disappointment to Didcot, to whom evidence of criminal conversation was a possible route to income from the cuckolded spouse. He considered passing on a bit of tittle-tattle to the Grub Street coves that wandered the London hotels looking for sleazy gossip and always willing to part with a sixpence, but decided against it; in time it might work out to be worth more.

Despite the letter telling them to call and giving a time, it did not seem to Dundas that keeping them waiting in an anteroom constituted bad manners, but for once Puisaye showed no sign of impatience; he expected powerful men to be rude and, it seemed, rated their ability to meet what was asked of them by their utter lack of consideration for others. This meant, Pearce surmised, that when the count did meet the man whom enemies and friends alike – he had more of the former than the latter – called the 'uncrowned King of Scotland', he would no doubt be impressed. Dundas controlled the entire body of Scottish Members of Parliament and used their block vote to support and sustain William Pitt's Tory administration, brushing off the continual accusations of influence peddling, and corruption, which were always attached to his name.

John Pearce had met Henry Dundas many times, the first in the company of his father, Adam – two men who, if they shared the fact of being Scottish by birth, shared nothing else, especially in terms of politics. Adam Pearce was a radical dedicated to fighting privilege, Dundas the ultimate party manager and upholder of state power. Their dislike was mutual, not aided by the very strong suspicion that the writ from which Pearce *père et fils* had been obliged to flee to France had been engineered by Dundas.

An hour passed in which neither explanation nor refreshment was offered until, finally, a rather superior clerk announced, 'Lieutenant Pearce, the minister will see you now.'

A supplicant look came from Puisaye, who knew what

was about to happen; Dundas would ask for a detailed assessment of matters in the Vendée so in some sense his subsequent supplications rested in this naval lieutenant's hands. All he could say, and the Frenchman took it entirely the wrong way, was that he would tell the truth. Pearce was barely through the door, satchel in hand, when Dundas barked at him, his accent as harsh as was remembered.

'What in the name of the Devil Incarnate have you been up to?'

'Obeying your instructions,' came the sharp and not very polite, if mystified reply, this as he conjured how he was going to tell Dundas to mind his manners.

'Does the name Raynesford mean anything to you?'

That stopped Pearce cold, but he prevaricated by asking why.

'I have on my desk a request from Sir Phillip Stephens seeking to know if there is anything of a secretive nature going on in the lower parishes of Hampshire? The only thing that could possibly come to mind involved you.'

'I fail to see the connection,' Pearce insisted, though given the use of Emily's maiden name the two had to be linked.

'A certain naval officer rolls up in Lymington, leaving behind him in a certain inn a paramour who has no right to be with him at all, given he is apparently, according to the lady, on some kind of secret assignment for the Government, at sea on a mission, for all love, vital to confound the nation's enemies.'

'Ah!' Pearce responded, having heard Emily's tale it was now possible to guess at what had happened. That old admiral she had confronted had continued to poke about, obviously not satisfied with what she had told him.

'How this has come about I cannot tell, but it has and I must deal with it.' Dundas looked at his desk, picking up and reading a letter. 'You know Sir Phillip Stephens quite well, do you not?'

'I would not say we were friends,' Pearce replied, trying to be jocular with his tone and change the mood, while also to cover for a mind racing to seek an explanation. 'Quite the opposite, in fact.'

'Probably because he dislikes you and makes no secret of it, which shows he's not entirely bereft of judgement.' Tempted to get up and leave, Pearce knew he could not; Emily was involved so he let Dundas continue. 'He seeks clarification from me, given anything of a secretive nature concerning France must emanate from my department, and I am obliged to tell him I have no knowledge of what he is talking about.'

'Which should be an end to the matter.'

'And if it is not, what then?'

'Tell him and swear him to secrecy.'

Dundas had a high colour anyway, the sort that comes from an over-consumption of claret and port, which passion did nothing to diminish and to that was added his hard Scottish voice.

'He is not that kind of person, Pearce, in fact he's a tiresome auld gossip and busybody. If he finds out what you have been up to on my behalf it will be all over the town and it will certainly be known to our political opponents in a day, and I hardly need point out it will not go down well with our fair-weather Portland friends either.'

Pearce was as aware as anyone of the needs of Pitt's government, since it was never out of the newspapers and was the stuff of coffee house discussions. They kept office due to the support of the Whigs led by the Duke of Portland. Lose them and the majority in the house became paper-thin to the point of ceasing to exist. Yet from what he knew, and he had to admit that was limited, Sir Phillip Stephens was not overtly political.

'I cannot see why he would concern himself.'

Dundas picked up the note and waved it; obviously it was the communication from the Admiralty. 'Somebody's been traipsing around Hampshire calling himself Lieutenant Raynesford and no such person exists, which hints at skulduggery. That may impact on the reputation of the navy, which is very much Sir Phillip's bailiwick, so I need to know if you and this Raynesford are one and the same person. Did you, Pearce, take with you a lady, and did ye book into a Lymington inn under an assumed name as a married couple prior to sailing to the Vendée?'

Pearce was in a bind and could not answer right away, only to be made aware by the knowing look he received that he had answered in the affirmative merely by his silence. 'The lady's name must be kept out of this.'

'By which I judge that she at least is married?' Pearce nodded and Dundas slowly shook his head. 'We must nip Sir Phillip's curiosity in the bud.'

'Surely a denial from you will suffice.'

'I cannot rely on it. You travelled to and from the ship, I take it from Lymington?' Another nod. 'Say he sends someone down to investigate and that leads to a certain vessel lying at Buckler's Hard and a crew who will be only too willing to tell of a recent trip to the Vendée and back under a certain Lieutenant Pearce.'

'He might make the connection anyway, it was he who supplied to me the temporary commission for HMS *Larcher*.'

'A request that emanated from this very building, which he will find out if he pursues the matter. This will expose the fact that I have been dabbling in things that would not find favour in certain parts of the administration, and so close am I to Billy Pitt it would be bound to drag him in as well.'

'Are you planning to enquire if the mission was successful?'

'Judging by the hints in your note asking for this meeting it was not, and who, any road, is this Count de Puisaye you mentioned?'

Pearce was on safer ground here, happier to talk about what he had observed than the problem of false naval officers. He gave a detailed account of what he had found in the swamps and forests in that part of France as well as his opinion of that which he had observed as he travelled to the edge of the region.

'It seems to me that they are merely being left to wither, confined to the region, which would be difficult to penetrate and no doubt cost many casualties, so it is, in effect a stalemate.'

'And the second part of my question?'

'I thought it best to bring back a representative of the rebellion, who wishes to make a plea to you for support.'

'I'm not sure that was wise.'

'While I am sure that it was unavoidable.'

Dundas sighed, but he did not request an explanation. 'And how do you suggest I deal with him?'

'I know you will find it hard to be polite.' That got Pearce a glare, which pleased him; he liked to score off Dundas – it somehow redressed the balance of what had been said earlier. 'He wants the British Government to launch a full-scale invasion and, in company with the Vendéen rebels, to take Nantes and, from there, to march on Paris.'

'A capital notion if only we had the means.'

'He believes the country is ready to rise up and help restore the Bourbons.'

'Which is not certain to be our desired aim.'

'These are not matters with which I am concerned,' Pearce said, reaching for his satchel. 'I have here what is left of the money you gave me. Since I had to sign for the full amount, I suspect I require your signature for the residue.'

'Residue?'

'Yes, I left six of your bags with the rebels, to facilitate their activities, and since I have had to travel the Count de Puisaye, I have used your money—'

'Government money!'

Pearce shrugged. 'Call it what you will and count it if you wish, but there is at my reckoning something like three hundred and ten pounds, though I cannot be sure due to the variation in coinage.'

'You've given away and spent two-thirds of what I entrusted to you?' The tone of the Dundas voice did not require John Pearce to enquire if his actions met with approval. 'This for a rebellion you tell me is likely to get nowhere?'

'I used my judgement.'

'As you did in taking your bonny lass to Lymington! It strikes me Pearce that you have exceeded your brief somewhat and, apart from that, I have only your word that the money you say was given out to the rebels is indeed in their hands.'

'It would be a bad idea, Dundas, to judge me by your own standards.'

That struck home; rumours of his light-fingered attitude to government money were the meat and drink of London gossip, added to the conviction that if he was not lining his own pockets then he was doing so for his loyal group of Scottish MPs.

'And as for proof, there is a man outside who can confirm my endowment.'

'A fellow I have never met, representing a group, according to you, I do not need?'

'It strikes me, Dundas, that you may have to indulge him somewhat.'

'Why?'

'To keep your secret, for the last thing you want is a French émigré aristocrat bleating all over the town about being fetched over from the Vendée in a naval warship to no purpose.'

'I asked if bringing him back was wise, I now know it was not.' There was a moment when, hands resting on the edge of his desk, Dundas was lost in thought. 'Best have him in.'

Pearce raised his satchel. 'Signature?'

'Can wait till I have had it counted.'

'Then I will leave it with you.'

'You will not,' Dundas snapped. 'You will stay where you are and aid me in dealing with this Puisaye.'

'I don't often see Dundas in a good light, Emily, but the man is a politician to his toes. He dealt with our count with consummate skill, a bit of flattery, a bit of reality. Had the old buffoon eating out of his hand.'

'To the point that he has not returned to the hotel?'

Pearce topped up both their glasses with wine as he replied.

'No, and he will send for his chest. The Government will play with him for a while, I suspect, and put him up in the meantime in some comfort. But I imagine they will be wanting rid of him and will contrive a very good reason why he must go back from whence he came to prepare the ground for something that, if my assessment is right, will never arrive.'

'Michael?'

'Has gone to visit some of his old haunts and will no doubt be drinking to excess, at which point he will probably fall out with some innocent and clout him.'

'You should restrain him.'

Pearce just laughed and spooned some food towards his mouth. 'Then I would be that fool. It is a fact that he would listen to you before he would listen to me.'

'And Amélie has gone now too, she left me a note.'

'She has been invited to stay with a party of French émigrés that have a house in Spitalfields. She also thought that it was wise to take up their offer quickly and I have to say I am grateful, for while she was here in Nerot's she was a charge on my purse.'

'As am I.'

'Emily, it is not the same and you know that.'

'I will need the address, since I must write to her from time to time.'

Pearce smiled across the dinner table. 'To enquire after more bad habits?'

'I would say your worst habit, John, is not talking about that which is most pressing.'

'Do you recall the first time we dined in this room? I think it was then that I first realised how attracted I was to your person, though I seem to recall you left in a hurry and rather flustered.'

Emily frowned. 'Another bad habit is your determination, when something comes up which you wish to ignore, to change the subject in quite so obvious a fashion.'

'Perhaps I fear what will come out of not doing so, Emily.'

'You did not then question Heinrich last night?'

'I did not feel it was my place to and you seemed so deeply engaged in conversation.'

'Yet you walked part of the way home with him.'

Pearce was dying to respond with a comment about her insistence that he should come nowhere near her room, but he held his tongue; matters were proceeding to some kind of conclusion and his cause would not be aided by references to his desire to make love to her.

'You did not ask, when you must be curious?'

'Oddly enough, Emily, if I was faced with physical danger I think I would react in a way that would smack of upright behaviour . . .'

'You have done so in the past, I have seen and admired it.'

'I do not want you to admire me for that.'

'Heinrich and I talked of happiness, or rather the impossibility of ever achieving such a state.'

'We talked of matters in France now and how many more of his perceived enemies, his one-time friends, Robespierre will guillotine. Heinrich and I share the opinion that he will one day fall to that himself. Who will take up the reins of power if he does was a subject for speculation, and if he does fall, will it bring peace?'

'And?'

'We came to the conclusion as I suspect did you and he – that is, no conclusion at all.'

'On the contrary, John.'

That surprised him but he did not speak.

'Heinrich convinced me . . . perhaps "persuaded me" would be a better expression, of how I should deal with the circumstances in which I find myself, deal with you, my husband and his threats. If indeed he did cause the offices of Mr Studdert to be broken into and burgled it argues that he will, as you say, stop at nothing to get me back.'

'It is not for love of you, Emily.'

'No, his pride is deeply wounded.'

'Hurt one man's pride or break another's heart.'

'Tomorrow I will reply to his letter and in it I will say that his attempts to ensure my return will not succeed and I will allude to that theft, while adding that it was a failure and that I still have the documents that will see him in court on a charge of perjury. I will then go on to tell him that my heart is spoken for elsewhere and though I do not mean to cause him pain, he will soon, no doubt, learn that I have taken up residence with you and observe that I intend to do so openly.'

Pearce reached over and took her hand. 'I will try to make you happy.'

'That is what Heinrich said, John – that only you could do that.'

'A noble sentiment from a fellow who carries a torch for you himself.'

The rap at the door of the private dining was unwelcome, the face that appeared even more so, it being Didcot bearing a letter, which got him barked at.

'Has anyone ever told you, Didcot, that your timing is appalling?'

'Can't be helped, your honour, not when a messenger comes from the Houses of Parliament itself, and I take leave to guess what he fetched will not brook delay in the reading.'

'Leave it.'

Emily laughed. 'You might as well open it, John, we are only halfway through supper.'

'Very well, give it here.'

Handed over, Pearce was breaking the wax when he realised Didcot had not departed, which got the crook-faced servant a hard look that had him withdraw, a sour expression on his chops.

'He probably knows what it says,' Pearce whispered

loudly before the door fully closed, pleased to see it jerk; then he began reading. 'My God, they have a damned cheek these politicos.'

'Am I going to have to get used to that kind of language?'

Still looking at the letter Pearce's reply had a vague quality. 'I daresay, Emily, but you would wonder at someone sending me a missive demanding my immediate presence at Westminster and at this time of the evening. Dundas can go to the devil!'

The door swung open again. 'Will you be sending a reply, your honour?'

Pearce looked at Emily as he answered Didcot. 'I will, to tell them that tonight I am otherwise engaged.'

Had she not had her back to him, Didcot would have seen her blush.

CHAPTER SIXTEEN

The shell from Fort Monteciusco could be seen and it was heading towards the redoubt set up to enfilade it from the western heights, yet no one moved or sought protection because this had been happening for weeks now, and since that included a pair of senior officers, a captain and the commodore, who stood rock still hands behind their back, it behoved everyone else to show the same indifference to potential danger. As a rule the fire from French cannon, required to elevate their guns to account for the marginally higher position of their British counterparts, landed just short, the odd one catching the rock face in the right way bouncing up to threaten the protective breastwork. This one was different; it grew and grew and did not even show any sign of dropping in its arc as it lost velocity.

'They've doubled the charge!'

That shout came from Captain Staunton, the man at present in command, and he turned to tell everyone to get down. The missile hit the top of the stone-built part of the rampart and sent the carefully arranged rocks flying in all directions, one of which, a large object, struck Staunton in the back. Others clanged into the quartet of 24-pounder cannon, dislodging one and setting off a noise like demented church bells with the others. Another rock seemed to bounce in the air before coming down to land not very far in front of Commodore Nelson, sending up from the ground a salvo of loose stones made too hot to touch by the sun, many of which struck him in the face.

From being an orderly location the battery redoubt was reduced to a place of seeming carnage. Staunton was face down and still, his hat a yard away from his outstretched hand, his back and side a mass of bright-red gore. The gunners, being the furthest forward and working the guns stripped to the waist because of the heat, had suffered badly from ricochets and a goodly number of the wounds seemed serious. A cacophony of shouts mixed with cries of distress filled the air and it was those that made Toby Burns move, but not before he had checked his body to ensure he was unscathed.

Nelson was shouting, one hand over an eye, with blood streaming through his fingers, 'Get any medical men up here, and stretchers too. Mr Farmiloe, man those cannon and fire off any that are primed and ready, we do not want Calvi to know we are hurt.'

'Sir, you are wounded,' Toby said, rushing over to him.

'I am ambulant, Mr Burns, see to those more in need.'

A voice called out. 'Captain Staunton's dead, sir.'

'Poor fellow, a loss to the service,' Nelson replied, removing his hand to show a mass of nicks around his eye, which was already looking flaming red, and above that a deep and copiously bleeding cut. 'There is a bit of linen in my right-hand pocket, Mr Burns, be so good as to fetch it out and tie it over my face.'

'The major wound will need stitching, sir.'

'Which means Surgeon Roxburgh and his damned needle,' Nelson hooted. 'Now there's a man who would struggle to make a living as a seamstress.'

That was Nelson all over and it irritated Toby: how can he make jokes at a time like this? There are men groaning and badly hurt, the French have humbugged us by using a double charge, which no one expected given they were as likely to blow apart their cannon as harm us, and now we are in mortal danger of a repeat blow. These were the thoughts that ran through Toby's mind as he did as he was asked, equally aware that two of the 24-pounders had been fired as ordered and they were being reloaded, this while the last one was inspected for damage.

Farmiloe, unbidden, was allocating men to fill the gaps and form as many complete gun crews as possible and one was short of a commander. 'Toby, take charge of one of the remaining cannon.'

The reply was automatic. 'Aye, aye, sir.'

'Dick will do, Toby, the lieutenant's exams are not yet sat and who knows, you and I may have our pass dates on the same day.'

God, Toby surmised, he's looking forward to the damned examination, which prompted an outburst of truth.

'I'm sure I am not yet ready and I cannot fathom Hotham's reasons for pushing me forward to take them.

He admonished me to study hard, and I have, but nothing makes enough sense to give any confidence at all. And how can we sit for lieutenant in the midst of a siege anyway?'

'But that's the point, Toby,' Farmiloe said, when the artillery duel had ceased and, sat in the shade, they were studying the books, mainly that fount of all nautical wisdom, *The Seaman's Vade-Mecum*. 'I admit we have to study for the technical aspects of the exam but I am reliably told by Captain Nelson that every candidate is expected to know their stars, mathematics, spherical trigonometry, sail plans and knots, as well as log keeping for stores and stowage. The vital part is the emergency, how we will cope when suddenly required to act on a situation of which we have not been forewarned.'

'They were forever setting exams at the school I attended,' Toby responded, gloomily. 'And I never did well.'

'Lord in heaven,' Farmiloe hissed, 'Captain Nelson has returned. I bet he has a corker of an eye under that bandage.'

'He's lucky he's got an eye at all, Dick, from what I saw.'

'Gentlemen, I see you about your labours.'

'Boning up, sir,' Farmiloe replied.

'Then I must ask you to bone less, for we cannot allow that battery yonder the freedom to do to us tomorrow what they did to us today.'

'An attack, sir?' Farmiloe asked, his face eager.

'To spike the cannon, not to hold the fortress, to seek to that would only invite a counter-attack we would find difficult to repel. I have asked Captain Walker to provide a party of marines for the assault but I need you two to ensure their cannon are rendered unusable.'

It was fanciful, on an early July day in the Mediterranean, to think that a chill hand had gripped the heart of Toby Burns, but that is what it felt like to him and he was back in Hotham's cabin as the old scoundrel explained to him that he was once more being sent to serve ashore under Commodore Nelson, his face as usual full of apparent concern, to mask what Toby was certain to be his insincerity.

'I admit to ulterior motive this time, Mr Burns, for it has been decided by Lord Hood, given the shortage of officers brought on by wear and tear as well as casualties, to hold a set of examinations for a lieutenant's commission. Naturally, all of those acting the rank, and there are quite a number after so much action, will sit, but so will those who have served a goodly time in the mid's berth, and you . . . well, with what I have seen despatched to other vessels you are near the top dog of that particular berth.'

He was not; in fact Toby knew he was far from admired and the cause was jealousy. 'I hardly feel I am ready, sir.'

Hotham came over avuncular, even to the point of a glistening in his pale-blue eyes, as though his memories warranted tears. 'Never met a mid who thought otherwise, but I have seen the same fellows pass with flying colours.' Then the voice became more brisk. 'Hence the transfer to *Agamemnon* for I know that when it comes to a siege Commodore Nelson will not oversee it from his deck. He will be ashore and in the thick of it and so will those who accompany him. Be assured the captains who sit in judgement on those who aspire to promotion will have in front of them the service activities of the candidates and, in your case, that can only do you good. To volunteer once is commonplace, to do so continually, as you have, is exceptional.'

For a midshipman who had never volunteered since he first set foot on a ship's deck that was a comment to which it was hard to avoid reacting, and that with plain disbelief.

'Mr Toomey has a letter for Commodore Nelson, so as soon as your dunnage is gathered I suggest you make haste.' That was followed by a grin Burns saw as wolfish. 'Be a damned shame if it was all done and dusted afore you arrived.'

'Sir.'

'Good day, Mr Burns, and good luck.'

He had taken the letter from Toomey as requested, wondering at the look in the clerk's eye, which seemed to contain a degree of revulsion. Of course he was Hotham's man, heart and soul, but Toby could recall no event that would have made his reaction to his presence one of personal affront.

'Mr Burns, are you with us?'

'Sorry, sir.'

'I daresay it is the heat that has your mind wandering. Did you hear what I said?'

Toby Burns had been aware of the piping voice, but lost in his own concerns and sure Nelson was talking to Dick Farmiloe he had paid insufficient heed. 'I am forced to admit I did not, sir.'

For once Nelson showed a hint of exasperation, which

was not generally in his nature, no doubt brought on, Toby surmised, by the pain of his wound, which must be acute.

'Then I would ask you to concentrate, young sir, for this is important. Fort Monteciusco mounts a battery of six heavy cannon, yet I assume, given they are of an age and have been plied much these last days, that there is only a single piece that they dare double-charge and that is the vital one, which must be destroyed.'

'Surely we should spike them all, sir.'

'Bravely advanced,' Nelson replied, in a tone of voice more common to his nature, 'but I doubt that practically you will be given time to do so. As soon as the marines assault the walls there will be flares aloft to tell Calvi that their south-western fort is under threat. That will bring out the French reserves to repel the attack and we will have limited numbers to hold for any length of time.'

'How will we tell, sir, which is the one to destroy?'

'Why, Mr Burns, each cannon I have ever seen is stamped with its date of casting.'

'Hard to see in darkness, sir,' Farmiloe said.

'Failing the ability to see the date of manufacture, the best cannon will take its ball tightly, the older long-fired ones will be loose.'

'Am I allowed to say, sir, that is not very scientific?'

'You are, Mr Farmiloe, and you are right, but it is all the indication we have.'

'Will the Bullocks not support us, sir?' asked Toby.

'Not in this lifetime; I have never known a body of men who take so much time to plan an attack, never mind execute it. Were we to rely on them it would be next week before we saw any attempt to give us succour and they would want a full frontal assault, no doubt.' Feeling perhaps he had been too harsh on the soldiers, the voice softened a little. 'General Stuart is having to cope with much debilitation in their ranks also. Bullocks are never as healthy as tars.'

Overheard by the sailors manning the battery that was greeted by much growled yet wholehearted agreement about the first part of Nelson's complaint. To the men who had slaved to get these cannon into position and done so over terrain the defenders of Calvi thought impossible, the tardy behaviour of the army, who seemed to envision obstacles rather than possibilities, had been a running complaint. Officers and men alike of the fleet thought them scrimshanks and bellyachers. When he added his rider about sickness in the ranks there was none of the sympathy so evident in the commodore's tone.

Books were put aside and preparations made, blades sharpened, pistol and musket flints checked and the weapons themselves cleaned and oiled. There was no shortage of cork trees and that burnt was used to blacken the faces of those taking part; each mid would lead a party of sailors who knew their guns, while the marines dulled the shiny parts of their weapons, discarded their white webbing and removed from their person anything that might make the kind of noise when moving to alert the enemy. Night came early and noisy with insects in the Mediterranean and since every bastion, French and British, was torchlit, the exit through the besieging line had to be made from a point away from the battery position.

Toby was afraid, but felt more calm than he had ever been going into action, almost in the mood to let whatever would happen take place, though he had a mind to wait till everyone else was over the walls opposite before he ventured to join them. That still left a risk and he accepted he had no choice. If it was not bravery it was indifference, for the man who held power over his future existence seemed determined that he should not have one. The night was hot and sticky for those crouched in the thick scrub that coated the island and everyone was looking forward to moving for one very simple reason – the breeze that would cool their perspiration-soaked clothing as they stood up. Above the sky was a carpet of stars, but the moon was new and no more than a sliver, high in the sky.

'Ready?'

The hissed demand was answered in like fashion and when Captain Walker was sure all had responded he gave the signal to move forward into the deep valley, rock and wood strewn, that separated the two batteries, leaving them unavoidably slithering downhill on screed until they reached the bottom. There Walker halted to allow the stragglers to catch up and so he could ensure that, when they moved again, they were doing so in the right direction, not easy, as surrounded by trees, there was practically no light.

That made more fiery the flash of the first musket and so disoriented were the assault party that there was no assurance it was not coming from behind rather than in front. It was Walker who shouted but he could not know if his command to get down was being obeyed because he could not see, this as an order roared out in French and a line of flashing musket pans and the flaring discharge indicated that they had perhaps walked into a trap; had the enemy suspected that an assault might be attempted to spike such a dangerous weapon?

'Mark those flashes, lads,' Walker yelled. 'Pick one out and aim for a foot below.'

Lying flat on the pine needles that covered the forest floor Toby Burns was aware, first of the musket balls cracking through the trees to eventually create a thudding sound as they embedded themselves, then of the illumination of the immediate area round him as the marines replied, then of the smell of spent powder mixing with the odour of human sweat, or was it fear? He could hear the man closest to him as he went though the mantra of reloading, which had to be slow and by touch and experience in the darkness.

'Bite charge,' that followed by a spitting sound, 'hammer back, prime the pan, ground weapon, powder in, ball in, ram home, cock the hammer, take aim, fire.'

That brought a long powder flash from the muzzle and another in the pan. Toby was crawling backwards as that was being repeated all around him, seeking to get deeper into the undergrowth so as to avoid what must surely follow, hand-to-hand fighting in the dark with bayonets, knives and clubs, combat at which he knew he would be useless. The forest was full of shouting, screaming and fusillades but he had no notion beyond that of what was happening and that went on for what seemed to his ears an age. Then it began to fade, the voices becoming, if not faint, more distant, the sound of discharged muskets beginning to echo all around rather than close, and thankfully no more balls cracking overhead.

Silence was slow to descend and he lay there, feeling the rivulet of fluid running down his spine and wondering whether it was safe now to move. About to get to his knees he heard a rustling sound and that induced near panic, for this Corsica was a strange place and who knew what demons and bloodthirsty creatures resided in these forests? To stay still was to face whatever was making the noise; to move might mean pursuit but it was the lesser evil so, on hands and knees, Toby began a slow crawl, he thought back the way he came, reassured when the ground beneath him began to slope and the treetops opened just enough for him to see the star-filled sky.

That did not show him the butt of the musket that clouted him on the top of his head; lacking a hat it might have killed him. As it was he was too stunned to react when a voice spoke a rough command and a hand grabbed his collar and sought to drag him upright. That brought forth a squeal and got him a hard slap on the face and a demand for silence. The word might be the same but the pronunciation was not; the man holding him and now shaking him ferociously was French.

'He could be out there wounded and in need of help, sir,' Farmiloe insisted. 'I do not ask that anyone else goes out, but I will.'

'I must forbid it, young man,' Walker responded.

'And I too,' Nelson added. 'We raise a truce flag when daylight comes and ask to be allowed to recover our wounded, the same to be granted to the enemy.'

'Do you think they will agree?'

'It is common practice,' Walker said, 'but it will depend, Mr Farmiloe, on their having people to search for. If they have none they may decline.'

'How long till daylight, sir?'

'A couple of hours, which you know very well,' Nelson insisted, 'so I suggest that you would be better served getting some sleep than standing around fretting and that I must make into an order.'

'Sir.'

'He's a brave young fellow,' Walker whispered as soon as Farmiloe was out of earshot.

'Aye, we ask a lot of our youngsters and in my experience they never let us down. The pity is you never got to spike the guns.'

'I cannot believe that they were forewarned, sir, though it is possible that they saw what damage their cannon did this morning and therefore anticipated that we could not leave matters be. My impression, and I admit it is only that, was that the French were as surprised as were we when we made contact. One musket going off in panic is what began the exchange.'

'Well, we came out of it relatively unscathed, did we not?'

'More scratches from the undergrowth than wounds, sir.'

'Then we are left to pray for the safety of Mr Burns.'

Sat on the cold stone floor the young man about to be the subject of their prayers was rubbing the top of his head, which was very sore and sticky with dried blood, not forgetting his other aches and pains, for he had not been gently handled by his captors as they dragged him back up the hill to Fort Monteciusco. There had been a brief and pointless conversation with an officer who did not speak English, and in failing to get much response from a groggy non-French-endowed captive the officer had ordered, Toby presumed, that he be tossed into this cell, all rough stone walls and lit by a single piece of smelly tallow.

He had shed tears at first, but pain aside it soon occurred to the youngster that he was, in this cell, which was well below the parapet onto which he had been dragged, a lot safer than being in the redoubt with his fellow Britons, given the cannon that had been used to such effect was no doubt being prepared to do so again and he was presumably to the rear of it. Then there were the thoughts based on opinions from his own side. If the French could not sortie out from Calvi and if the outer British perimeter was held, lacking relief it was only a matter of time before they would be obliged to surrender.

If that happened he would be freed and surely the French would feed him in the meantime, though they might, and this was a worry, employ torture. Yet they had showed no desire to that yet and as he ruminated on the pros and cons of being a prisoner it occurred that he would be more likely to survive in a deep cell than out on the battle area. And incarcerated he could not study for his examination, which he dreaded. Being a captive had to give him an excuse to decline to take part.

At dawn, when the request was made for a truce to recover any wounded, the French were very decent; they admitted they had as a prisoner a young officer and that although he was wounded it was superficial and he was not in any serious danger, though any notion that he should be paroled to return was declined. An English speaker was found to inform Toby Burns of this outcome and the youngster had to struggle to look crestfallen, though he was, in truth, pleased. Where he was, he felt, left him secure and safe for the first time since he had set foot aboard HMS *Brilliant* and come under the tutelage of Ralph Barclay.

'It is, Sir Roger, a travesty and an insult to my professional standing and I demand to see Lord Howe to have the matter redressed.'

'His Lordship has retired to Bath to take the waters.'

He'll need a stiff brandy when I am finished with him, Barclay thought angrily, what was being thought upon in his head very obvious on his countenance, a fact which certainly registered with Admiral Curtis. The fog of war had cleared somewhat and it was now known for a fact that towards the closing stages of the 1st June battle that the elderly Howe, exhausted, had retired to his cabin to rest, leaving the quarterdeck of his flagship, and consequently direction of the battle, to his captain of the fleet, before whom Barclay was now sitting and demanding answers.

'For a fleet commander he seems strangely reluctant to carry out his responsibilities.'

Sir Roger Curtis had very pronounced, black eyebrows, which moved up significantly at such a remark from what was a mere captain. 'I will pass on to

His Lordship your opinion of his capabilities. I am sure he will appreciate it.'

'You may also pass on that I, and I am not alone, demand that some kind of despatch be sent to support the original communication to the Government which gives full praise to those officers left out, and thereby diminished, and now see their reputation in question.'

'Captains who were slow to obey orders?'

'I complied with my orders with as much alacrity as circumstances dictated.'

Curtis sat forward. 'I was on the deck of the flagship at Lord Howe's side, Captain Barclay. It was I who ordered, on his instructions, that the requisite signals be sent aloft and I can tell you from where I stood you took a damned long time to get into action, when you were quite specifically directed to close with the enemy.'

'Which I did as soon as it was prudent to do so.'

'Damn you, sir,' Curtis exploded. 'It is not your place to be prudent, it is your duty to obey and do what you are told.'

Ralph Barclay refused to be cowed. 'I waited to avoid being caught in the fire of the flagship, which would have done more damage to HMS *Semele* than that inflicted by the enemy. Or would you have my hands die under the balls of your cannon? The vessel I engaged, I would remind you, was so successfully handled that it sank. And since you are chucking around accusations of being slow, I am bound to ask why nothing was done to pursue the French fleet, which was beaten and vulnerable, which given Lord Howe was no longer directing the battle, must fall to your lack of strategic grasp.'

Curtis was on his feet before Ralph Barclay was finished. "This interview is at an end.'

Barclay stood too. 'It may well be, Sir Roger, but I will tell you now that the matter about which I came to complain is still very much in play. It seems to me, sir, that you have heaped praise upon those who would fawn on you personally and damned by omission anyone with the audacity to stand up to you and identify your errors of judgement. Good day!'

'The man's arse is bruised with the act of being kissed! As for Howe, I suspect he is asleep somewhere, up to his neck in Bath salts and convinced he is a hero.'

That got nods around the groaning table ashore, where Ralph Barclay had convened a meeting of those officers who shared his concerns, including Captain Molloy, whose conduct had been deemed so shameful he was close to demanding a court martial to clear his name, an option also being considered by the senior man present, Rear Admiral Caldwell, who had shared the supervision of the centre squadron of Howe's fleet, not that he had received recognition for it, and it was he who spoke.

'How are we to reverse it, Barclay? The King esteems Howe and praises him to the skies, as if a man at home on a farm conversing with his trees knows anything about fighting at sea.'

'Perhaps his great knowledge comes from his son, William,' hooted Albemarle Bertie to general amusement; the Duke of Clarence might be a post captain but he was generally held to be a useless one and that was as nothing compared to his arrogance and condescension.

'I had what I thought was a bright idea, that we set up a fund to pay for stories supporting our case. The written word will play harder on the Government than any amount of bleating by us. They are, after all, struggling to keep their majority in the house and if we can get some peers on our side . . .'

That did not need completion. 'And I also suggest we pay for some cartoons to bring Curtis down a peg or two. With that great nose of his and those eyebrows he should be easy to caricature. In short, gentlemen, I think we should dig deep into our purse and subscribe to a campaign.'

Just outside the dining room door, Cornelius Gherson, who could clearly hear this suggestion being approved, swelled slightly, for it had been his notion. That Barclay did not credit him was not a consideration; positions reversed, he would not have ascribed it to his employer.

'Then, gentlemen,' Barclay said, standing and raising his glass. 'I shall proceed to London to get the campaign under way. To our future recognition, I say, and damn those who would do us down.'

That got the room up and drinking deep.

CHAPTER SEVENTEEN

The fellow who turned into Downing Street – a subsequent message from Dundas had been sent to tell him to attend there – had a lift in his step so jaunty that he would not have been angered to be hailed a sailor, and in truth John Pearce might even have broken into song. If not everything in his life was rosy then he could at least say that the most important aspect was; Emily Barclay was committed to him and from there all things were possible, though he asked her not to reply to her husband, telling him of her intentions, until the matter of Charlie and Rufus was resolved – any mention of his name would not aid matters.

Such a mood did not survive when he entered the door of the First Lord of the Treasury, to find a pair of weary-looking and bleary-eyed ministers. William Pitt and Henry Dundas were seeking, with a hair-of-the-dog bottle of claret and a copious breakfast of fish, fowl and red meat, to recover from a bruising session in Parliament and the prior consumption of wine that had both preceded the night sitting and sustained them throughout the small hours.

'We have another mission for you,' Dundas said, through some heavy chewing.

'Do you, indeed?' That got a hearty nod. 'Then I must disappoint you for I will be obliged to decline.'

It was William Pitt who responded, and softly. He did not have either the Dundas high colour or the brisk Caledonian way of expressing himself; called upon for a description Pearce would have said he had lazy eyes and an almost translucent pallor to his skin hinting at a lack of robust health. But he would also have been obliged to add that here was a fellow who had risen to the highest political office at the ridiculously young age of twenty-four and had held it through many a crisis for over ten years. That suggested remarkable powers of political guile and a strength of character not replicated in his physical appearance.

'You feel you have the ability to do so, Lieutenant Pearce?'

Pearce chose to be flippant in his response. 'Is not freedom of choice the right of every true-born Briton?'

'Perhaps if we were to remind you of previous writs,' Dundas responded.

'Previous and, given my father is no longer with us, surely spent.'

'Ah, spent,' Pitt exclaimed, playing with the fish on his breakfast plate; he did not look like a trencherman. 'You seem to have a talent for that, Pearce, given what you used of the funds entrusted to you.'

'For which I have accounted.'

'We want you to take a message to Lord Hood in the Mediterranean, as you did previously.'

Pearce looked at Dundas as he said that and found himself staring at the bottom of a glass in the process of being drained. 'You make me sound like some kind of ever-at-the-ready post boy.'

Dundas replied, once he had swallowed his wine. 'I would hate to flatter you by elevation, Pearce.'

'I believe my father, even if he did not give credence to religion, often had occasion to tell you to go to hell.'

'Your father—'

Dundas got no further than that; a held-up hand from Pitt was enough to stop him.

'Please, Harry, let us not go there, to where you two will find nothing but dispute. Your father is no longer a trouble to the Government, for which I am grateful, while having said that I am bound to add he died in the most appalling fashion and we are sorry for it.'

'I can believe you might be, sir.'

Dundas just shrugged at the obvious exclusion of himself as Pitt continued. 'We are required to communicate with Lord Hood, as we did before, outside the normal channels; in short, to pass to him a letter that only he knows has been delivered.'

'Send someone else.'

'Someone we know we can trust?'

'I'm not sure I am that person.'

'We want to send you, and not on the mail packet this time but in a ship that you will command.'

'Which,' Dundas added, 'has the advantage of

removing you from any chance of what you got up to in the Vendée becoming common knowledge.'

'Is that what this is really about, for if it is, my lips are sealed?'

'But not those of your one-time crew,' said Pitt. 'They could still set us a problem.'

Pearce was surprised, but he made the connection after a minimal pause. 'You want me to take *Larcher* to the Med?'

'Two birds with one stone, Pearce! You still have yet to turn in the temporary commission giving you command of HMS *Larcher*, and from what we can glean the fellow you replaced is about to go under the knife for whatever ailment it is he is suffering from, which implies at least a long convalescence.'

'You see us,' Pitt interjected, 'in the midst of one war, when in fact we are mired in two and the second one is of such duration as to have no beginning or end, for it is politics. In order to pursue the actual conflict with France, Dundas and I spend days, and as in the case of the last twenty-four hours, many hours of the night, fighting a shadow political one to keep up the struggle.'

'Do you believe,' Dundas, demanded, 'that we have to defeat the dark forces that exist across the channel?'

'Of course I do, though given I am in the presence of a very dark force indeed, I take issue with the word "we".'

'You're a serving naval officer.'

'And you know just how I feel about that!'

'So you intend to disappoint us?'

'I have other plans.'

'To do with the lady who is, like you, staying in

Nerot's Hotel, perhaps the same one who was sharing your accommodation in Lymington?'

'Have you been spying on me, Dundas?'

'Don't sound so shocked, Pearce, it's what I do and the country is safer for it.'

Pitt stood and Pearce noticed that his pale cheeks had a touch of rouge. 'I will leave this to you, Harry, if that is all right.'

'Fine, Billy.' As soon as Pitt had exited Dundas spoke again. 'A delicate soul he is, not one to enjoy unpleasantness.'

'Is that what I am about to experience?'

'What did the man I send round to Nerot's learn, eh? That the place has gossipy servants, but who does not? That you have an attachment to a certain Mrs Barclay, which on further enquiry turns out to be the wife of another naval officer. Promises to be messy, I suspect.'

'You are wrong, Dundas, it is not messy, it is about to be the very opposite. Mrs Barclay has repudiated her marriage and hopes circumstances will allow her to live happily with me.'

'True love is it?' Dundas sneered.

'Something that can be given to most people, although I doubt you are aware of it without the use of a mirror.'

'Your father was wont to exercise his wit on me, laddie, and I would advise you to recall where it got him. A married woman running off with one sailor, and leaving behind to grieve another. Now that would make a tasty morsel for the morning papers, would it not?'

'I told you she had to be kept out of it.'

'So you did.'

'And I would remind you,' Pearce barked, 'that I have all the details regarding my mission to the Vendée and so am in a position to retaliate should you break that requirement.'

'Where you managed to pocket some substantial sums belonging to the Government.' Dundas reached into a coat pocket and produced a document, which he made great show of opening and reading. 'Here it is, specie to the value of a thousand guineas, signed for and dated by Lieutenant John Pearce on Buckler's Hard.'

'Monies for which I am prepared to account and I have a witness in the Count de Puisaye as to how the majority of it was employed.'

'I wonder what the count would put first – you in Newgate for debt, since I don't think you have a spare sum to make up the losses, or a promise from the Government to provide help for his rebellion? Still, you'd have Mrs Barclay to come and visit, which would be a comfort as well as food for a right good scandal.'

Dundas stood now, a wolfish grin on his rubicund face. 'I will leave you to cogitate on that, Pearce. Help yourself to some wine if you need it, but know this. I am no a man to trifle with and if old Adam were here he would tell you that too. It's a wee trip to the Mediterranean or . . . ?'

'Has anyone ever told you that you are lower than a snake?'

'Every day, Pearce,' Dundas replied from the open doorway, 'and, laddie, it is water off a duck's back.'

The mood of the earlier part of the day was gone now, to be replaced with gloomy reflection, for he had no doubt that Dundas would carry out his threat; he was not a man to make such in idle fashion. There was a moment when he wondered what could be so important that it had to be carried by hand all the way to Lord Hood, but that was not a thought on which to linger; the paramount one was the public shaming of Emily, for there was a vast difference between the likes of the *Hampshire Chronicle* and the much more numerous papers printed in London.

She would become the butt of public disgrace, and that in newspapers that were distributed throughout the whole country, for if the people who printed them claimed high moral values they would sink to the gutter in a trice for a salacious story of marital infidelity. There would, no doubt, be some artist only too happy to do a very accurate pen and ink likeness and he would not put it past Dundas to distribute pamphlets so the chances of escaping ridicule wherever she went were slim.

The threat of Newgate he had to think was real; again, Dundas was not a bluffer and it would be his word against that of a minister in high office. Even if he talked of what he knew, the experience of the Government, which he had observed his father having to fight, was plain: when they decided to play dirty they did so very seriously indeed. Adam Pearce had never been able to get anything he wrote published in the newspapers, or make a case for his freedom of speech, the very simple reason being that men of power had no trouble making it plain to the editors and proprietors that there was a line they must tow if they wanted to be on good terms with Downing Street.

Oddly, Pearce suspected if he put the case to Emily, despite her fears, she would probably tell him to resist.

It was part of what made him love her, that part of her personality that he had first observed when she had stood up to her husband over punishing him and had then, when she found out that he was a both a tyrant and a liar, caused her to move from his cabin to Heinrich Lutyens' hospital in Toulon. Emily Barclay had a rod of steel in her, added to an innate kindness to go with her outstanding beauty. In short, he was a lucky man and he would not do anything to see her unhappy, and if that meant acceding to the recent request, so be it.

Sailing to the Mediterranean was not all bad for by the time he arrived the high summer heat would have faded to something very pleasant. Toby Burns was there and so, as far as he knew, were the other people with whom Lucknor had corresponded. It was a chance for him to gather evidence of his own, facts which would further enhance his ability to silence Ralph Barclay and truly cow him, for he had in mind something he had not dared even mention to her, the notion of launching a parliamentary bill for divorce. That it was hard, going on impossible, to get such a dispensation was no reason not to try.

Turning his mind to the proposed mission he was not sure that an armed cutter like HMS *Larcher*, being cramped, was a vessel for such a long voyage. She had been built for inshore work and even the trip to the Ile de Noirmoutier had taxed her ability to carry enough stores to cover for unforeseen eventualities like being held back by foul weather. Mentally he began to calculate what would be required to facilitate a voyage to Gibraltar, where he would be able to revictual, then from there to where the papers told him Hood was, off the northern tip of Corsica.

Lord, he thought, it is so cramped too, that tiny cabin, and that set off another train of thought. It was the sound of Pearce laughing that brought Dundas back and he looked as if he thought him deranged.

'You have your post boy, Dundas, so prepare your communications and let me know when to collect them.'

'I am curious to know what made you change your mind?'

'Certainly you are, but you will never know and I suspect never guess. Now I bid you good day, I have other matters requiring my attention.'

A few miles away, in the City of London, Denby Carruthers was closeted with the Tolland brothers and demanding to know how they had got themselves into such a bind. If the explanation he received was not the entire truth, it was plain that they had put a private matter of retribution against this fellow called John Pearce ahead of what he saw as their duty, which was to get back to their trade and begin to repay his investment, a point he made forcibly.

'I will not let it rest for all time, Mr Carruthers,' Jahleel said, which had Franklin nodding too and vigorously. 'I will have that fellow's blood, but I see I must set it aside for a while until you and we are in profit and you know you have chosen well.'

'Of course I must deduct the cost of your freedom from our first transaction.' Seeing the elder Tolland's eyes narrow, Carruthers added quickly, 'Unless it imposes a burden, in which case it can wait until payment does not sting.'

'Fair enough, but one request, and I promise not to act on it without you being informed. We need an eye kept on the Pearce fellow and we need to know that when the time comes we can gift to him what he has coming his way.'

'Which is?'

It was Franklin who ran a finger over his throat, then said, 'And this time we will not stop to talk. The time for that is past.'

The alderman's next words were tentative, for he had just been informed that the notion of committing murder was not one to trouble these two before him. It had not been something about which he had harboured much doubt but there was a great deal to be said for outright confirmation.

'I do have in mind another way to settle that debt and perhaps even add to it a payment.' Denby paused for a couple of seconds then added, 'A substantial payment.'

'How so?'

'If I were to say that I have certain people who trouble me, as much as this Pearce fellow seems to trouble you, people whose removal would add to my contentment, I am wondering if I could engage your services to rid me of them?'

Jahleel Tolland just shrugged.

'That is good and I will bear it in mind. Now, when can you take possession of the ship I have purchased and when can we set sail?'

'We?'

'Yes. You cannot fill its holds without you spend money, my money, and it is a habit of mine when that happens for me to be present.'

'This is not a game, Alderman, we deal with some right hard bargains and suspicious as hell with it.'

'Then I shall look to you to protect me and our investment. I ask again, when can we begin?'

'Got to gather a crew first. Can't sail a ship without we have hands to man the barky.'

Carruthers frowned. 'How long will that take?'

Jahleel laughed. 'No time at all, Mr Carruthers, the coast is teeming with those willing to do the work, men who know how to hand, reef and steer and never be taken up by the press neither.'

'A week at most,' Franklin added.

'Then I suggest today is a good day to begin looking.'

'That I agree to, but it would be best we look over what you have purchased first.'

The scraping of chairs had Isaac Lavery scooting back to his high desk and by the time the door opened he was over his quill and scratching away. He had not heard everything, only those words made plain when voices had been slightly raised, which left him wondering about this John Pearce fellow, for that name when first used had been near to a shout and accompanied by a loud slapping sound – he assumed a hand on the table. The name resonated, for he had been sent weeks past to visit the Strand offices of Edward Druce, his employer's brother-in-law, to find out where that very fellow was serving.

'Lavery, you are to remain here, do you understand, until I return. No errands.'

'Certainly, sir, and can I say to where you have gone if anyone enquires?'

That got him a glare. 'No, you cannot.'

With that Carruthers followed the Tollands out of the door.

'Fishing in dangerous waters seems a strange expression to use Mr Lavery, are you sure it is the right one?'

Looking into the corn-blue eyes of Catherine Carruthers the clerk saw innocence mixed with naivety and it was to him a charming combination. This woman, trapped too young in an unsuitable marriage, could not even begin to make a true assessment of her husband's nature even if she had shared his bedchamber. She saw him in the domestic setting and if that was strained through past indiscretions on her part, it was, nevertheless, conducted in a polite way. In his business dealings Denby Carruthers was very far from that and, now it seemed, not satisfied with the coups he regularly achieved in legitimate trade, he was about to dabble outside the law.

'He is mixing with some very strange people and of excessively low character.'

The nod, along with pursed lips, looked like sage acceptance; in truth, Catherine Carruthers could not care less what her husband got up to, outside his need to care for the upkeep of a style of living to which she had become accustomed, and if he got harmed in the process so be it. She listened to this grumbling regarding his activities only to ensnare Lavery to her true purpose, which was to find and reconnect with the man who filled her dreams, Cornelius Gherson, Lavery's predecessor and the person who had so strained that domestic harmony.

'It is good of you to keep me informed, Isaac, for it would never do that my husband should overreach himself.'

'I will seek to ensure he does not and certainly forewarn you of any risk . . .'

The sentence was plainly unfinished and there was a fear then that he might call her Catherine, but thankfully the moment passed, that being a favour which would have to wait. Her task was to play the old fool, and each step in allowing him familiarities had to be carefully graded so as to avoid anything that might force her to reject him, a game in which she was well practised. Catherine Carruthers had been a precocious beauty and learnt very young how to use her gifts to gain her ends; nothing blinded a man, even a clever one, as much as sexual desire. Lavery would be no different, and if she handled matters correctly he would do her bidding. Having softened him up she could now proceed to the real question to which she required an answer.

'How goes our search?'

'I confess, not well.'

'Then it must be stepped up, surely – widened.'

'I fear your husband has laid constricts upon my ability to act on your behalf. I must seek his permission to do so.'

'He has no idea of the nature of . . . ?'

'None.'

'Then how are we to proceed?'

It was a bold step to take her hand, and a nervous one that did so, though the charge of electricity that ran through Isaac Lavery's body was a thrill which he had never before experienced and he looked at Catherine Carruthers for a sign she had undergone the same, taking her frown as evidence that she had. Rationally explained to anyone with sense, his suit would have invoked hilarious laughter – he, of middling years, strained income and no great beauty, making love to a ravishing young woman, and a rich one? But in Lavery's imaginings all things were possible and here, running up his arm, was proof positive. He had nothing to fear from Cornelius Gherson; if the fellow had held a place in her affections once it had been replaced now.

'With caution, my dear lady, but proceed we must. I will find Gherson and deliver to him your concerns for his well-being.'

She had been tempted to withdraw her hand and show some displeasure, for which, she was sure he would react like a whipped dog. But in the end she let it rest in his fingers for, to find the man she loved meant everything, the man who would rescue her from her unhappy situation of being wife to a man far too old to understand her.

CHAPTER EIGHTEEN

'A voyage to the Mediterranean?' Emily asked, turning away so he could not see her face; was she troubled or pleased?

'And aboard HMS *Larcher*, the very same vessel that I recently commanded. The crew are in the main splendid fellows and since I must go—'

'Why must you?'

'Let us say a combination of duty and a debt.' Turning to face him she looked unconvinced as he added, 'And since I fear to leave you alone in London, I wish you to accompany me.'

'What?'

'I cannot just leave you, Emily, for at sea I cannot protect you. We have already established that your husband will stop at nothing. Well, that might include abduction and incarceration, from which no force of law would be able to release you. Justice is iniquitous in the subject of matrimony and all the rights rest with the man. He could keep you chained in his cellar and nothing could be done short of violence to free you.'

'I could go somewhere and wait.'

Not having mentioned Dundas's threat – and he did not trust the man one inch – he felt the need to press. 'Like Lymington, which is no different to any other town in the country and a damn sight better than most. A strange woman alone, you will be a subject of interest. What will you do for company, and will you be comfortable with the lies you have to tell, for people will probe?'

'You are asking me to embark on a very bold step.'

'I am asking for your companionship on voyage to and from the Mediterranean, to make life more bearable than separation, and you can depart in secrecy – no one will know you are aboard whom we do not wish to have that knowledge.'

She finally smiled; it was not acquiescence but a sign of a break in her resistance. 'Run away to sea, as boys do in tales of adventure?'

'Think of it in the nature of us getting to know each other.' Pearce produced a wide grin then as he recalled how he had come to the thought originally; it had been none other than the notion of that little cabin and the propinquity its size would force on two occupants. 'Which we will do even if disinclined, for the cabin we will occupy is so very tiny we will forever be in each other's way, from which I for one will take great pleasure.'

That got a becoming blush. 'Is it fitting, John?'

'It's a damn sight more discreet than taking a house in some out of the way place while I fret that you might be in danger.'

'And when we get there you will have duties to perform.'

'Only one, to deliver a private letter, and then it is a happy return.' He could see the flaw and so could she – her presence would be known throughout the fleet as soon as he joined, so he came close and embraced her. 'I will drop you in Leghorn, proceed on my mission, then sail back to collect you when it is complete.'

'You have such freedom.'

'I would like to see the fellow who could infringe on that.'

The knock at the door was this time anticipated and Pearce opened it to the hotel servant, who had come to grumble as well as respond to a summons.

'That big Paddy of yours is in the stables a'sleeping on hay an' snoring fit to wake Lucifer. There's not a soul in the hotel willin' to seek to rouse him, for he was threatenin' to mince them when he barrelled in last night an' he might have done them in if he had not passed out.'

'Tell them that, when sober, he is a lamb.'

'Never in life – wakin' him is a task for you, sir.'

'Very well, Didcot, I will see to it shortly. Now I wish someone to begin to pack my sea chest – Mrs Barclay's trunks and valise too – to be ready for departure either tomorrow, or I think at the latest the day after.'

'You is leaving, your honour?'

'We are.'

'An' might I ask to where you is headed?'

'I am off to sea gain, Didcot, but Mrs Barclay is going to King's Lynn in Norfolk.' The intimation that he had said too much was well performed as he dropped his voice. 'But I would be obliged if you would keep that bit of knowledge to yourself. I'm sure I can trust you.'

'Lips is sealed, your honour,' Didcot responded, mentally rubbing his hands while in fact touching his forelock. 'I shall see to it that all is clean afore it is packed away, an' all.'

'Good man,' Pearce said, slipping him a coin.

Door closed behind him Emily began to shake with laughter, Pearce with a finger to his lips to insist she should not do so out loud lest Didcot hear her.

'You are so sure he will let on?' she asked, still not fully in control.

'Near certain,' Pearce replied, again keeping the Dundas business to himself, 'and maybe I would be the same if I had his life. It may mean nothing, yet it may also send your husband on a wild goose chase if he seeks to find you. Now I must go and rouse out Michael and tell him we are off to sea again.'

If, when he woke, Michael had a sore head, he also had Celtic powers of recovery, aided by the swift despatch of a tankard of ale, so that washed and shaved he looked to have no ill effects from his nocturnal debauch; his eyes were as bright and his grin as wide as ever. The day was spent in preparation, with the Irishman acting as escort and protector when Emily went shopping, carrying a small club, not so very different from a marling spike, inside his short blue coat. Pearce received from the Admiralty, by hand messenger, not only confirmation of the extension of his commission, but also the order and flag that would see him sail under their pennant, which precluded any other officer from impeding his passage all the way up to admirals.

With his papers he went to the Victualling Board to enquire as to where he could draw supplies for HMS *Larcher*, very little of which would be available at Buckler's Hard. He departed Somerset House with a sum of money for purchases plus the written authority he required to draw on any naval stores at any dockyard en route, including Gibraltar. His last call was at Downing Street to pick up the communication he must carry and another bout of traded invective with Dundas, who seemed afire to know what he was going to do with his lassie.

'I have told you twice now, it is none of your damned business.'

The man could not help himself; he had to show off and there was a lopsided smirk to go with it. 'A nice quiet place in the county would suit, I hazard. I hear Norfolk is bonny at this time of year.' Seeing the look that got, he added, 'Oh, your secret's safe with me, Pearce, but it does mean there'll be no backsliding or finding reasons not to complete your task.'

'Don't you repose trust in *anyone*?'

'Not many and certainly no one bearing your name, so put that letter in a weighted sack and if anything should happen to make you think it might fall into the wrong hands chuck it in to the briny. Until then, guard it with your life.'

'Perhaps I will sell it to the Whigs, the proper ones, of course. I am sure Charles James Fox would excel himself in the house with sight of it.'

That got him a look of thunder, which was pleasing,

for it indicated that he had hit home. Fox was a fearsome debater, but more than that he employed the kind of wit that tended to squash opponents across the floor of the house and Dundas, too often the butt, hated him with a passion.

'Do that, Pearce, and you'll spend the rest of your days in a prison hulk off the Medway Marshes! And stick to your duty, for I never met a naval officer yet that did not whore after a prize or two.'

Ralph Barclay was testing the use of a stick to support his wounded leg, this for his journey to London, a trip he had insisted to a reluctant Sir Roger Curtis was necessary for him to consult the very best physicians. He was stomping to and fro when Gherson brought him Davidson's letter, the clerk exchanging a glare with his employer's so-called servant Devenow, tall enough to have his head touching the deck beams and broad with it. He now had his arm in a sling as well as a still swollen ear given to him just before the 1st June battle, though it was not as bloody and as gory as it had been right after it was inflicted. The sling at least stopped the cack-handed buffoon from trying to do any of the tasks that fell to a servant, for it was an area in which he was worse than useless.

Gherson and Devenow loathed each other as much for their differing manner as for their competition for the captain's attention. The clerk saw Barclay as a means to an end, while Devenow was slavish in his devotion, a man to follow Ralph Barclay from ship to ship and, it had to be said, into the cannon's mouth; indeed he had turned up in Sheerness to join him aboard HMS *Brilliant*, though at that time his presence had been seen as a mixed blessing. He had been welcomed but with reservations.

Not anymore; it was Devenow who had carried Ralph Barclay to Heinrich Lutyens' hospital when the captain had taken the ball that shattered his left arm, subsequently amputated. If he had not changed from what he was – a lout, a drunk and a bully – then he had risen in Barclay's estimation to become a very necessary aide, if not a confidant, and there was only a modicum of true regard. In truth, neither was Gherson a confidant, but he did handle things of a private nature, even down to arranging investments for the large sums of Barclay prize money already earned. The safe investments were in Captain Barclay's name, the very risky ones, which might go bad and lead to writs for repayment, were in the name of Devenow; Ralph Barclay reckoned the ruffian could stand a debtor's prison more easily than he.

The name on the letter Barclay recognised, for if he was represented by Ommanney & Druce, he yet knew the name and reputation of every person who traded as a prize agent for the officers of the Royal Navy, their various abilities a common subject of conversation as well as their failings when it came to settling cases; like most captains Barclay had one mired in the courts for a well-laden merchantman recaptured off Brittany in his first week at sea.

'Surely he is not soliciting my custom?' he said as he broke the seal and began to read, his head slowly beginning to shake. 'I cannot believe that a man of his standing is worried about a couple of tars.'

'Sir?' Gherson enquired and Barclay passed the letter

over and after a short perusal he provided an explanation. 'I think you will find that Davidson represents John Pearce, sir.'

'Of course, damn it, I did not smoke the names.'

'Do you recall sir, that absurd soubriquet, the Pelicans?'

That got a low growl from Devenow; it was Charlie Taverner who had split his ear and he had suffered at the hands of those Pelican sods before that, the worst being Michael O'Hagan.

'Why would he offer four prime hands, it says here they are ex-smugglers, for two such creatures?'

'They have a bond, sir, and I fear he thinks you might ill use them.'

'Give me half a chance, Gherson, and I will do so. The slightest slip on their part and I'll see them at the grating for a round dozen each.'

That had the clerk smirking at Devenow, who obviously had not told the captain the truth of his head wound – Barclay had assumed he had been drunk and fallen over. The look Gherson got back was full of bile. But soon Gherson's attention was back on Barclay and he wondered if he should tell him that between decks Charlie Taverner and Rufus Dommet had a mess that would act to protect them. Indeed he half suspected that was the root cause of Devenow's damaged ear.

'Well I'll be damned if I'll oblige Pearce.'

The letter was handed back. 'Four good hands in place of two, sir.'

Barclay waved the paper with some irritation. 'You're not suggesting I do?'

'Wouldn't be right, your honour,' Devenow snarled.

That got him a rebuke. 'This is none of your concern, man, please stay out of it.'

Gherson was strong on self-preservation and he could recall very clearly the scary tales he had been told when he too was a pressed seaman. If others eventually saw that the older hands were playing upon them, Gherson had taken to heart their tales of how easily a fellow aboard a ship at sea could come to harm – the most frightening, for a man who had been tossed by Denby Carruther's thugs into the River Thames to die, was the notion that on a dark night any unpopular cove could so easily go over the side.

Vanity, and he had a great deal of that, did not prevent Gherson from the knowledge that he was not much loved by his fellow man – he despised most of them in return and made little secret of it, the only exception being his propensity to grovel when he needed their help. Having no idea how Devenow had got his split ear it was not too far-fetched to suppose it had come from either the Pelicans or the members of their mess, and if they would attack and wound a big sod like him, what would they do to anyone else against whom they had a grudge, he being the most likely?

'I think it would be safer if they were off the ship, sir.'

'Safer?' Barclay demanded.

It's all right for you, Gherson thought, secure here in your great cabin with a marine sentry at the door and every eye on you when you go anywhere, never mind that Devenow is ever by your side. What about me? I dare not go on deck after dark, and who is to say that daylight renders me safe?

'Sir,' he said, trying to sound sage, 'they are troublemakers.'

'Not on my ship.'

'They are cut from the same cloth as John Pearce and he has caused you no end of nuisance in the past.' That being reminded did not go down well was obvious by the expression on Barclay's face – he looked like a mastiff who had swallowed a wasp. 'I am merely suggesting that it is not prudent to allow these two individuals to remain aboard when you have an opportunity to remove them and stop them from fomenting disorder.'

'It seems to me, Gherson, that you have some indication that they have been at that already.'

'I took it upon myself, sir,' Gherson lied, 'to warn them against it, but can I be sure they heeded me?'

'By damn, they'll heed me.'

'Ask Devenow how he got his ear.'

'What?' Barclay asked, turning to the man in question.

'You thought he was drunk, sir, but I know he was not, so how did he come by such a wound?'

'Well, Devenow, how did you?'

'I'd not like to say, your honour.'

'No doubt,' Gherson advanced, his tone mocking, 'because of a spirit of comradeship within the lower deck.'

'Who was it, Devenow?'

'Can't rightly say, your honour. It were dark and it came out o' the blue.'

Gherson surmised he was lying, he being reluctant to admit that he had been bested in a fight.

'Just the kind of trouble, sir,' he droned, 'that no one wants aboard a ship of war.'

It was interesting to watch Barclay ruminating, for he was fighting an internal dispute, between obliging John Pearce, which he hated to do, as against having trouble brewing under his command, which, like every officer in the Royal Navy, he dreaded. In concert with the likes of Gherson he neither sought nor needed popularity, but he did need efficiency and between decks feuds were inimical to that.

'What are they like as hands?' he asked, after a long silence.

'Mediocre, sir, I am told.' Gherson had no idea and would not have been able to give an opinion even if he had watched them; when it came to being useless in the art of sailing he was top of the class. 'You could enquire of their divisional officer.'

The response that such a notion was stupid nearly came out – no captain who valued his dignity would ask such a question of anyone but his premier, and having equal to his regard for his standing now, he made a great play of reading the letter again.

'They are of insufficient interest to me to care. If Pearce wants them so badly let him have them and we will profit by it.' Thinking perhaps that he might be giving way too easily, Barclay actually barked, 'But the replacements better be as he says, or I'll have his guts.'

Even Devenow, devoted as he was, seemed embarrassed by that idle boast.

'Detail one of our mids to rig out the pinnace and take this pair up-channel to HMS *York*. Best take a quartet of marines also; we don't want any trouble on the return journey. Now, is all in order for my journey to London?'

'Your barge is waiting, sir,' Gherson replied.

'Then let us be off.'

'I will just gather my investment portfolio, sir.'

That cheered Gherson's employer up no end; if Ralph Barclay had possessed two hands he would have rubbed them, sure as he was that the money he had put into various projects should by now be beginning to show handsome returns.

Ralph Barclay was not the only one on the move; when it came time to take a hack to Charing Cross, there ostensibly to put Emily Barclay aboard the northbound coach, the whole trio were in a joyous mood. Pearce had gone round the hotel tipping the various people who had seen to his needs, for along with Didcot there were the maids who cleaned and made up the beds, the people in the kitchen, and even the stuck-up sod who manned the front desk, the same fellow who had presented a bill that made the recipient's eyes water a little.

'I do hope you will grace us with your custom again, sir.'

'I will if I take a Spanish plate ship.'

'Which, sir, I surely hope you do and recommend us to your fellow officers.'

Pearce was tempted to say that a recommendation from him in that quarter was likely to lead to bankruptcy, but held his tongue and he went out to the waiting hack calling out loudly their destination, that being changed as soon as they were out of sight. The hack took them to the same person from whom Pearce had hired transport to take him originally to the New Forest, with Michael riding on the box seat with the driver.

'We are free, Emily,' Pearce said as they passed the Bishop's Palace at Fulham.

'For now, John.' Seeing his crestfallen face she took his arm and squeezed tightly. 'Let us enjoy it while we may.'

The crew of HMS *Larcher* were mightily pleased to see him again, and given that their previous passengers had been odd no one raised an eyebrow to the fact of a woman, and a very pretty one at that, being brought aboard. Emily, if she was surprised at the paucity of accommodation, hid it well, praising it as cosy in such a way as to win the smiles of those who overheard her, that to the accompaniment of nudges, nods and winks regarding the rakish nature of their master and commander, who was brisk about his business once she was settled.

'Mr Dorling, we will sail to Portsmouth to victual from the dockyard.'

'And then, sir?'

'Then we will sail down-channel, and when we are out of sight of land I will tell you where we are going.'

The Admiralty pennant was inside his coat; that would not be lifted to the masthead until no one could see it from the shore.

'If anyone asks in Portsmouth what we are about, tell them we are casing smugglers.'

'Could become a habit that, your honour.'

CHAPTER NINETEEN

HMS *Larcher* took on board what she could from Buckler's Hard, especially fresh provisions such as bread and greens, but there was no way they could supply salted beef and pork, as well as the quantity of peas, small beer and rum and general stores that the vessel would need for such an extended commission; that could only be found in a proper naval dockyard, likewise spare canvas and yards, which were too steep for the funds Pearce had. As soon as all was loaded that could be acquired the anchor was raised and the ship drifted down on the tide and the rudder into the Solent, where sails could be set to take advantage of the prevailing westerly wind.

The quartermaster weaved a course through the dozens of warships anchored off Spithead: 100-gun Leviathans, abundant seventy-fours as well as numerous frigates and sloops. Emily Barclay was confined to his cabin, in which he had admonished her to stay until the armed cutter was fully loaded with stores and anchored away from the shore. The surprise for John Pearce was when Michael O'Hagan approached and asked that he be allowed to stay out of sight as well, seeing he knew the intention of where to tie up.

'It was from here myself, Charlie and Rufus ran and I fear that the press gang you overheard might be based at Portsmouth too. Sight of me and they might just want to take me up on that warrant, and that does not speak for those in pursuit of the reward.'

'Which I would not let them do, and I would point out, Michael, that if they know you by your description they do not know your name.'

It was a stroke of good fortune that had the Pelicans on a vessel in which they had never been mustered; it was a frigate that had rescued them from the ocean and a ship that had caught fire and sank, leaving them drifting in an open boat.

'And since we are going to pack every spare inch of space with victuals, where would you hide?'

'I daresay Mrs Barclay would not object to my sharing your little cabin for a while.'

'No she would not, and if it makes you feel secure, so be it, but we will miss your muscle when it comes to shifting barrels.'

'Port admiral's boat approaching, your honour.'

'Best get out of sight now, then.'

It was not, of course, the admiral in charge of Portsmouth Dockyard in that launch, but one of the officers employed by him to keep in order the busiest naval base in the world. The town sat on the best and safest anchorage on the south coast and had grown from a small port to a sizeable conurbation entirely due to the presence of the fleet, replacing the Nore, once of equal importance and still a major base. When the Dutch had posed the greatest danger to the nation the mouth of the Medway had been the vital location for the fleet but for nearly a century the threat had shifted and stayed with the French. Not only did it provide ample space to anchor – the whole of several fleets could assemble here – it also, for the purposes of shore leave and a way to put a lid on discontent, abutted the Isle of Wight, which held the two satellite bases of Ryde and St Helen's. As an island it was a place that allowed for shore leave.

Portsmouth might be on the mainland, but it had an added advantage: the city stood on a series of islands, was traversed in its entirety and entered and exited by a series of bridges. Given the propensity of Jack tar to desert that meant a few well-placed marines could stop the flow – necessary, for once in open country the men of the sea were hard to catch in a nation whose sympathy extended to those perceived to be oppressed. Indeed there were many old hands who boasted they could travel the length and breadth of the country and never be taken up by those seeking deserters.

The fellow who clambered aboard was, like Pearce, a lieutenant so the lift of the hat was to his commission in command of the ship rather than his rank, and he gave his name as Pettigrew. Under normal circumstances it would have been in order to offer him some refreshment, a glass of wine and a biscuit perhaps, as well as a period of conversation in which the hunt would be on for mutual acquaintances; that, with his fugitives occupying the cabin, was not possible and for once, and against all common custom, John Pearce did not merely introduce himself by name alone.

'You will have heard of me, I am sure, given I was assigned my rank at the insistence of King George himself.'

Pettigrew's face took on that look folk have when they are memory searching and it was not long before enlightenment replaced the furrowed brow; the case of John Pearce had rippled through the navy with most officers deciding that such an elevation, even by royal hand, was an insult to a service which prided itself on its professionalism. That a man could be made a lieutenant by a mere stroke of the pen at the base of an Order in Council flew in the face of all precedent and it was only long-serving and getting-nowhere midshipmen who saw a possible avenue to advancement.

'I would invite you to take a glass of wine with me, Mr Pettigrew, but—'

The other man cut across him. 'I would have to decline, sir, as I have too many other duties to perform.'

Since Pettigrew would not meet his eye it was probably a lie, but having achieved his aim, Pearce could allow himself to look hurt, which produced on the other man's face a hint of satisfaction; he would be able to tell his contemporaries, and quite probably his superiors, that he had put the upstart John Pearce in his place. For all he had set out to produce that result, there was still the temptation to reverse matters and that could not be put aside, which led to a very pointed and long look at the city of Portsmouth all the way down the shore to Southsea.

'A nice safe billet you have here, Mr Pettigrew, not much chance of being required to face shot and shell in a safe anchorage. Tell me, what kind of interest does it require to get you such a comfortable posting?'

'Your orders?' the man snapped, holding out his hand.

These were passed over to be examined in a manner that implied they might be forgeries, which told Pearce just how successfully he had got under Pettigrew's skin, then followed the list of stores Pearce required and that got a lift of the eyebrows.

'Where are you off to with all this?'

'I am not obliged to respond to that, sir.'

'I do think my superiors will want to know.'

'Then, sir,' Pearce said, 'I will decline to tell them.' The face changed yet again to a 'you would not dare' look. 'Now please be so good as to advise me at what point I can berth alongside the storerooms and load.'

It could only have been malice that brought the reply, as well as the sneer that accompanied it. 'I do not think an armed cutter warrants a berth at an overworked dockside where vessels are queuing to load. No, you anchor at a buoy and we will send out hoys from which you can take your stores.' Spinning round he pointed to one of the farthest from the actual shore in any direction. 'There, number forty-seven seems a likely spot.'

That angered Pearce for it would make the task for his crew ten times as hard – loading when afloat was much harder – and for those doing the supplying it would be even worse. They would not be pleased to have to get a flat-bottomed hoy loaded with supplies out so far into the anchorage. There were none so spiteful for anything that engendered effort as dockside labourers, and Pearce had heard too many tales of their ways of taking revenge on sailors to just let this pass. There was a very strong chance he would get meat long in the cask and closer to rotting than fresh, and that would be before he was supplied with short cables and poor canvas.

'Please wait there a moment.'

'Whatever for?'

That got him a held-up hand as Pearce disappeared into his cabin, a finger to his lips to induce silence and, despite his words to Dorling about secrecy, he took from a casement locker the red and gold Admiralty pennant. Back on deck he showed it to Pettigrew unfolded.

'You will find me a dockside berth, sir, for if you do not your intransigence will be reported to the very Board itself and, if I have my way, to the King. In short, consider your career, sir, and if your superiors ask why you have been so kind as to advance my place in any queue you may tell them that you were overwhelmed by my charm. What you will not do, on pain of censure, is mention this pennant.'

There was a moment, in fact several, while Pettigrew calculated the loss of self-respect in acceding but his career won out and he nodded, though he spoke through pursed lips. 'Word will be sent to you as soon as I have cleared a space.'

'Thank you, Lieutenant,' Pearce replied, lifting his hat as the man spun and went over the side.

The loading, when it took place, was done with the ship tied head and stern using shore derricks and a long gangplank, that traversed by a veritable stream of willing hands and every item checked aboard by Dorling. Pearce, having sent a couple of hands in a wherry over to HMS *York*, made his way to the Port Admiral's offices to extract from Pay Office the wages due to his crew, which had not been forthcoming for months even on home service. He demanded their money as well as his own, all listed, submitted and signed for – though not without a series of laments from the Revenue Officer doling out the coin regarding the lack of available specie – to make what he insisted upon, a cash transfer. Pearce had declined to accept chits that local traders would take as a discount.

'Have you any idea, sir, what it takes to get gold and silver enough sent down to pay the fleet?'

'I do, sir; it is the need to find enough folk to transport it without they charge a fortune for the task.'

'That sir, would be a fine contract to possess, one and one half of a per cent of the value of the specie carried.'

Pearce could not resist it; he leant forward and whispered, 'Would you, sir, like a guaranteed way to be able to secure such a contract?'

'I most certainly would.'

'It's easy,' Pearce responded in a louder voice, 'just grease well the palm of a man called Henry Dundas and it will be yours, for that is how those who presently make a killing get their payments.' With that, his muster books and a bag of money, Pearce walked out, calling over his shoulder, 'You'll find the grasping wretch in Whitehall.'

When he returned to HMS *Larcher* it was to find an impatient Pettigrew harrying his crew and the dockies – he had a ship of the line and an irate post captain waiting for the berth. His ship lay very low in the water, so many stores loaded that some meat barrels had to be lashed to the deck under tarpaulins, and still the last item, water, was being pumped into the 'tween decks where the carpenter, Kempshall, was filling and sealing barrels – given such a small vessel did not run to a dedicated cooper – while others in the crew struggled to move and stack such heavy receptacles.

Going halfway down the companionway Pearce called out, 'Never mind that sod shouting at you on the dock, lads, take what time you need. I saw a man killed doing what we are about now and I do not want that repeated on this ship.'

Then he went to find the men he had sent on his errand, his heart lifting when they told him the result. Next it was to Dorling to get from him a list of those men it would be safe to let ashore. 'With the caveat that I cannot afford to lose any to tardiness or an attempt to run.'

'There are one or two I would not trust, sir, but I would hazard they are such lazy sods as to be no loss.'

'I still need a boat crew.'

'There's enough men serving of a religious nature, your honour, who see Beelzebub as residing in such places as Portsmouth. They would not go ashore if offered, lest it was to a chapel.'

'Then find me a pair.'

'Word from my brother, sir, he reckons if we take on much more in the hold we'll be supping sea water.'

'Very well, Mr Kempshall, stop the pumps. Mr Dorling, I then want the men assembled for I have their pay.'

'By the mark, Mr Pearce, that will lift them.'

Pearce pulled a face. 'Since they are going ashore it is more likely to debauch them than lift them. The elevation will go to the whores of Portsmouth.'

'Only some of them, sir,' Dorling replied with a grin. 'We ain't owed that much pay.'

'Then prepare to cast off,' Pearce responded, before calling, 'Buoy number, Mr Pettigrew?'

That had the lieutenant making an over-obsessive look full of worry at the board he had in his hand. The number that came back was twenty-four, which Pearce assumed was the closest one he had free to the shore. The lines were taken from the quayside bollards fore and aft, the gangway slipped onto the hard and sweeps used to open a gap before the boats took up the strain on the cable that, lashed to the stern of the cutter, towed the ship out to its buoy. This meant Michael could make an appearance, which he did to many a jibe about the way he had skipped the labours of the rest, by which it was time to pipe the crew to their dinner, food taken by Emily and Pearce in his cabin, with a couple of planks over his sea chest serving as a table.

'We shall raise sail at first light, Emily, and then you can come on deck. I am sorry your confinement has been so long but I fear with my reputation there might be those come down to the shore to use a long glass to espy the ogre.'

'It was not all arduous, John. I had Michael for company and he was most informative about you.'

That got her a wry smile. 'I am not sure that you should be quite so curious as to ply people for facts about me, finding out for oneself is so much to be preferred.'

'You would not say that if you had heard his paeans to your character.'

'We are fond of each other and I suspect he over-praised.'

'John, it is more than that. I do not think you know how much you have gained in respect for your never giving up in your fight for the rights of others and not just your own.'

'A burden it would be good one day to put aside.'

'I think you will never do that, for if you would scarce admit it, you have too much of your father in you.'

'To hear you say that, were he here, would shock him. We used to argue a great deal about his notions of the way matters could be improved for the poor.'

'You must tell me all about him.'

'Not now, my dear, for we will be at sea for weeks and have ample opportunity to talk of such things, for you, likewise, must tell me of your past.'

'I'm not sure I have one of any interest.'

'You do, everyone has things that act to form them.' He leant over and kissed her on the head. 'But the very fortunate few have a future to look forward to.'

The crew had not lingered at their mess tables over dinner, but set to at dressing for going ashore. It was blue jackets, clean ducks, a striped kerseymere blouse topped off by a gaily coloured bandana and, for those who had one, a black and shiny tarpaulin hat. Pearce, who acted as purser as well as commander, was called upon to sell to his crew lengths of ribbon for their pigtails and new socks to adorn their legs, as well as blacking to get a shine on their shoes. When the last man had been seen to he went to see the cook.

'Mr Bellam, I want you to go ashore and buy enough food for six.'

The man's round face fell. 'I do not want you to do more, since I perceive you wish to visit the fleshpots of Portsmouth. So let it be a cold collation and just leave it by your coppers and I will do the serving.'

'Six hearty mouths, or six light, your honour?'

'O'Hagan will be one of the party.'

'Then I'll buy for eight, 'cause your Irishman can eat for four on his own.'

The boats plied to and fro to the shore, some hired, for once the local wherrymen spotted a ship allowing shore leave they were like flies around a honey pot. The noise and gaiety were loud, occasionally interrupted by a prayer from the holy types who seemed to want their God to make sure that no pleasure was had by their shipmates and that perdition, which surely awaited them, should be left in abeyance. Once the noise died down, John Pearce and Michael O'Hagan set off for HMS *York*, with two hands to help row. Once there, and leaving Michael on the main deck, Pearce went to see Moyle in his cabin.

'I fear your two followers think they are being sent to serve where my whim takes them, Mr Pearce.'

'You did not tell them of our arrangement?'

Moyle was shocked and his voice in reply was abrasive. 'I will tell no one, and that especially to a pair of loose-tongued men of the lower deck. I ask that of you too, tell them nothing of our arrangement!'

'Of course, it is a matter best not talked about, but did not the men who brought them here let on?'

'I doubt they had knowledge of it. The midshipman who came aboard with them asked only that I sign for their arrival. All I did was stick them in an upper deck cell with barely a how d'ye do. They asked questions, which I ignored.'

'How fare the men I brought you?'

'You were right about a pair of them needing to be taught their manners.'

'I am tempted to give them a hello, just to depress them further.'

Moyle responded so hastily he ended up tripping over his own words.

'Never fear, they are low enough and I would not want that the sight of your face should raise in them the will for a contest that will rebound on my men.' Having said that he seemed to recover somewhat his composure. 'In fact, I would have to forbid such a thing.'

'So be it.'

'So one of my men will take you to the right cell.'

John Pearce had in him a strong streak of mischief and now it came to the fore, aided by the fact that the light was fading and it was now getting dark outside; he could see lights twinkling on the shore.

'Could I ask, then, that you have your men bring them to my boat, and it would be an aid if they were a little rough and aggressive in their handling, as I mean to play a game with them.'

Moyle tried and failed to hide the fact that he was dealing with an odd sort of fellow and nodded. 'Makes no odds to me, Mr Pearce.'

'Then I will get in the boat and wrap myself in my boat cloak.'

He was huddled in that, with Michael sat in the bottom of the boat to disguise his height, when they heard the rough voices of Moyle's guards abusing the men as they brought them out to the top of the gangplank. With lots of pushing and shoving it was rough handling indeed, but truly not harmful if you excepted the spirit, that was until they were, chains struck off, virtually thrown into the boat, which produced cries, if not of pain, then of dented pride.

'Get sat down the two of you,' Pearce growled in a manufactured voice.

'Where we goin'?' demanded Charlie Taverner, always the more vocal of the two Pelicans.

Pearce replied in the same kind of disguised voice. 'To a hell ship, that's where you're going, for Barclay has seen to you good and proper, with a man in command who loves nothing more than to wield the cat with his own strong hand and nothing done to warrant it.'

'That's agin the laws of the navy,' Rufus said.

Michael, behind them, tried to disguise his voice too, though his brogue was evident. 'Bugger the laws of the navy, we are a law to ourselves.'

It was one of the other pair, the men brought to help row the boat, who broke the deception. 'Could you tell me, Mr Pearce, what in the name of our Blessed Saviour it is you're on about?'

'Pearce?' said Charlie, his tone full of mystification.

'Sure, fellow, he is our commander.'

'And I believe,' Pearce said, emerging from his cloak, 'your good and loyal friend.'

Michael heaved himself up and stuck his head between them. 'And, sure, boyos, he's not alone in that.'

'Pinch me, Rufus, 'cause I think I'm dreamin' now.'

'Not so, Charlie; the Pelicans are reunited.'

Back on board, they ate the cold meal left by Bellam, and Emily renewed her acquaintance with Charlie and Rufus, who were shy in her presence, particularly the youngster, and somewhat at a loss to see that her relationship with John Pearce had progressed to the point of consanguinity and that they would all be sailing together to the Mediterranean. Charlie still had about him a bit of that roughish charm which had sustained him as a sharp working the Strand and Covent Garden and it was he who proposed a toast to her, with which none present could disagree.

'Ma'am, I hereby propose that you be inducted as an honorary Pelican.'

The glasses were up and drained and Emily was delighted. The last act of the night, with drunken men coming noisily back aboard in ones and twos, was for Emily to write a letter to her husband with Pearce helping, his opinion being, and she took it, that to mention him was to fuel a fire already burning heartily enough.

CHAPTER TWENTY

When HMS *Larcher* sailed over and plucked out her anchor she was not the only vessel about to put to sea; the Tolland brothers had been true to their word and had gathered a crew in no time at all – rough-looking fellows that men gave a wide berth to when out walking – bringing them up to London to man the *Percy,* the ship Denby Carruthers had purchased, and they set about getting ready for sea with all the expertise of blue-water men, reefing and roving, bending on sails and taking in the stores needed for a short voyage.

The man himself had gone to consult with his brother-in-law on an unrelated matter and in doing so had put Edward Druce in an uncomfortable position; he had previously supplied to Carruthers men to deal with Cornelius Gherson, having been told the fellow had cuckolded his employer, a couple of Impress Service toughs of much muscle and little conscience when it came to turning a coin. He had no actual idea what they had done for the alderman, only that it was unlikely to be pretty and Druce had ever since regretted putting the risk of family disgrace to the forefront of his reaction when asked for aid, really to spare his wife embarrassment, without examining the likely consequences.

In some sense he had been relieved when Gherson unexpectedly turned up in his offices in the company of his client naval officer Captain Barclay; at least it implied that he had been beaten for his sins rather than anything worse, which had been a worry. But here was his wife's brother once more sitting in an armchair, drinking his wine and seeking more help and this to find the same fellow.

'I tried to fix him with the Bow Street Runners, Edward, but he managed to wriggle out of that somehow. That matters less than the notion he will turn up to trouble my marriage once more, so I need to find him so that I can keep a watch on his movements.'

'Find him,' Druce replied, his hands arched like a church steeple.

He was prevaricating, for he had on his desk a letter from Ralph Barclay saying he was coming to town, bringing his clerk with him, and desired a meeting to discuss the state of his present investment, as well as how to proceed with the expected payments from the 1st June battle. It was a double worry that they both might turn up when Carruthers was still here, for he had lied to his brother-in-law when asked a few months past about Gherson, saying he knew nothing of the fellow, when he knew very well he was serving as the captain's clerk aboard HMS *Semele*.

His reasons were complex and tested on them he would never have admitted to the truth, which was that in Gherson he recognised a fellow keen to profit personally from his employer's ventures and willing, if asked for advice from Barclay, to advance the schemes of Ommanney & Druce. In short, he was a source of profit now and potentially much more in the future and that was the paramount concern of a firm of prize agents who made most of their returns by speculating with their clients' money.

'It could be like seeking a needle in a haystack, Denby.'

'Not quite, Edward, Gherson goes where there is money to be made.' The nod was inadvertent and quickly stopped. 'So that narrows matters, and I know he is London born and I suspect this is where he will plough his furrow, probably a felonious one, for the city is the place of opportunity to rogues like him.'

'I'm not sure I can assist, Denby.' That made his brother-in-law stiffen. 'Ask me for the whereabouts of a sailor and that I can do by a simple enquiry to the Admiralty, where we maintain strong contacts.'

'I must find him,' Carruthers snapped, his face closing up enough to tell the man at the desk just how much hatred was in the sentiment. Obviously Carruthers knew it too, realised he was being obvious in his loathing and perhaps even in his intentions, so he sat back and modulated his tone. 'To stop him visiting mischief on another as he visited them on me, of course.'

'Quite, quite, but would not a thief-taker be a better prospect?' Seeing interest Druce went on. 'You say your man is a thief—'

'And a satyr, for all his tender years and innocent looks.'

That was a barked interruption, from a man Edward Druce had always thought too strong in his passions, the kind of thing that led him to marry such an unsuitable bride. And Druce had a duty, which was to deflect his interest in Gherson and even to send him on a wild goose chase if necessary. Serving on a ship, the man was relatively safe, rarely ashore, in London only on the odd occasion, and if things went as normal HMS *Semele* would be at sea for most of the time; a warship at anchor was not a proper use of assets even for an indolent commander addicted to taking the waters of Bath such as Black Dick Howe.

'Let us stick to larceny, Denby. If you are looking for a fellow who steals money, then that is a job for a man who takes up criminals and, I might add, I know of no one who searches up and down the land for infidelity, it is more a local interest. I do have knowledge of a fellow who might take the work, for the Bow Street Runners and their successes have made his occupation less profitable than it used to be. One of his gifts is that he is well connected and seems able to use a network of people to search far and wide. He would, of course, require funds to proceed and a payment for success.'

'I am not bereft of the means to fund that.'

'No,' Druce replied with some feeling: well heeled and successful as he was, he could not hold a candle to Denby Carruthers. 'So would you like to know where to find him?'

'You find him Edward, will you?'

'Me?'

Carruthers stood up. 'Yes, I am going away for a few days, perhaps a week. Get hold of your fellow . . . what's his name?'

'Hodgeson.'

'Retain him, Edward, and I will see him on my return.'

'Where are you going?'

'People keep asking me that, as if it is any of their business.'

The manner of that rejoinder, so cold and dismissive to what was a very simple question, eased the conscience of Edward Druce; he did not like lying to his brother-in-law even if he felt it necessary. But he was not to be treated like some busybody. Lord, he might even tell Gherson that Denby was seeking him out! There was, however, no desire to let his feelings be known or have a proper falling out, certainly not with a powerful city alderman and a brother to a wife who esteemed him highly, so the response was polite.

'Well I hope it is successful, Denby.'

'Sir Phillip, I believe Lord Howe was humbugged. We chased that frigate when we should have gone in search of those American merchantmen.'

'You may well be right, Captain Barclay, but I do not see how I can bring to the Board such a supposition. And if I did I doubt they would act upon it.'

'What I am saying, sir, is that the despatch which Sir Roger Curtis wrote at Lord Howe's behest does not detail all the facts, and there are men suffering from finding their contribution to victory ignored.'

'The King was cock-a-hoop when he heard the news,' Sir Phillip Stephens said, rather wistfully. 'Felt vindicated, for you know Lord Howe only got the Channel through his insistence. Lord Hood was livid.'

Damn them both, Barclay thought, pulling out a letter written by Gherson.

'Nevertheless, I wish to lay before the Board of Admiralty that all was not as stated and that if accolades are to be given, they should be given equally to all the captains engaged.'

'Very well, Captain, I will see it is as you wish.'

Bustling out of the building, his stick rapping a tattoo on the flagstones, Ralph Barclay supposed Sir Phillip to be right. But he had achieved his aim, had laid his evidence in what was now the public domain. Time to get on with the defamation of Sir Roger Curtis, for he was easier to attack than Howe; any assault on him might be seen as a criticism of the monarchy. He made his way to Covent Garden and a coffee house where he had arranged to meet with Gherson. His clerk had been given the task of finding out what newspaper people might take a payment to promote their case as well as an artist to begin drawing Curtis in an unflattering light. It would have been nice to engage Gillray, but he was too steep in price.

Sitting down beside Gherson, Barclay could not help his nose twitching. 'God, man, you smell of the whore you have been with!'

'She was not a clean creature, that is true,' Gherson replied, unabashed, 'but she was cheap.' He then handed over a list of names, with the various coffee houses at which each could be contacted, and it was a long one;

it seemed those who wrote for Grub Street were keen to accept payment and truth was not a fixation. 'I doubt you will have trouble, sir, in defaming Sir Roger, and I have it on good authority Lord Howe as well, if you so desire.'

'Not a good move for a man's career, I think, given the King esteems him. We will talk of these tonight, now we must go and find out how well I am doing.'

It was but a short walk to the Strand and the offices of Ommanney & Druce.

It was a good hour later when Edward Druce was convinced he was having what the French called *déjà vu,* and something more than that after his corpulent partner, Ommanney, having gone through the present investments and potential future ones of their client while supping fine Burgundy wine, had left him alone with Ralph Barclay and Cornelius Gherson. During that hour, Barclay could not but recall a previous visit to these offices when, with a ship after five barren years, a new wife and orders to get to sea, he had sought an advance on prospective prize money from the two partners. The level of condescension they had shown then matched their fawning on him now, and to make him feel better still, he could look at the great portrait of the most famous victory of his much loved Admiral George Rodney which he watched unfold from a distance; there it was, at torn sails, bursting cannon and an angry smoke-filled sky, the Battle of the Saintes.

'An investigator, Captain Barclay?'

'Yes, to find my wife.' Seeing the look in Druce's

eye, he felt constrained to explain, his voice slightly overwrought. 'My wife Emily is much younger than I and has had her head turned.'

Was that what could be said about Catherine Carruthers, Druce was thinking, that her head was turned, which made him glance at the culprit, who was watching his employer with a very slight smirk on his face. So was this another young and pretty woman who had fallen for his charms, for he was a handsome devil, with his soft skin and near white hair? What was it about the tender sex that they could not see in such corn-blue eyes as Gherson possessed that the only thing for which he had true affection was himself?

'For reasons I have yet to completely establish she has decided to desert the marital home and take up residence elsewhere. I must add that she has done that entirely on her own – there is no other party involved.'

'And if you find her?'

'I will, of course, seek to persuade her of the error of her ways, and beg that she comes back to be the dutiful wife I married and have deep affection for.'

Gherson's reaction then, the widening smirk seen out of the corner of his eye, convinced Druce that Barclay was not telling the truth, not that such a fact was any of his concern. But there was advantage in this; he could recommend Hodgeson for both tasks that had been brought to his attention this day and hope that he only succeeded in one of them. Damn me, he thought, I should charge the fellow commission.

'I do know of someone who might be able to help.'

'And how do I find him?'

'Let me do that for you. I take it you are, as usual, staying at Brown's?'

'I am, so send him to me there.'

'Actually, Captain Barclay, I think it would be best if you met in my office, with me present to introduce him and to offer, should you be at sea, to monitor his activities, a duty I am happy to undertake with no charge upon your tariff.'

'That is kind of you, sir.'

'I take it Mr Gherson will be coming by for a more thorough examination of your portfolio?'

'Tomorrow, if that suits, Mr Druce,' Gherson replied.

'Fine, I look forward to it, but I would suggest you meet Hodgeson on your own, it is after all a personal matter.'

'I agree,' Barclay said, throwing a glare at Gherson.

And, Druce was thinking, I have the whole of tonight to think how to play this game.

To be at sea was blissful; the weather was warm, the sea, albeit with a strong Atlantic swell, presented no threat and, once past the Lizard and heading due south the ship was eating up the miles with a potent westerly on its beam. With yards trimmed near fore and aft the bowsprit was the main driver and the deck was canted like a shallow roof, which made movement interesting and meant no food would stay still on any table. The crew seemed not to have changed in any way, they treated him as they always had, with respect and what looked like regard, so it took time for John Pearce to realise that the crew of HMS *Larcher* had resentments when it came to Charlie and Rufus.

New men in a settled crew always had a hard time bedding in. In what could be years of sailing together few mysteries remain as to how a man would think, never mind speak or act. A scratched nose was a signal some fellow wanted a pipe of tobacco, moods and tempers were related to the state of the moon, the crew had a vernacular of their own, based on common navy slang but subtly altered by their shared experience and the common jests that became like old friends; his Pelicans had none of that.

They had accepted Michael because he had acted as a servant; no more, he was content to be part of the lower deck and treat Pearce as what he was, the man in command, which did not allow for too much familiarity. The fact that the other two had dined with the captain and his lady as soon as they had come aboard was seen as suspicious: were they set to spy? They could not help themselves for being a bit familiar and that was before Pearce himself dented his reputation by chastising one of the crew merely for telling a vulgar tale in the hearing of Emily.

It was a problem having a woman on board in a ship with no proper heads to speak of, saving a slops bucket tossed over and washed, and it stood to reason a lady wanted to be clean, so it was rig a sail every couple of days, fill up a butt of water and let her do her necessaries to the back of that and no hands allowed aloft, though there was no way to avoid the surreptitious looks for the hope of spotting a flash of bare flesh, even an ankle. Most of the crew were under twenty-five years of age, many of them younger, and they were as red-blooded as any of their years. But unused to company of that nature, one hand forgot that he was stitching eyelets in a sail hard by where Emily was doing her ablutions and he was not quiet in his tale-telling.

'That Black Cath, mate,' he crowed, 'I ain't never seen the like. There's me so full of ale I was erect and as hard as that Indian teak, an' I reckoned I could piss a mile an' sets a challenge for a contest. Up jumps Black Cath, eyes flashin' like Lucifer's cat, and says a shilling piece that I can out piss you any time. A woman, says I, never in life!'

Other crew members, picking up that there was yarn-telling afoot, had slowed their own work to listen, which encouraged the teller to raise his voice.

'We go into the alley and I hauls out old Harry, an' by Christ did I give it length, twenty feet for certain. Well Cath has just downed a pint of mead in one, which could be counted as comin' it high in the cheating line, but gent I am, I let it pass. Over she bends, back to the target, hoicks up her shift and let's fly.'

'She a one, Black Cath,' came the shout from one of the younger crew, a noise that brought Pearce from his logs to see what was going on.

'Well,' says the sail stitcher, 'I don't know what she's got in them private regions of hers but I hope I don't get caught in there for I'll be a gelding if I am. She out pissed me by more yards than I care to count, a stream as straight as an arrow and still kicking up a foot of dust when it landed. Stronger in them parts than our barky's fire engine, I reckon.'

Pearce looked hard at the culprit and then at the screen. Emily was behind there and must have heard every word.

'Bosun, take that man's name, and I want him before me within the hour.'

'Aye, aye, Captain,' Birdy responded, without much enthusiasm. He was looking at the screen and so was everyone else, that was until Emily pulled it back and, head down, made for the cabin. Suddenly they were all busy.

'I apologise for that, my dear.'

'Why?' she whispered as she slid by, 'I have no right to be here, the men have.'

The collective behaviour of his fellow humans had ever been a mystery to John Pearce; he had seen people praise and cheer every word his father uttered in a stump speech, only to throw clods of turf at him seconds after he had finished. Mobs were fickle things, but so was collective opinion and it was very obvious to a man sensitive to such things to notice that the atmosphere had changed and seemingly in a blink: the crew were discomfited and Emily thought she was the cause. He knew better, knew that his Pelicans and their relationship to him lay at the root of the problem.

'It is my fault, John, and the fellow forgot I was there.'

'No it is not and he should have remembered. Tilley's damned lucky I am no lover of a flogging or he would have had half a dozen.'

'Will you stop cursing!'

'No, I will not!'

'You should not have stopped his grog.'

'You know nothing about discipline. A captain must act to curtail poor behaviour or who knows where it will lead?'

'It will lead to you being as bad as my husband.'

'That is unfair.'

'I wish to apologise to the crew.'

'And I forbid you to even think of such a thing.'

If you could not have a quiet conversation on a ship, you certainly could not hide a full-blown row and with decent movement all of the crew might have heard a portion that pieced together would constitute a whole if they had not been prevented from doing so.

'Sure, boyos, you'll be coming away from the after part of the barky.' That stopped a few in their tracks and the wiser heads were already moving to get below, for if Michael was the jolly Irish giant normally, he had a face like thunder now. 'Seems to me that a man and his woman ought to be able to dispute in peace.'

'Not a soul is like to interfere.'

The ham-like fists came up, not all the way but enough. 'Happen if I stop up a few ears no one will know what is afoot.'

'Anyone not employed,' Dorling called, 'down below now.'

Odd that the voices in the cabin became muted, as though they realised even through the bulkhead that it was not proper to so loudly argue. But it was not silent and it was obvious the matter was not settled, until Pearce came on deck and ordered all hands to be assembled.

'I have several things to say to you, first about the men I fetched ashore in Portsmouth.' That had heads turning to partake of collective agreement. 'I sense you feel they are too familiar to my person, or is it the commission I hold?

Many of you must have wondered at the connection and I assume they have not told you of it, so I shall.'

And he did, from the Pelican Tavern to their volunteering to save his skin, finishing with this. 'I owe these men a debt of gratitude I cannot pay, for they have stuck by me as I hope I have stuck by them. Now you know this coat I wear is a fluke, for if matters had gone another way I would still be a hand, probably a poor one too, unable to tie a decent knot. They see me as one of them not a blue coat who will flog at a whim, a threat, I must tell you, they have faced more than I.'

He paused and slowly looked over the crew, seeking eye contact. 'When I say I owe them, I owe you too, for the way you have served me since I came aboard, for which I am profoundly grateful. Having a lady aboard imposes certain restrictions which I would ask you to observe, but I cannot oblige you to do so, which has been pointed out to me by the person sharing my cabin. She wanted to apologise to you for any inconvenience, when in truth it is my request for forgiveness to make. I ask of that now, and, Tilley, your grog is herewith reinstated, but I tell you, keep your voice low if you wish to keep it.'

'Three times three lads, for Mr Pearce.'

That accolade he took before diving into his cabin, glaring at Emily and snarling, 'Now I feel less a fool and ten times more a fraud.'

CHAPTER TWENTY-ONE

Hodgeson was a bear of man, not tall but with heavy shoulders and arms that even covered one knew to be strong. He was also quiet, a listener rather than a talker, a fellow of few but acute enquiries, an observer, not the man to take centre stage, and he was doing that now to Ralph Barclay, who was having some difficulty in holding back what he wanted to keep to himself, namely that his separation was due to matters not for discussion and that even someone he engaged had no right to dig too deep.

'Am I to understand, Captain, that your wife, should I find her, will not willingly return to you?'

'She may require that some truths be explained, for instance that she will be denied bed and board if she refuses, but I do not see it coming to that.'

'But you feel sure you are able to persuade her?'

'I am, just as soon as I can get her alone.'

'So once I have found out where she is residing . . . ?

'Tell me and I will take matters into my own hands,'

said Barclay, standing up. 'Mr Druce knows where I am and will communicate with me when you have fulfilled your assignment.'

They were in the coach back to Plymouth when he raised the subject with Gherson. 'I'm not sure I can repose faith in this Hodgeson fellow, he seems to lack fibre to me. I want you to think on another way to proceed; let us give him a week or two and if he finds her, well and good Then you and Devenow can do what is necessary.'

'Me, sir?'

'She's a frail woman, by damn, surely you are not afraid of that too?'

Determined to refuse when the time came, Gherson just acceded to keep the peace, as Barclay continued. 'Mind, if he fails we may need some of your low-life contact again, like that fellow who helped you burgle my wife's solicitor.'

The man was called Jonathan Codge and he was the last person Gherson wanted to ever see again, he being a man who would sell his own mother down the river for a copper coin, then want the body to sell to Surgeon's Hall.

'I think him ill-suited to such a task, sir.'

'Then think of someone else man, someone from your black past. Now, you spent time with Druce, be so good as to tell me what he told you about my chances of profit, and spare nothing, we have a journey of some thirty hours.'

The more he thought about the prospect of ridding himself of his wife, the more it appealed to Denby Carruthers; it sustained him through the bout of seasickness that came upon him as soon as the *Percy* exited into the wide Thames

Estuary and hit the North Sea swell. Likewise, having observed the crew, he was sure he had the instrument to hand that would release him from all sorts of problems, in particular a fellow called Codge who was blackmailing him – he had tried to have him arrested by the Bow Street Runners in company with Gherson, who would have been transported or strung up at Tyburn; somehow they had both talked their way out of it.

Three disappearances, and with Gherson definitely gone and he would be free to take another wife, this time one with money instead of beauty, though he would seek both – perhaps a widow with an inheritance which would become his to do with as he wished once they were wed. Druce would engage the man he had named and he, the instigator, would stay well out of it. Let his brother-in-law handle matters and, if anything went wrong, nothing could be traced back to him.

'He is not telling the truth, Mr Druce. I suspect if I find Mrs Barclay the captain will seek to take her forcibly back to their home and keep her there.'

'And this troubles you?'

'I have known these things go wrong, sir, and I have seen death be caused by it.'

'You're surely not suggesting Captain Barclay would murder his wife?'

'How to know what harm will come of trying to take her if she is not willing?'

'There must be ways, man.'

'There are methods to ensure it is quiet, and those to ensure it is successful, sir, but without wishing to imply a lack of judgement on your part, it is not the way that navy men are accustomed to behave. It requires guile, not brawn, and patience, not the bull at the gate.'

'Then I shall persuade the captain that your expertise should be employed.'

'Good, I have my description and her name, and she sounds a rare beauty, which makes matters easier. Plain ladies are much harder to locate, they being so numerous.'

'I had you listed as a thief-taker, a man who chased felons and murderers, yet you seem to know a great deal about the gentler sex?'

'It would shock you, Mr Druce, just how many of those I have pursued were women. Do not think them gentle, sir, for they are not. When it comes to cold-blooded crime they are a match for us men.'

'Good. Now I want to talk to you of another case, a fellow to find this time. He is called Cornelius Gherson and I have here a description: dark hair, black eyes and a stooping walk. He is a money thief and too fond of women, especially those who are wedded to his employer.'

'Singular name.'

'It is,' the prize agent replied, thinking that was the one thing he dare not change. But with luck and that description Hodgeson would not get within ten miles of the man. Let him drain the Carruthers purse, for that was no concern of Edward Druce. His task was to keep Gherson alive and seek to earn both himself and the company money.

Catherine Carruthers would never have tried to follow Isaac Lavery if her husband had not been away and, in truth, she was nervous of doing so now. But he had said he was taking the opportunity, brought on by the same absence, to make a wider than normal search and talk to more of the kind of people who might know Gherson. It was odd how quickly he disappeared into a nearby coffee house, one used by city traders and not the sort of low creatures that Lavery was supposed to be questioning. Even more alarming was the time he stayed.

'Boy, come here.' The urchin obliged, for the well-dressed lady had a coin in one hand, which she pointed at the coffee house. 'For this I want you to go in yonder doorway and look for a fellow with large ears and a purple nose. He has too quite large bags under each eye and is dressed in black, I doubt you can miss him.'

'And what then, missus?'

'Just come back and tell me who he is talking to.'

The boy shrugged and ran off, to disappear through the door. He would not be allowed long, for he was grubby and not the type for such a place; they would rate him a pickpocket if they noticed him at all. As it was he was out in less than a minute.

'He's not talking to no one, missus, just sitting reading the newspaper over a pot of coffee and a dish of steak pie.'

The coin left Catherine Carruthers' hand before she even noticed it or the boy were gone, he scarpering in case she changed her mind about payment, no doubt, leaving her to ponder on what she had just been told. One thing was plain: Lavery was not doing what he was supposed to do and had he ever done so? The thought that he might have just been leading her on was hard to contemplate at first, but in truth, over weeks and much of her spare household budget, the man had not provided a single clue to where Cornelius could be. It was a sad woman who made her way home, her mind in turmoil.

When Lavery came back he was quick to find her and all flustered, relating that some of the places he had visited were so full of villainy that he had more than once feared for his life, places where people had no shoes, barely any clothes that were not rags, and where the possession of a handkerchief was considered wealth enough to get your throat cut. He had, too, acquired a cough he was sure indicated some kind of malaise he had picked up from the air he had been obliged to inhale.

'But was it fruitful?' Catherine asked.

'Alas,' came the reply and a hand reached out to touch her fingertips. 'But we must not despair, we must take the opportunity of your husband's absence to progress things properly.'

Suddenly he took a firm grip on her hand and she knew what he meant by progress, and it was a notion that made her blood boil. But she pretended to be faint to cover her confusion, vapours that Lavery took for an excess of passionate attraction. Then he was on his knees.

'You know, dear lady, that I would go to the ends of the earth for you.'

'Mr Lavery,' she gasped, in a fair imitation of a woman in distress, 'the other servants.'

'Of course,' he responded, raising himself up with a groan that testified to less than fluid joints, and his voice sounded just as weak. 'But you must understand how easy it is for me to forget such constraints.'

'Yet remembered they must be, for if my husband was to find out . . .' That did not require to be completed and the thought of what might happen rippled through Lavery's weak frame as she said feebly, 'In truth, Mr

Lavery, I do not feel entirely well, perhaps that malaise you spoke of has afflicted me.'

That stymied him; having made such a play of it he could not now dismiss it.

'I feel I should retire to my room to rest, please aid me to stand.'

'My dear lady,' he said, but he did as she wished. Then his voice recovered its strength to take on a note of hope. 'Perhaps you would like me to accompany you and see you settled.'

'No, I can manage.'

And I can mange you, she swore to herself as she climbed the stairs to her room, a seething mass of hatreds, crushing disappointments and plots for revenge. But Catherine was not a fool; she knew she could not just turn on Lavery and tell him she knew she was being both cheated and led up a garden path. Who knew what mischief would fly from such an act. A better plan would have to be formed, and before it was time for the maid to bring in a candle she had the outline of one.

'Mr Lavery will ask for me, Molly, and I would like you to tell him I am weak and unable to be up and about.'

'Yes, Madam.'

'And he has agreed to undertake some errands for me. Please be so good as to pass on how happy it would make me if he carried them out.'

When Molly had departed, Catherine Carruthers began to dream if not to sleep; it was not a new one but a common one, in which she was in a sunlit meadow, reunited with Cornelius Gherson and happy to become his willing lover there and then amongst the sweet flowers.

* * *

'Gherson!'

Barclay's shout echoed though HMS *Semele*, carrying timbers and decks with ease. The man called knew what it portended for he had seen the sender's name of the letter delivered and had fretted ever since as to what it might contain; it was worse than he feared.

'She mentions the burglary, by damn, but tells me she had removed the court martial papers beforehand.'

'Please sir, your voice.'

'What?'

'The whole ship will hear you and that was a crime.'

'It was your crime, Gherson, not mine. I've a good mind to hand you over to Devenow and let him have his way with your brains.'

'If it was my crime it was at your behest, sir.'

'You dare to threaten me?'

'No, I merely point out that we are part of the same act in the eyes of the law.'

That changed Barclay's tone; his voice dropped several decibels. 'You mean she might tell a magistrate?'

'What does her letter say, sir?'

'That I am to leave her be, that she has gone off to the country and I am not to pursue or seek to find her.'

'It seems to me a too flimsy matter to trust to her word. I think we must up the search and once she is found ensure that she cannot speak.'

Still nursing a limp, Barclay threw himself into a chair and put his head in his hands. 'She has the means to ditch me twice over now, thanks to you.'

The clerk took that without murmur, it mattered not that it had been his employer's idea to steal the papers, the thing now was to find a way to silence Emily Barclay, and Gherson's thinking did not rule out the notion of doing so on a permanent basis. Not that he would suggest such a course; he knew his man too well; Captain Ralph Barclay, brave as a lion on a battling quarterdeck, did not have the stomach for a quiet bit of removal.

'The search, sir, perhaps we could put more people on to it.'

'Yes, we must. And we must pray to God for deliverance from the malice of all those people who hate me.'

Just pray for you? Gherson thought, his bile rising; thank you very much, you old goat – what about me!

Denby Carruthers was both surprised and delighted that doing business in Gravelines was so easy; nominally under French control they had done nothing to interdict the trade between Flanders and England – as the Tollands said, they needed the gold. If the people he was called upon to deal with were capable of violence they also had a good grasp of how to do commerce – quickly and without fuss – and he felt, weapons apart and without the strain of menace, right at home, as if he was doing his normal day's exchanges in London.

The efficiency extended to supply and loading, and if he had a slight worry he might be cheated, both the attitude of the Tolland brothers and the speed with which his purchases were supplied laid that to rest. The wind had been fair on the crossing to Gravelines, it was less so on the return but they got within reach of Ramsgate inside a day's sailing, where a boat was lowered to take him ashore.

'Get yourself set for the night, Mr Carruthers, and take the coach back to London on the morrow.'

'I will do that, Tolland, but, you know, I am tempted to ask, should I not come with you to land the cargo?'

Jahleel Tolland's polite tone evaporated then. 'No one who is not needed to sail this ship of yours gets to see where we land, nor who we spread out the sale of the goods to. You go back to your house and wait for us and we will bring you the money we earn to the farthing.'

'Please do not think I don't trust you.'

Looking at each other in the light of a lantern, both men knew the truth: mutual trust did not exist. The only reason Denby Carruthers would not know this night, and never know on any other where they landed their cargo, was because that was the only card the Tollands still held and it tied him to them.

He took to the boat and even in oilskins he was wet through when finally it was run up in pitch black onto the Ramsgate beach.

Hodgeson the thief-taker had contacts amongst the Grub Street hacks and they, because of their trade, knew every fly-by-night character in London, Westminster and half the counties of England. A tot of brandy here, a tumbler of wine there, and when pushed to it a coin passed over, soon had the word out that he was looking for two people and news came back within forty-eight hours about a certain Mrs Barclay staying at Nerot's Hotel, now gone to Norfolk it was believed, who had been of interest to someone at the Home Department of Henry Dundas.

That took him to Nerot's but not that he enquired

within its walls; there were a few taprooms around Jermyn Street to which the staff would wander when they got a chance, anything for a quiet bit of imbibing not under the eyes of their employer, and he soon established their favourite haunt, one they shared with the like-minded servitors in the St James's Street gentlemen's clubs.

To spot a man who will tell you something for a palmed coin is a skill, and a good guide is the fellow who moans incessantly and likes the world to know his grievances, yet loudly protests his honesty. So picking out Didcot was not as hard as a layman would have supposed and it took no time at all, once he knew there was payment to be had, for the hotel servant to give chapter and verse.

'You reckon Mrs Barclay has a paramour, then?'

'No doubt about it. Now I don't say he was rogering her there and then, but it was at the top of his mind, and if it hadn't yet happened she was gettin' ripe for the fall. It were in her eyes.'

'And it was this Lieutenant Pearce who let slip about her going to King's Lynn?'

'Did too, 'cause he trusted me, ye see, knew an honest man when he saw one. Why you asking, any road?'

Hodgeson slipped him a half-guinea, which was felt rather than looked at for its value. 'What do you care?'

'Don't give a toss, friend, but I'll go to another tankard afore you light out for Norfolk, 'cause you don't have to lay it that you is looking for her. Stands to reason if she's Mrs Barclay there's a Mister somewhere about, who would not be happy to see his wife – and she is a beauty, take my word – rolling in the hay with a good-looking cove like John Pearce. And he is not backward either, not when he's getting letters from Downing Street.'

'And they left together, you say?'

'Service at sea for him, I reckon, Norfolk for her.' That was followed by a wheezy laugh. 'Rumour has it they still paint their faces blue up there.'

That was the last place Hodgeson would go looking, for Didcot was an old fool who did not have a clue when he was being joshed. If Mrs Barclay was in some kind of liaison with a naval lieutenant, regardless of how far it had gone, he would be an easier person to find than a woman who could be anywhere, especially if he was serving in some capacity. And where he was she would most likely be, or close by.

As a time to interrupt Denby Carruthers his wife could not have chosen worse. He had not long arrived from Ramsgate and had a mass of papers to look through, bills, proposals for insurance and reports on some important investments. But disturb him she did, as soon as Lavery was sent out to deliver some share certificates, to tell him of the way he was being betrayed by his clerk.

'Lavery came to me with information about your affairs, husband, and I fear he did so in order to seek a way to gain my affections.'

The alderman nearly blurted out, 'At his age?' but he actually said, 'What information?'

The head went down and her hands were twisted around her embroidered handkerchief, this to demonstrate how reluctant she was to reply, while the catch in her voice was one she had used often on a very indulgent father, as well as one employed to discourage disappointed suitors prior to her marriage.

'He told me that a man had been in touch regarding a certain individual whose name, were I to mention it, would cause you upset.'

How did he know about Codge? It mattered not, Lavery did and that was that. 'It pleases me you are aware of the hurt it causes.'

'And I hope you believe I am still penitent,' she whimpered.

Catherine Carruthers' motives were, to her, quite straightforward: Lavery had failed in his task of finding Gherson and his protestations that he had tried hard were nothing but lies. But in the process of letting her down she had shown him a certain degree of encouragement which, should her husband ever realise, would be fatal to her future. She knew her beloved Cornelius to be alive and in time she would find him; until then she must have both the security of her home and her husband's income.

Lavery could not be trusted and if he let anything slip about her desire to find Cornelius then all hell would break loose and she might be cast adrift. Better he was dismissed and much better that she, having spoken first, would render any excuse he gave for his behaviour both invalid and unlikely to be believed.

'Why did Lavery do such a thing?'

She looked at her husband then, her eyes damp. 'I think he harboured thoughts inappropriate to a fellow of both is age and appearance and that made him volunteer to me things which I had no knowledge of and no desire to hear. That a man like that should have designs beggars belief, I know, but—'

She knows Gherson is alive, he thought, but enlightenment in that matter did not in any way provide the same clarity as to what he was going to do about it. Denby Carruthers was wondering if in agreeing to keep his shame secret, on advice from his brother-in-law, Druce, he had done the right thing, while deep down he knew he had been left with no choice. Still, matters were in hand for him to find Gherson and when he did . . .'

'I should leave it with me, my dear, and I will take care of it.'

'Lavery will be dismissed?'

'Not immediately, my dear, we do not want the old fool blackening your name in revenge, for he will be aware where his trouble has come from.'

'You are so wise, I don't know what I'd do if I did not have you to advise me.'

Right at that moment Denby Carruthers, though he was smiling indulgently, was thinking he had seen chucked over the parapet of London Bridge the wrong body, or perhaps there should have been two instead of one. He had been a fool to think that someone as young as Catherine could come to love him. All his experience in business told him that there comes a time to cut your losses in a failed venture. Not that he would do so suddenly, even if he thought the Tollands at hand to do the deed. As in a trading loss he would withdraw at a careful pace, hoping to pass off to some other hand the majority of the liabilities.

'My dear, it is your beauty that makes you so vulnerable

to such advances, I know for I am not immune to that myself.'

'I have wounded you, I know, but I will work hard to make good that hurt.' Catherine Carruthers approached her husband and laid a soft hand on his shoulder.

'As for Lavery, humour him, but you must not worry your pretty head about the old booby again.' In using the words old booby, Denby Carruthers wondered if he was talking about himself.

CHAPTER TWENTY-TWO

They were on the latitude of Ferrol when the first dull boom came floating across the ocean; so faint it was impossible to tell if it was real. Pearce was on deck at the time and it was not only his head that became cocked as he wondered if he had heard correctly. It was also the case that no one wanted to be the first to seek to identify it in any way lest they make a fool of themselves.

'Mr Dorling, given our position would we be able to hear land-based gunnery?'

'No, sir, we are too far from shore for that.'

'Thunderstorm over the horizon, I reckon,' said one of the hands.

The next boom was not so faint, and taking his own judgement and adding it to the direction the men before him were recoding the sound, he had it nearly due south, just a few points off his bowsprit.

'Mr Dorling, let's get more sail aloft and increase our speed.'

That got a satisfied grin; Pearce had refused to crack on before and if he progressed at a reasonable rate it was also sailing easy and Dorling had been afire to test the top hamper. Soon the decks were full of men, the rigging too. He left what was set and went to the master, aware almost immediately that the heel of the deck had increased and so had the amount of white water scudding down the side. The actual effect would have to wait till the log was cast and that he would also leave to Dorling, for in the young master he had a very competent seaman, much more so than he. All he took responsibility for was the sending of a second lookout aloft so two men could more easily scan the whole horizon.

He entered his cabin to find Emily at her embroidery doing what she had done for her husband aboard HMS *Brilliant*, though she had never admitted that to Pearce – making cushions with the name of the vessel in the stitching.

'I hear the sound of padding feet, John.'

'Yes, we're increasing sail. We heard a sound like gunfire but it may just be weather.'

'Do you wish me to desist?'

'Not yet,' he replied with a smile. 'It will turn out to be nothing at all.'

Sound is one thing, pressure on the ears quite another and when another boom came, just as he stepped back onto the deck, Pearce was sure he could feel it on the drums, but also knew the power of imagination. By now Dorling had everything aloft that HMS *Larcher* could carry, without overdoing the driving sails, which would press her head down and be counterproductive by increasing the drag on the bows. But the fourth boom, when it came, left no one in any doubt: it was cannon fire and dead ahead. Calmly he re-entered the cabin and told Emily to cease her sewing.

'We will have to clear for action, which means this cabin will become a fighting space. Thank God we ate enough of the stores to free the deck. Let's hope there's enough room below for the furniture.'

'It will not require much.'

Emily was looking at what Pearce meant by 'furniture'. Most of the space was taken up by the bed they had used, for there was no pretence this time; he slept in his cabin and was awoken from there to take his turn on the watch. There was his sea chest and her trunk, the clocks and the tiny desk he used for writing up his logs.

'It suddenly occurs to me that you do not carry a surgeon, John.'

'No, that's another duty which falls to me, with aid, of course, from the cook and anyone else who can stitch.'

That had her holding up her unfinished cushion. 'Then I know where I should be, for did I not learn from Heinrich in Toulon how to look after the wounds of fighting men?'

'I hope you do not have to deal with anything like that on this ship. I have strict instructions to avoid anything that interferes with my mission, and even if there is an exchange of gunfire over the horizon I should sail on by and ignore it.'

That was when it came, not a single shot as before, but a salvo loud enough to carry and press on the senses.

Pearce was on the deck in a trice. 'Gentlemen, we will clear for action.'

This had been rehearsed almost daily on the way south, well out to sea from the Bay of Biscay, and the crew had smoothed out any gremlins. Each went about his duties without being told, striking certain artefacts below, removing a couple of bulkheads, the gunner making up charges for the guns while the captains collected and affixed the flintlocks and all the while the sound of gunfire grew.

Emily had donned an apron and was directing some hands that had completed their tasks to set up a temporary sickbay by Bellam's coppers, already bubbling with useful hot water. She had also found in the holds a store of medical equipment, not least a supply of medicinal brandy. Some aboard spied her and kicked themselves for not finding it sooner; show a British sailor drink and he would consume it and never mind that one day later he would be lying on a board dying for that same drink to ease the pain of surgery.

'Gun captains, we shall not run out the cannon just yet, open ports will slow us down, but make all ready to run them in for loading. Aloft there, can you see anything yet?'

'Nothing yet, sir,' said one, this while the second man threw out a hand. 'Belay that, we can see a set of topsails three points off the starboard bow.'

'Quartermaster.'

The man nodded and eased the wheel a few points, this as Michael came up and presented him with his pistols. He would stay at his side, while Charlie and Rufus, now fully accepted, had each been given the captaincy of a cannon.

'Gun flashes, your honour.'

The sound and pressure followed hard on the heels of that shout from the masthead, which had Pearce grabbing a telescope and heading for the shrouds, to climb up and have a look for himself, now that there was something to see. As he looked aloft he saw his Admiralty pennant, which brought back to him the words of Henry Dundas.

'Sod Dundas,' he said to himself, 'there's a fight going on and it can't just be ignored.'

You never lose sight of the first time you clamber up a set of shrouds and Pearce could recall it now; the grey waters off Ramsgate, the loud voice of the bosun, Robert Sykes, who had turned out to be a decent type made cruel working for that bastard Ralph Barclay. How many times had he done it since and how much was it now so easy, when the first time he had known a real dose of fear. Near on his back he went over the main top and on up a second slimmer rope ladder to the very top, where he could sling his leg over a yard and, once steady, lifted his glass and examined the scene.

'Three ships, your honour, and we reckon one fightin' a pair.'

The gunfire and flashes were steady now, which spoke of a duel being fought at range. He swept the scene and took in the two vessels closest – the third was obscured by smoke – their flags streaming out red and gold.

'They cannot be Spaniards, they are our allies.'

'Never in life, your honour.'

'They might be French privateers under false colours.'

'And what are they attacking?'

On a fluke of wind the smoke cleared enough for Pearce to see the third ship and he had to steady his glass to get the view properly.

'My God, it's the *Lorne*, postal packet.'

'You know her, your honour?'

'Well, and her captain too, who I hope is still with us.'

'A Falmouth packet carries more metal than we do.'

Pearce nodded in agreement as he swept the scene again to register that the vessels *Lorne* was engaged against were likewise two-masted brigs of some twelve guns. They would not be as sleek as the ship on which he had sailed with Captain McGann, yet his opponents likewise were larger than *Larcher* and better armed. Here was an old friend in a fight and that meant his orders could go hang and likewise the risks. It was time to be back on deck so he grabbed a backstay and slid down, pleased to note that they had closed so much the entire action was in plain view.

'Mr Dorling, we will need to be nippy to confound these two . . . what I assume to be Frenchmen.'

'Spanish colours, sir.'

'There are not many vessels that have the legs of a Falmouth packet so I suspect a ruse to get close to a brig that could show them a clean pair heels, indeed they were designed to avoid a battle rather than engage in one.

'Spain might have declared war on Britannia since we weighed, but it makes no odds, there is a British vessel in distress and we must give her aid. Those two are between *Lorne* and us and what I aim to do is get past them and coordinate my actions with the packet. They will not want to fight if we are acting in unison, they will want to disengage and we must help them do so.'

'We should shorten sail, sir.'

'Make it so – let's get the headsails in as well as the lateen and go down to topsails. Gun captains, as soon as we have shortened sail get your cannon run out and loaded, both sides.'

'They're bigger and heavier than us, sir, they won't expect us to come on.'

'Well they are in for a surprise. I want those cannon trained right forward and the bow chaser to fire as soon as they have a range that might do some damage. Mr Dorling, keep an eye on the sods; I want to know if they alter course to impede us or come right about to give us a broadside.'

Time can seem to stand still at sea; even with all the action going on over the bow the act of closing with whosoever were the enemy seemed to take an eternity. Having loaded and run out both sides he had split the men needed to fire them and he also had to make sure they did not all go off at once in case the ship's timbers could not bear it. The only way to control that was to take charge himself and he went to the bow, talking to each man as he passed him, giving reassurance.

'You all right, Charlie?'

'Never better.'

He turned to ask Rufus the same question, to be met by a steely look in a man who had, when he first met him, been so much of a callow boy. There was no need to question him, and that applied to the majority of the crew, because this was what they trained for. Then, of course, there was a tradition of victory at sea: Britannia Ruled the Waves, so they expected victory almost as a right. The one person Pearce had not considered was himself and he realised that he too had blood coursing through his veins, had eyesight seemingly more acute than normal along with the knowledge that he was actually looking forward to a fight.

'Enemy to starboard has put down his helm, sir, and is turning to meet us.'

'He's too late,' Pearce replied, wondering how he could be sure, but he was.

The swinging ship had held his course too long thinking that a smaller fighting ship would not attack but, more likely, only seek to bluff in order to get him to draw off from the packet. Now he had realised he was wrong and he was acting to prevent it. Pearce could see men rushing across the deck to run in and load guns which had not yet been employed, and that became crucial. Could they get them into use before he could rake them? If he won the race the first bout was his, if not this deck would be a mass of bloody broken flesh in less than a minute of mayhem.

'Bow chaser, see if you can slow their loading.'

The starboard cannon spoke almost before he had finished giving the order and he kicked himself for not loading it with grape. Yet it had an effect, called down from the masthead for he could see nothing for smoke. The enemy had shied way from their guns, probably because they expected a mass of small metal balls to sweep across their deck. As it was, the round shot hit the bulwarks and broke off a serious amount of wooden splinters.

The man in command obviously realised that he was going to lose the contest to load, but then he compounded his original error. To seek to escape by turning to port proved to be the worst choice of all, for he had only two cannon – stern chasers – with which to meet a full rolling broadside from HMS *Larcher*. If that was not much compared to a ship of the line his adversary was still presenting the most vulnerable part of his ship to his enemy.

'You've got him, your honour,' Dorling shouted.

There was a scene of panic on the enemy deck; they knew what was coming just as they knew there was nowhere to hide, for on the up roll *Larcher*'s cannons could rake the deck, on the down roll she would put her round shot right in through the stern lights and they would run the length of the brig killing anyone in their path, and that said nothing regarding the damage to the hull and her internal construction. The crack of musket balls whizzing past his ear reminded Pearce he had forgotten about that. Luckily Michael O'Hagan had not: he and a quartet of others let fly to keep down the heads of their opposite numbers, now trying to reload.

'Number one. Fire!' Pearce took three steps as the ship dipped into the swell. 'Number two. Fire! He kept walking; if he had stopped to look he would have seen the transom of the enemy brig disintegrate on the second ball, with a great crashing sound as it went through the flimsy wood, huge flying splinters following in its wake. Even over the sound of guns, the screams could be clearly heard of those who worked on the lower deck, but he was soon disabused of an easy success.

HMS *Larcher* shuddered as though she had hit a wall. It was not return fire, but a broadside from the second enemy vessel, which had ceased now to bother *Lorne* and directed her attention to saving her consort, which had suffered so badly her head had fallen off and she looked to be rudderless; cannon number four had seen to that part of her steerage gear. Aboard *Larcher* thuds and cracks indicated some of her scantlings were stove in, but a quick check got the message from below that there was no water entering to flood the lower decks or gaps so wide that daylight could enter.

'*Lorne* is attacking, Mr Pearce, sir.'

Pearce looked to where a finger pointed and there he could see that the packet had raised a tad more sail to close with the enemy and he was not alone in the observation; the fellow who had just delivered that broadside and was preparing another saw it too, to realise that if he did not move swiftly he would be trapped between two fires. That he was a good sailor became immediately obvious as he abandoned his cannon in favour of canvas, getting enough aloft, and quickly, to outmanoeuvre those trying to close with him under scraps of topsail.

Better still than that, he swept round *Larcher*'s stern and had a cable ready to take his consort in tow, at which point the packet gave up on the fight and that had to apply to the armed cutter, she being too small to continue alone. But the fight was over and the cheering started – so loud was that, it seemed it might be heard in England.

'I always thought you'd make a fighting tar, John Pearce, and by the Good Lord I was right.'

McGann, small, bright-eyed and with ginger hair,

was indeed still in command and there were many other familiar faces to greet and shake hands with. But *Lorne* was Falmouth bound and carrying both mail and specie, so to linger was not possible; speed for the post was of the essence. Unusually, Captain McGann took an on-board drink to toast their victory, for he was abstemious at sea and the opposite on land. He also had fulsome compliments for Emily Barclay and a wink for John Pearce to tell him what a rogue he was, and too soon they parted company to the sound of repairs being made to *Larcher*'s damaged hull.

'I am glad he is going north, Emily. The last time I was with him in Gibraltar McGann started a brawl. In drink he is convinced that he is an object of uncontrollable desire for any woman on whom his eyes alight.'

'What, that nice old gentleman?'

'You should observe him in drink, he makes Michael look saintly.'

'Which I am to the toes, your honour,' his friend said, right by his shoulder.

'Mr Dorling, let's get our sails set again and resume our course.'

There was no more than a touch at Gibraltar to top up the water casks and to allow Brad Kempsall to make more serious repairs to the hull than had been possible at sea. Then it was a cruise in an ocean now controlled by Britannia and Spain. Blue skies met blue waters, the sun shone in the day, sometimes too hot, but the nights were comfortable enough for Pearce and Emily to sit up late on deck and have him identify for her the stars.

Then the day came when he had to ask Dorling a favour.

'You are the only other person on the ship who keeps a log?'

'I am, sir.'

'Well, I want to go to Leghorn and drop off my lady and I don't intend to write up my course to there and back to Corsica. It is no great distance and the stores consumed will not tell anyone I have gone astray.'

'And you wish me to do the same?'

'I can ask, but you know you have no obligation to comply.'

'Makes no odds to me, sir, if it is discovered they will break you and I will say you threatened me with a loaded pistol.'

Having said that with a grave countenance, and seeing Pearce react in a like manner, Dorling suddenly grinned. 'I believe I had you there, sir?'

'I believe you did.'

There were a mass of British vessels in Leghorn, a few navy, but mostly privateers, for this was the base for the wolves of the Mediterranean Sea who went out only for profit and justified their activities as aiding the war effort as Letters of Marque by their interdiction of trade. Through a shore-based naval officer they found a house where Emily could stay and to which Pearce promised to be back in a few days. Having been together and so close for weeks their parting was difficult and all the old anxieties, put aside for the voyage, resurfaced for Emily Barclay, for if they had talked much they had tended to avoid the most serious subject.

'I will not be long and let us think to talk when I come back, and instead of doing that which we have – skirt round it – let us move on from speculation to a proper plan for our future.'

Pearce was not the only sad face when they sailed for San Fiorenzo, where Lord Hood was anchored. Emily had grown on the whole crew – even those superstitious coves who had predicted disaster if they took a woman on board were sad that she was no longer with them, for she had been kind to all, with a ready smile and a willing ear for a tale of a life too hard to bear, or a wife and bairns back home who lived on the meagre pay the navy allowed.

Sighting HMS *Victory* lifted Pearce's spirits; all he had to do was deliver his letter, then up anchor for Leghorn again, to collect Emily and set off on what would be a less than speedy voyage back home. Life was at that moment as sweet as it could be.